Moon Shadows

A Halloween Anthology

Editor: Veronica Moore

Laurel
Highlands
Publishing

Cover by JosDCreations
http://JosDCreations.com

Laurel Highlands Publishing
Mount Pleasant, PA
USA
http://LaurelHighlandsPublishing.com

ISBN-13: 978-1-941087-11-4   ISBN-10: 1941087116

Table of Contents

The Lightkeepers

Renny Kalp

My day started like any other. Nothing indicated that the direction of my life would change forever.

The autumn leaves had turned the mountains into a canvas of beauty. A chill in the air made me wonder if there had been a frost that morning. That wouldn't be uncommon in the Appalachian Mountains, for we expect frost in the month of October. All that was left of our garden was a few pumpkins and our dear, old scarecrow we called "Squatch." I remembered looking at him as I skirted the garden for my routine morning walk.

My walks had become important to me. They gave me time to clear my head and allow my imagination to exercise, too. Sometimes, my sister would join me, but more often, I was alone. I loved the company, but walking alone allowed me to set my own pace, both with my feet and my mind. For some reason, on that chilly morning, I decided to change my usual route. Instead of taking a path through the woods at the edge of our property, I went downhill toward the valley below. A stream-fed lake provided a stopover for geese and swans on their migratory route.

With the plan in mind, I took a quick look back to see if anyone was around. I only saw Squatch, with his one raised arm that seemed to be waving good-bye. As with all plans, they could change in an instant. When I set out on my journey, I noticed the ground was softer underfoot than I liked. Not wanting to get my feet wet, I decided to walk along the firm edge of the road and pick up the valley trails further ahead.

As I descended into the valley, the ground mist rose to mix with a light fog; obviously not the best walking conditions. I no longer could see the path ahead. I stayed on the firm shoulder of the road, as it gave me the best surface and kept me from losing my path. I was somewhat annoyed that my pace had to be slowed and my attention had to be on my unsure footing. But one thing became clear to me, when it's foggy and you can't see well, hearing becomes your better sense.

It was too early for any appreciable amount of traffic, so I was surprised when I heard a car approach. Because I couldn't see it, I stopped to determine its direction. As I turned around, a large white car screamed by, forcing me to jump out of the way.

My jump to safety led me into the arms of a huge oak tree, just off the side of the road. Had the limb been a few inches higher, I could have avoided a headache. Literally. As I recovered my composure and checked myself all over, I decided I could continue my walk.

While I had been jolted, the car stirred the fog, allowing me to see the road ahead once more. With determination, I set out again toward the lake. I remembered picnic tables artfully placed near the water and I hoped to rest there and gather my wits. I stayed with the road to the bottom of the hill where it came to a crossroads. Normally, I would have chosen to go left, towards the lake. But the scene before me shocked me.

An old, abandoned youth hostel had been renovated. There it sat, beautiful, inviting, and obviously under new ownership. The last time I saw it, its decaying exterior was boarded up with ominous "No Trespassing" signs. The lake I had been planning on seeing, was part of this property, but locals paid no attention to the "Stay Out" signs. Trails blazed through the tall grass surrounding the lake and the grass was actually worn away around the picnic tables.

Now, the lawns were mowed; the sign by the road said, "Welcome." I could actually see the lake from where I stood. I was awe struck. Some minutes had passed before I realized a women stood in the opened front door, framed by firelight, motioning me to come in.

The hostel set back off the road with a circular drive. Low lights outlined the drive and while trees surrounded the building, the ground was free of leaves. All was in order. Shrubs were neatly trimmed and the hostel itself was newly painted. I raised my hand in greeting to the unknown woman as curiosity moved me up the drive.

When did all this occur? Who bought the property and how long was it under repair? So many questions crowded my mind and I was still smarting from the crack to my head. My eyes were drawn to all the many decorations on display. After all, it was Halloween. Groupings of pumpkins, some carved, some painted, peeked out from beneath neatly stacked hay bales. Cornstalks tied in bundles were placed near barrels of fall flowers. I could hear wind chimes tinkling and the sounds of falling water from a beautiful fountain nearby. There was even a scarecrow that looked like our Squatch, pointing the way up the path.

I wanted to spend more time taking in all the niceties around me, but the woman motioned me to come in, so I made my way to the opened door. I ascended three wooden steps up to an expansive porch, where my new neighbor awaited me.

"Hello," I said as I extended my hand in greeting. "My name is Eva and I guess you'd say I'm your neighbor since I only live about a mile away." My voice trailed off as she clasped my hand in a firm and welcome handshake.

"Hello," her soft voice returned. "I'm Sophia and welcome. Please, come inside and have a look around. You must be curious about the old hostel and our grand opening."

"Grand opening?" I asked. "You're opening as a hostel again?"

"No," she replied. "But it makes a great bed & breakfast and we still serve the public."

"How wonderful," I returned. "I can't tell you what a surprise this is to me. I had no idea anything was happening here."

She smiled with no reply. Then, she decided to respond with, "It's amazing what can be accomplished when you have the resources and the contacts."

I nodded and wondered whom she might know. I slipped off my shoes at the door as she offered to escort me inside. I apologized that my shoes were quite dirty as I'd been forced off the road into a soft-bottomed gully; hence, the knot on my head and the dirt on my shoes.

She smiled kindly and said, "You can warm yourself by the fire and if you like, I can make us something to drink. Perhaps coffee or tea? I have a wonderful new blend of herbal tea I'd like to share. Would you mind?"

"No. Of course I'll try it, but don't go to any trouble for me," I said.

She was already heading into an adjoining room as she said over her shoulder, "Make yourself comfortable. I'll only be a moment."

I moved to the fireplace to warm my hands and noticed the beauty of the carved wooden mantle. A gold gilded frame surrounded a haunting, nighttime seascape. A full moon provided the only light that rested on a young woman with a child in her arms. She gazed out to the open sea; searching, waiting, perhaps for her lover to return. I could feel the deep longing of that young mother.

I turned to gaze around the room. With my back to the fire, I faced the doorway. To either side of the door, a series of masks were on display, the kind of masks you might see at a masque ball or Mardi Gras. Feathers and jewels resembled cat eyes, with long slender stems to hold them. Antiques graced the room. Delicate teacups were arranged on a side buffet with Egyptian artifacts dominating the room. A bust of King Tut was used as a bookend. Golden figurines of Isis and Osiris and a miniature replica of the Ark of the Covenant were visible in a barrister bookcase. Lots of leather-bound books and plenty of book shelves made the room warm and inviting.

Sophia returned with the tea and took the chair to the right of the fireplace. The tea was welcoming on the chilly morning. I settled back in my chair and allowed the aroma to fill the air around me. I took deep breaths and the warm sips chased the chill away. We engaged in small talk at first. Then, she turned to me in earnest and asked, "How do you like what we've done with the place?"

"I'm speechless," I replied. "So beautiful, yet cozy. I can't help but wonder how all this could be accomplished in such a small amount of time!"

"Ah, yes. Time," she said. "Well, most of the work was on the inside. We completed our work here first. Then it was only a matter of establishing order on the outside. Besides, we wanted the place ready for All Souls Evening. The Lightkeepers will be arriving soon."

"Lightkeepers," I queried. "All Souls?"

"Well, tonight is Halloween or All Hallow's Eve. These next few days the veil between the living and the dead is the thinnest."

My look of confusion encouraged her to explain. "At this time of year, the souls of those who have died can be attracted to visit those they loved or hated. It's a very sacred time and it's possible to be visited by the departed."

"And the Lightkeepers?" I asked.

She replied with, "The Lightkeepers protect the living

souls. They travel with them. They guard and protect both the living and the dead."

"Why do they need protection?" I asked.

She looked at me for a long moment then continued. "We all have guides that assist us at the time of birth and at the moment of our death, because we are most vulnerable at those times. They act much like tour guides that show us the way and keep us out of trouble. Then, there are times they feel the need to look in on us. Perhaps we are in pain or we cry out for help." She rose from her chair and walked to the door. "You see these masks here?" I nodded and she said, "Well, masks are designed and worn to hide the identity of the person beneath. The Halloween tradition of wearing a mask was to scare off demons who might be looking for an unwary soul. It really isn't much different from what we do in our day to day lives. We put up a facade. We want the world to believe we are someone we're not; perhaps brighter, more important, prettier, more confident. You see what I mean?"

Again, I nodded, then asked, "But the Lightkeepers, you know them?"

"Well—yes. I'm aware of their presence," she spoke thoughtfully.

I knew that our conversation was taking an unusual turn. Who talks about other worldly events on their first meeting? How did our conversation go awry? Yet, I couldn't stop myself from pressing her for more information.

"Do you mean they're not visible?" I joked.

"Well, some are—some aren't," she said seriously. "There are many things about this time of year that are part of the great mystery. But, I like to believe that the Lightkeepers know they are welcome here. I make it known that this is a place of rest, so I try to create an atmosphere that will attract them. I also think of my own father and those who have gone ahead of me and invite them, too. It's just a feeling—but I believe I contact them. I send them my love and let them know they are missed and remembered."

I remained quiet, just listening and trying to understand my strange, new neighbor. I finished my tea and fussed about the time that passed and I had to get on my way. She expressed her understanding and rose from her chair to walk me to the door. As we passed a side table, she picked up a beautiful stone from a small bowl. Heart-shaped, it was smooth and had a shade of milky rose. She turned it over in her hands, then said, "Here, I'd like to give you something to remember our visit. Think of it as an amulet, or a good luck piece."

"Why, thank you," I said. "I truly appreciate this."

Then she said something that didn't make sense at the time. "Everything will be all right, you know."

I looked back at her and said, "Of course." But I didn't really know what she was talking about. I thanked her again for her hospitality and set off in the direction of home. The fog had lifted and the road was quite visible. My walk had been interrupted, but pleasantly so.

I had a lot to think about and as I approached the tree where my morning mishap had occurred, I noticed something was not right. There was ash on the road from burnt out flares. There was a rescue vehicle with two paramedics visible near the open doors. A fire truck with firemen directing traffic around an obvious accident scene slowed my breath. I stopped, hoping to catch a glimpse of who was on the gurney. No one tried to keep me back; they rather ignored me. So, I kept my focus. I was trembling all over as I made my way to the gurney, yet I knew who would be there.

A week later, I learned all the details of the accident. I had been hit by the car and must have sustained a head injury that kept me unconscious for at least a week. I tried to tell everyone about my experience with Sophia, but they insisted I hadn't gone anywhere. What's more, the hostel remained abandoned and boarded up. I felt saddened by the whole event. I felt a genuine loss, as if I had lost my best friend. But every time I tried to speak of my visit, my husband would look frightened. I didn't want him to think I was crazy.

I could tell by the questions of the doctors that hallucinations would keep me in the hospital a lot longer than I wanted. They would ask me about Sophia and try to act unconcerned when I would launch into my story. Then, I'd be scheduled for more tests and more interviews. I caught on soon enough. They were treating me like Dorothy from the Wizard of Oz. I had to deny my visit in the old hostel and pretend it never happened.

I was anxious to leave the hospital and revisit the hostel. Surely, there had to be some proof, some evidence that she was there. I played the role of patient-cured and soon I got the response I needed. Time to go home.

The relief in my husband's eyes was enough for me to bury my story. I had no one to talk to; no one with whom to share my story. It was maddening. But I was determined to go home and mend on my own. The stay in the hospital allowed me time to go over all the details of that fateful day. I could even taste the tea Sophia had prepared for me. It was then I remembered her parting words, "Everything will be alright, you know." Somehow, I felt relief. Everything *will* be all right. I made those words my mantra as I conquered my anxiety. There was something so frightening about not being believed.

Finally, the day arrived for my departure. My husband arrived early that morning. He was unusually positive and trying hard to keep my spirits up.

"It's okay," I said. "I'll be fine for now. No more headaches. No more hallucinations."

He seemed so relieved. He set off to find the doctor to sign my release. While he was gone, one of the aids brought me a plastic bag with my things—shoes, clothes, etc. I thanked her and looked at the battered clothing. I was still depressed until something caught my eye. There, at the bottom of the bag, was my stone. The stone Sophia gave me! Such joy enveloped me that I nearly jumped out of my chair. It was real; all of it. I did visit with Sophia. I did have tea and I heard about the Lightkeepers. But I knew something else, too. It was my story. I'd have to keep it close to myself. I would protect it, else they would make it to be just another crazy story.

I made it home that day and within another week, my husband walked with me to the hostel. It was still overgrown and abandoned. We stood in front of it a few minutes without speaking. He watched me from the corner of his eye. Finally, he said, "You okay?"

"Of course," I replied. "No need to worry. I had quite a shock, but what a beautiful place this could be. I know. I saw it." He smiled and humored me.

My spiritual journey began.

I don't talk about my encounter anymore. I keep my stone in my pocket. Every now and again, I'll rub its surface and say to myself, "Everything will be alright." Now every Halloween, I watch for the Lightkeepers. I send out a thank you to Sophia and all those who have gone before us. I know that she has been my guide and probably protected me when I arrived and will be there when it is time for me to leave. I am no longer afraid.

Happy Halloween, for indeed it is.

Stranger Nights

Jacob Lambert

"Hey, lady, are you going to give me my change or what?" a man with a thick, salt and pepper beard said, his red, nondescript hat pulled down over road tired eyes.

Mimi Sanders didn't hear him, nor did she register his continued query. In fact, as she stared past the man at the counter, through the glass doors behind him, and out into the darkness beyond, the only voice she heard was Dr. Peters, his tone flat and indifferent: *Six months.* It had been like receiving a death sentence, and in many ways, she thought, it was, but there had been no trial, no evidence of guilt. There had only been her and Dr. Peters, she the defendant—he, the judge and jury. There had been no fear at the time, but now…. Now there was plenty, and those two words, echoing in her exhausted mind, made her crave one thing, the very thing responsible for her emaciated frame and the shooting pain in her right side: a drink.

"Look, are you going to give me my damn money or do I—"

Feeling the man touch her shoulder, Mimi snapped out of her daze and pushed his hand away. "You might want to watch yourself, son. I might be old, but I still got enough teeth to bite every last one of them fingers off and wear 'um for a necklace."

The man's eyes suddenly became tea saucers, but the shock didn't last long. Seconds later, a wide grin appeared on his face, laughter working its way up his throat. "Well, I am sorry, ma'am, but I've been asking for my change for about ten minutes, and you just kept staring out yonder. Thought you were having a stroke or something."

Mimi didn't return the smile. Instead, her upper lip quivered and pulled away from her tobacco stained dentures, producing a snarl. "I don't care what you thought! You're damn lucky that I didn't press this little red button behind the counter, and get you locked up for assault."

"Assault? Hell, lady, all I did was tap you on the—"

Interrupting him, Mimi leaned over the counter and squinted her eyes, making her face resemble, to the man in the red hat, a shaved Yorkie with a ragged bowl cut. "Aren't you Janet Monroe's boy, little Tommy?"

"That's my mother, why?" the man replied, the smile vacating his face.

"Cause I'm going to call that old hag and tell her what kind of a son she has, that's why. And if I see you in here again, I'm going to call the police. That make sense to you, or should I call your boyfriend and have him remind you?"

An indignant flash come over the man's face, his cheeks reddening.

"Oh, don't act like that, son. We all know about your little habit down at the Zip, how you sneak into the bathroom with them men. Heard it only takes two shots to get you good and friendly. Maybe your mother told me that. I really don't remember. I get faces and things mixed up these days," Mimi said, pushing away from the counter and folding her trembling arms over her chest, a smile replacing the snarl.

Without saying another word—or retrieving his change—the man walked to the door, stopped, and though it looked like he might turn around, he continued through, disappearing into his truck and driving away. The sound of his tires squealing made Mimi's smile only widen. She took a deep breath, and looked at the clock hanging on the wall beside the cigarettes. It was 10:34, four minutes past closing time, and two hours until Mimi would actually leave for the night. She could feel her side aching, the pain now slithering up to her head as she rounded the counter, locking the double glass doors and shutting off the lights surrounding the pumps.

Was it going to get worse, and if so, by how much, she thought, staring through the glass, out at the empty street—those two words reoccurring: *Six months*. Mimi's hands started trembling, and she felt a wave of heat cover her body, creating both sweat and gooseflesh. That couldn't be true. It just couldn't. Sure, she had drunk most of her life, but no more than anybody else had, and liver cancer...? How was that even possible? Her own mother had died of, what Mimi assumed would also kill her, a heart attack, but cancer didn't exist in her family, at least that she knew of, so, again, how was that possible? She didn't know, but evidently that didn't matter: a person doesn't have to understand in order to die. It just happens, regardless, like a child reaching out to touch a flame. Ignorance doesn't take the burn away, and Mimi, now staring down at her spotted sixty-one year old hands, felt not only her chest burn, but that familiar desire creep up her dried throat. It was time for a drink, and, coincidently, also to stock the cooler.

She looked through the glass one more time, and then started toward the register, intent on removing the drawer and taking it to the security room in the back. After, it was off to the cooler. And as she did, a funny image came to her mind, momentarily shutting out Dr. Peters droning death sentence. It was of Tommy, the man in the red hat, pulling his overweight butt up on a bar stool, his crack, partially hidden by a faded pair of Levis, serving as a sort of advertisement to the rest of the queers scoping around for something a little more satisfying than a shot of Rumple Mints.

Unable to control the impulse, Mimi laughed, dropping a roll of quarters onto the floor.

"At least I ain't that bad, Lord. What do you say?"

Like she expected, there wasn't a response, only the sound of the icy machine churning by the coffee maker—and, of course, there was Dr. Peters' voice, but that would soon fade, along with the fear. After three or four beers, the only thing Mimi would hear, hopefully, was silence. Both internal and external.

Thanks to the large, grey, wool jacket Margret, the district manager (or clown face, as Mimi called her), had left in the security room, Mimi didn't have to rely solely on the alcohol to keep warm, but it *did* help. She had managed to stock most of the bottled sodas, waters, and energy drinks—a thing that boggled her mind—and was about to move on to the beer, when she had decided that it was time to have a drink. It didn't take much, a whopping four beers (two chugged, two finished moderately slow), and now, sitting on one of the twelve packs of *Bud Light*, Mimi popped the top of her fifth, but only sipped it once and sat it down. She didn't want to chance it, possibly end up puking in the cooler. That had happened once, and by the time she got around to cleaning it up, the vomit had frozen to the smooth concrete, making one hell of a mess. No, this time she would finish stocking the cooler, and after, if she still felt the need—which she always did—she would have another.

Standing, her knees feeling strong but mostly numb, Mimi grabbed one of the six-packs and bent down, the heavy grating sound of the fans above and the box scraping against the concrete the only noises attacking her ears. She didn't even, like she expected, hear Dr. Peters' voice anymore, but the pain was still there, only now it had worked its way into her back, but—

Nearly dropping the six-pack, Mimi stopped, her eyes drawn to a set of muddy black boots ahead, the owner standing directly in front of the cooler window, but he couldn't see inside, or at least Mimi hoped. Her heart, which had been at a steady thump, now began beating into her ears, her eyes nervously shifting from the beer, to the boots, and then back. Her first thought, other than call the police, was that it might be the man from earlier, Tommy, but Mimi had seen him leave herself, and she had locked the doors, hadn't she? Yes, most definitely. But what if he had broken the glass? That boy seemed a little off, now that she thought about it, but wouldn't she have heard the glass shatter? She didn't know. After all, it was loud inside the cooler, and she hadn't exactly been listening. The thought made her shiver, but the beer (thank God for the beer) was still doing its job, for now at least, and as Mimi watched the boots walk away, toward the front, she scooted and, quietly, placed the six-pack on the floor—and stood, rubbing both hands together.

What was she going to do? If she could get out of the cooler and over to the security office, she could check the monitors, but what if whoever was out there caught her? Mimi turned around, seeing her opened beer resting on one of the twelve packs, and deciding that she didn't care. Maybe it was the alcohol in her system that made her feel that way, but she doubted it. If she stayed in the cooler, she might die; if she opened the door, the result could be the same, so what was the point, really? There was none, and that much she knew. But if it *was* that queer out there, Mimi wouldn't let him kill her quick, not until she took out at least one of his perverted, thieving eyes.

"Let's see what you got left, you old heifer," she said, reaching down and grabbing her beer, chugging it, and, after tossing it to the floor, she opened the cooler door and stepped out, the scent of charred coffee and pungent cologne stinging her eyes. But there was no one there, nothing, and if it wasn't for the muddy boot prints on the tan linoleum (*whoever is out there is lucky that I didn't mop before going into the cooler*), Mimi might have believed she imagined the whole thing.

Mimi, leaving the door open, darted into the security office, the wool coat suddenly feeling very heavy, and once inside, she looked up at the monitor, its tinted green screen displaying the opposite of what she had anticipated. There was, once again, nothing, only the empty counter and booth beside the double glass doors, which, she noticed, weren't broken, meaning that Tommy wasn't inside the store. Mimi sighed, her wiry body relaxing, but when she was about to walk out of the office, she paused. If it wasn't Tommy, who was it? Someone had to be out there, she thought, rubbing the side of her face and feeling the numbness slowly diminish from her cheeks. The beer had done its job, all right, but evidently, she hadn't consumed enough: her joints and side ached again, but the voice, that of Dr. Peters, still hadn't resurfaced. At least there was that comfort. But what next, make a run for the door? *That was ridiculous*, Mimi thought.

If whoever was out there didn't kill her, slipping on the linoleum might. Besides, she hadn't run anywhere in years, and the thought of even making the effort made her light headed. The best route, she decided, would be the exact opposite: she would walk, staying close to the left wall, and press the little red button behind the counter. And if that didn't work....

"Then it doesn't matter, does it?" she whispered, taking off the jacket and leaving the security office, the trembling in her hands returning, along with a new problem: a massive head-ache, one right behind her left eye.

Nearing the counter, Mimi could see the mirror above the doors, the one pointing toward the register and coffee pot (the one with a broken camera behind it). There wasn't anybody in the refection, so she continued forward, her back to the wall, her eyes staring in the direction of the counter, where the red button waited. For the first time that night, or any other that she could remember, as she moved along the wall, her mind was clear—the effects of the beer suddenly gone, a clarity so profound that her eyes simply scanned, seeing all but taking in nothing. Her mind was hers', the joy of emptiness, but when her hand touched the counter, resting on its smooth, cool surface, peace vanished.

"Excuse me, do you work here?"

At first, Mimi wasn't sure if she had heard anything, but when she turned her head, her body still clinging to the wall, there he was, standing in front of the counter, elbows leaning on its surface. Her mouth seemed stapled close, the pounding in her chest now boisterous, but she remained calm—the ache in her side piercing sharp, almost forced her to the floor.

"Hello, ma'am, are you okay?"

Mimi turned, facing the new voice, and forced a smile. Though it was semi-dark, she could see the man's shortly cropped brown hair and ashen face, a single scar running from his forehead to his right cheek, where it spread, forming a crowfoot around his lips and jaw. But his eyes are what attracted most of her attention: light blue, intense and soft. Inside, Mimi wished that she had seen eyes like those years ago, before she had given up on marriage and kids—or indeed men altogether. It wasn't lust that made her think that about the stranger. Those days had long since ended. Something about the man's eyes spoke volumes about his character, his soul, and Mimi found herself releasing the wall and turning the corner, stepping closer to him.

"How did you get in here? Oh, dear, I must have locked you in, I'm sorry, Mr....?" Mimi asked, surprised at the earnestness in her own tone.

Tilting his head and laughing under his breath, the man replied, "There's no mister, ma'am. It's just Roy, that's all. And I guess you did. Sorry, I should have been paying attention."

That was it! She had simply locked him inside the store and hadn't noticed. Mimi wondered how long he had been ambling around, looking for someone to let him out, but didn't ask. Instead, she smiled—a genuine display this time.

"Well, just give me a moment, okay, and I'll unlock the door, but—"

"That won't be necessary, at least not yet. I actually need to purchase a pack of cigarettes, if that's alright with you?" Roy asked, pushing away from the counter. This time, Mimi saw something odd about the man: his face was more than ashen. It looked drained of all color, leaving all but a ghastly white. And if Mimi wasn't mistaken, she thought she saw hundreds of blue varicose veins underneath the surface of his skin, but that couldn't be right, she thought. Yet, there they were, bulging and unmistakable.

"I'm sorry, but I've already closed the register down and put the money away. I can't even get back in the damn safe, though if I could, I would. You understand?" Mimi said, walking around the counter. But as she did, the man spoke. This time his voice sounded slightly irritated, leaving Mimi thinking, *Please don't, please?*

"Alright, well, how about something else?"

To this, Mimi stopped, her smile gone. She turned to the man, her customary, abrasive scowl returning. "Look, if you're about to try and sell me something, I'm going to get pissed real quickly. I hope that's—"

"Calm down, ma'am, and just hear me out. I propose a trade, that's all."

"A trade?" Mimi replied, her voice uneven.

"Yes, if you give me a pack of those Camels over there, I'll answer *one* question for you, anything you like, okay?"

Her first inclination was that the man was crazy, and had somehow escaped from the mental hospital down on the south side of town, but her second, and more apt, was pressing the little red button on the side of the counter. And she would have done just that, but her eyes caught something right before she could: the double glass doors—there wasn't a reflection in the glass, except, of course, her own. Immediately, Mimi stood bolt upright, her heart, once again, picking up pace, and in that same instant, she imagined that if her blood rushed any faster tonight, her chest might explode.

"How did you get in here, cause I know that there wasn't anyone in here when I locked them doors?" Mimi asked, scared to look directly at the man.

"Is that you question, ma'am? If it is, hand them cigarettes over and—"

"No, that's not my question, mister, uh…"

"The name is Roy, and there's no mister. So are we at an agreement?" Roy asked, holding his hand out, but not for a handshake.

Mimi walked over to the left, her eyes never leaving Roy, and removed a pack of Camels, placing them in his hand. She watched the man unwrap the pack and place a cigarette in between his thin lips, light it, and inhale. "Man, did I need that. I haven't eaten in days, and these are the only damn things that will curb my appetite. Anyway, I didn't catch your name."

"Mimi," she replied, her voice low and harsh.

"What a nice name. I wouldn't say beautiful, cause it isn't, but certainly nice. So what's your question? Or do you not have an idea yet?" Roy said, backing away, toward the red and blue booth next to the doors, and sitting.

She had never remembered being this scared in her entire life. Not even the cancer in her liver made her palms sweat this much, her throat tighten, and the headache behind her eye had spread to the other, making her face throb and temples burn. What was going on here? Was this really happening, or had she actually slipped inside the cooler, hit her head, and was now lying there bleeding to death?

Mimi reached down and pinched her arm, where it quickly turned a bright purple. Nope, she was here, alive, but if that was true, what did that make Roy?

"I… don't know yet. How much time do I have?"

Roy looked down at his wrist—there was no watch—and smiled, exhaling smoke through his nostrils, a human dragon. "I'd say you have two hours, ma'am, and then I have to be on my way. Is that enough time?"

"Okay, yes, that should do just fine," she said, and walked over to the cooler, removed a *Bud Light* tall boy, and opened it, drinking deeply until she couldn't feel the burning in her throat.

Roy snubbed another cigarette into the ashtray, beside the four other butts surrounded by the increasing mound of ash. He then sighed and looked over at Mimi, who was staring down at her hands, small streams of tears falling from her wrinkled cheeks. Perhaps, it was the gentleman in him that brought him to his feet and over to the counter. He didn't know, but he did it anyway.

"So, have you decided on a question?" Roy asked, removed yet another cigarette, and lit it.

Looking up from the counter, her arms shaking, Mimi nodded and tried forcing a smile, but it didn't work. "I think I have, but I'm sure *you* have heard it before."

"Try me."

"Okay, when my mother died, I remember her saying that she saw some kind of light, but I didn't believe her, you know? Just thought she was trying to calm me down. Anyway, I wanted to know what happens when you die, if it's anything like what I imagine."

Lowering his head and propping his hand on the counter, Roy sighed, frustrated. "You're right, ma'am. I've been asked that same damn question for over two-thousand years, and let me tell you what I've told everyone else: I have no clue."

"What do you mean?"

Roy shrugged and took another drag, "I mean exactly what I said. When I died, sure there were people there, but then there was darkness, nothing; and then I was back, you know, back *here*. As for what happens when *you* die, I have no idea. Trust me, I wish I knew. If I could shed this carcass, I would have done it a thousand years ago. But to be fair, ma'am, that question wasn't right, considering the fact that I couldn't answer it. Go ahead, you've got one more, and don't make me w—"

"*Why* do we have to die?" Mimi asked, her voice dropping off at die, the strength departed from her lips.

Turning around, his back to her, Roy walked to the door and leaned on the booth. In the back of her mind, Mimi thought to tell him that smoking inside, the last time she'd checked, was against the law, but opted against it, deciding, instead, to wipe the tears from her eyes and listen.

"That one's easy: things die cause that's the natural order of things. We're born, we grow, and if we're lucky, we die. That's the human condition," he stopped, squinted, and continued, "It's like the tip of this cigarette, you see? In a few moments, it will turn to ash and fall to the floor, and I think life's that way; it *has* to be that way. Trust me, death's not that bad. I've at least felt *that*, but like I said, the part afterward is a total mystery to me, but I assume you'll know before too long. Am I right?" Roy asked, tossing the cigarette to the floor, half-smoked, and stomped it out.

Mimi didn't reply. She continued staring at her hands, rubbing each of her knuckles, and trying to make sense of what Roy had said, but she couldn't concentrate. Every time she tried, the pain in her right side caused the answers to float away—hiding somewhere she couldn't reach. "You don't have to be so cruel about it, but yes, I guess I will."

As if ashamed, Roy looked down at his own hands and said, "You *know*, you don't have to die, ma'am. There is another option. Have you considered that yet?"

"I have, but I think I'll just wait it out, and see what happens next," Mimi said, finally looking up and meeting his gaze.

"I'm sure that's the best choice anyway, ma'am. Take it from me: you're lucky."

"Do you need me to open the door?" Mimi asked, an odd smile forming on her lips.

Roy smiled back and shook his head.

"No, thanks though. I think I can let myself out," he said, and before Mimi could reply, Roy walked through the glass and out onto the street, lit another cigarette, and continued down the road. Eventually, after a few moments, he vanished, leaving Mimi, though in pain, feeling better. And for the rest of the night, as well as the succeeding three months, she never again heard Dr. Peters' voice in her head, nor did she see find Roy waiting at her counter—but none of that mattered. Right now, Mimi Sanders needed a drink, and if she wasn't mistaken, she had a few beers in the cooler. Of that, at least, she was sure.

Masquerade

Patrick MacAdoo

They stared down at Brad. The contours of their noses and divots of their eye sockets manikin-ized the otherwise unbroken black sheer alienating their faces. Hoods concealed the rest of their heads. The four of them held court from behind the scarred wooden table. Brad sat in the tiny chair, his knees an inch from grazing his chin. He awaited their judgement.

He drummed his fingers on his kneecaps. Their masks might scare a little kid if all their hoodies matched the black nylon, and if Rusty's chest didn't sport the Mustangs' logo. The daylight drifting into the attic killed the mood, too, exposing the cardboard backdrops, and the moth-eaten sheets that hung from the rafters and created the corridors of the 'labyrinth.' They'd put up the exact same hacky scenery of last Halloween's failure.

His *younger* sister, affecting a deep, supposedly sinister

monotone, said, "The Secret Four have ruled. Because of your violation last night, for the duration of the Spooktacular, you will play the Thing under the Blanket."

Brad gaped. His sister and her two buzzard friends didn't move a muscle. Rusty squirmed, but didn't say a word. Brad said, "Screw it, I quit." He shot up, his momentum overturning the kiddy chair. He stomped down the stairs and blasted out of the house.

He slitted his eyes against the October glare. The unseasonable heat tweaked his boiling blood. *The Thing under the Blanket.* Grabbing ankles. A nothing role. So what if he went off-script last night. He'd had a great idea that scared the heck out of some kids. And they had the stones to punish him? He shook his head without looking both ways as he crossed the highway. They'd just been itching for any excuse to get rid of him, because they wanted the spotlight all to themselves.

On autopilot, he traveled the route with the least chance of bumping into anyone, taking the alley, then veering towards the walkway between the firehouse and the public pool. He glanced at the blue plastic tarp covering the drained pool. A hodgepodge of single-story buildings formed the facility's opposite border. From the playground beyond, little kids shrieked. The stillness of the deserted pool clashed with the park's midsummer-like turbulence, which irked him as much as the last time he went swimming, when, as usual, scads of brats ran around, screaming like maniacs, and the Krew were playing their dunking game, sharking in on a victim and taking turns holding the unlucky runt underwater while one of their gang distracted the lifeguard. That last time, Brad spotted them circling Rusty's little bro, so he dove in and busted through their ranks, making such a ruckus that the lifeguard noticed and banned all of them from the pool for the remainder of the season. The Krew was still giving him the stinkeye in the hallways. He'd wanted more than anything to put those rich jerks in their place by making this year's Spooktacular the best thing ever.

He crossed the street and cut through backyards till he hit the big ditch that wended to the railroad tracks, tracing his secret path to the northern edge of town. He stole through a stretch of dry weeds and vaulted a barbwire fence that as late as last Halloween used to snag the cuff of his jeans on every jump. With a snarl on his face, he padded over the pasture's tall grass towards the creek. Last Halloween, after his sister's haunted attic had revved up the town for a couple of nights, the Krew created their own haunted house that put his sister's bowls of peeled grapes and sheet-covered 'ghosts' to shame. This year, he'd suggested an expansion to the basement and the backyard. He'd come up with the freak show, the games of chance, and the zip line. They should've made him Spookmaster General.

He waded into a thicket that surrounded a humongous tree on the creek's bank. He found the hidden end of a knotted rope. The rope's other end coiled around a thick branch that extended over the creek. The starbursting leafage obscured the rope's middle section. Soon, when too many leaves fell, he'd take the rope down in order to maintain secrecy. He Tarzan-ed over the muddy, foam-dappled waters to the opposite bank and cinched the rope to another tree. All the easier crossings to the island led to well-worn and oft-traveled paths.

He edged into a clutch of dense bushes while holding his sleeved forearms up against the itchweed. He followed a trail imperceptible to anybody else and halted in the fringes of tall weedage just outside his personal clearing. Skeeters buzzed. Sweat trickled down his temples. In the distance, a corn-threshing tractor rumbled. No sign of pursuers, nor of intruders.

He permitted himself an evil smile. In a small town, everybody knows everything about everybody. Except for this.

He avoided the muddy patches—footprints being a dead giveaway—and leapt onto the downed tree in the center of the shady clearing. He straddled the bole before a cluster of stunted branches. He examined the crumbly bark. The hairlines remained faint, but he knew he'd have to find another hidey-hole come winter time.

He gripped the two sturdiest branches in the cluster and lifted, easing the entire section upward, revealing a notebook-sized cutout in the dead tree's trunk. He placed the lid further up the trunk with great care lest he splinter its edges and thus leave clues for snoops. He removed a black trash bag from the cache.

He fished a small pack of baby wipes out of the bag and sterilized his hands. He took one last look around. He pulled a second black bag out of the trash bag. From the second bag, he removed the mask.

He'd made it when he was in the third grade. He'd read about papier-mâché, and over one long October, starting with a paper grocery bag and the cardboard tubes from a few rolls of toilet papers, he based his totemic design on the monsters from

Where the Wild Things Are. The trudging middle-school years had faded the black and orange paint job, but somehow, the discoloring only served to increase the mask's magic.

He slid the mask over his head. Its rough sides abraded his ears. He aligned the eyeholes. The mouth hole beastialized his breathing. He sprang from the trunk and landed in a crouch on a grassy patch at the far side of the clearing. He snaked through the thickets to the banks of the other creek.

From the brush, he scanned the lush, shadowy green. Satisfied that no interlopers lurked on either shore, he crept out onto the sandy flat and gazed into the placid waters of a demi-pool, which curled into a nook off the lazy-flowing creek. Waterbugs skimmed the surface, tracing the very figures that inspired ancient geomancers, but their patterns did not disturb his murky reflection.

Two garish faces glowered back at him, one stacked on top of the other. He ignored their savage expressions. He shifted the mask upwards, so that he peered out from between the upper face's fangs, so that he breathed through the lower face's eyeholes. After a moment of disorientation, the secret face coalesced, the upper face's goatee becoming a pointy nose.

The cunning visage smirked him away, then it turned its attention to the dumb show playing out on the water's façade, the flickering shadows and sparkles and the wakes of waterbugs revealing the solution.

✳

"Wait here," Brad said, "and give me the high sign when he's up."

Tad and Chester, lackey-level Krew members, mumbled 'yah-yah's as they slouched sideways from him. Brad frowned. They looked like they were already forgetting their promise. He gave them KG jerseys, one Celtics green, the other Timberwolves black, both of which used to hang on his bedroom wall, which they *might* deign to wear while bumming around their houses.

He picked his way through the crowd. Halloween was still over a week away, but the Spooktacular was hopping. Mothers and babysitters herded rambunctious little kids towards the games, bobbing for apples and balloon darts and all the other kiddy crap. Teen cliques struck bored poses outside the shed that housed the freak show. Unsupervised tweens hogged the zip-line route, which started from the attic window, the only escape from the Things in the Attic, and zoomed to the treehouse, the domain of the Nameless Thing, then another line did a hard right towards the neighbor's backyard, descending over the Box of Monsters, another of Brad's creations, a giant open-topped crate with seven-foot walls, high enough to keep ground-level busybodies from peeking over, and with a riser inside lifting the costumed performers within reach of the zip-line rider, so that the monsters could snatch and grab as the victim passed overhead. The zip line ended at the neighbor's clothesline pole, where the rider could flop onto a mattress or tumble across the grass. Brad had a different landing in mind for a certain rider.

Nobody paid him any mind on his way to the big oak that

supported the treehouse. Seemed like half the town had turned up. *Good.* The more witnesses the better. He took a last look at Tad and Chester, who were hitting on some sixth-graders. He didn't really need them as lookouts. The mask showed him that he needed them to testify to the rest of the Krew that he was the one who did it. To everybody else, it would look like an accident.

He resisted the urge to glance around. He tried to present a semblance of routine. Most people probably didn't know that the Secret Four had kicked him off the carnival. He began to scale the oak, climbing the hard way, branch by branch, instead of using the slats he'd nailed into the trunk himself.

He exhaled half his tension when he rose into the cover of the leafy branches. He followed familiar handholds and toe-holds around the trunk to a position outside one of the tree-house's hatchways. From his shadowy perch, he spied the zip line running from the attic to the treehouse. The eyebolts securing the other zip line were within his grasp. He waited for Jason.

A spasm kinked his bowels. He winced, then clamped his teeth together. Had to be done. Collateral damage. Jason was all right. Brad vowed to make it up to him somehow later on. Jason's heft would hard-sell negligence.

Two giggling kids zipped into the treehouse, where they screeched in the black-lit chamber of the Nameless Thing, then burst out of the hatchway on the second zip line while his sister reeled the first zip-line bar back to the attic window, before Jason plunged out of the same window. His double-extra-large frame caused the line's angle to sag nearly parallel to the ground, and he swayed back and forth, the backswing slowing his pace to a crawl and threatening to bring him to a standstill.

Bitter acid rose to the back of Brad's mouth. He closed his eyes. Jason stranded mid-line. Jason's grip weakening, then giving, then Jason dropping a story and half, then splatting onto the knobby grass below. No way to convince the Krew that he arranged the accident that shut down the Spooktacular.

Brad opened his eyes. The silly grin lifting Jason's chubby cheeks did not waver, his braking, penduluming progress did not degrade to a full stop. Once Jason entered the treehouse, Brad reached out from his leafy concealment and clamped his pliers on one of the eyebolts. He swallowed the bitter slime in the back of his throat. He tried to block out Jason's giggles and squeals. All the kids were gonna blame the poor schmoe. His hand went ice cold on the pliers as Jason began his excruciating descent from the treehouse. He fingers relaxed, the pliers loose in his grip, as Jason neared the Box of Monsters.

Brad blinked. Hurried, a little slapdash, sure, but with the Krew's resources … the kids would forget all about Jason's fall.

He squeezed the pliers and twisted the eyebolt free, then stabbed at the next one, but before the pliers touched it, the line tautened then ripped the rest of them from the tree. He whipped his head around in time to see Jason plummet into the Box of Monsters.

Brad climbed. Girls screamed, parents shouted, the commotion helping to disguise his leaf-rattling scramble. He clambered onto the three planks of the crow's nest and flattened on his belly. He pressed an eye to a crack between the boards.

Rusty, his torso still in the tentacled Thing costume,

poked his naked head out of the hatchway. The mask hadn't shown Brad this part.

Don't look up.

Brad held his breath. Rusty was the only other one who knew about the crow's nest, high up in the oak's upper branches. Three summers ago, after they had the treehouse's floor and frame secured, a few assholes, charter Krew-members, started using the half-built clubhouse as a place to sneak their cigarettes at night. Eventually, Brad's mom found butts, and threatened to make them tear it down. Of course, Brad didn't dare snitch on the Krew, and none of those rich snobs stepped forward. Rusty sucked it up and took the blame, even though he never ever touched a cigarette in his life. His mother grounded him for most of the summer, and Brad's mother forbade Brad from hanging out with Rusty for almost a year, but the treehouse survived her wrath. He swore that he'd find a place for Rusty in his new carnival … even though Rusty betrayed him first.

Rusty peered upwards. A tremor rolled down Brad's spine. If Rusty climbed up here, then everybody would find out that Jason's accident was sabotage. Nobody would say that if they hadn't kicked out Brad, who designed the course and checked the zip line every day and night, then it never would've happened.

From the grass below, Brad's sister called out Rusty's name. Rusty continued to scan the treetop. She called again, louder, plaintive, and Rusty snapped out of it and began to climb down the slat-ladder. Brad exhaled.

He waited until Rusty was all the way down and the crowd was thickest around Jason, and then he hurried down the opposite side of the trunk. He padded into the other neighbor's yard and circled around to the alley. Tad and Chester, and the rest of the grinning, high-fiving Krew, occupying their usual patch of gravel in the alley, where they killed evenings by ripping on the carnival goers, welcomed him into their ranks with backslaps and bro-shakes.

Fit to burst, Brad took a deep breath and reminded himself to play it cool, and that this was just the first phase of the plan. Somebody said, "Let's blow this Popsicle stand," and the Krew swaggered toward the park.

Brad tensed. He wanted to get straight to work. He wanted to have his Halloween carnival up and running by tomorrow night, to fill the void left by the undoubtedly doomed Spooktacular. *God* he always hated that name. But the mask had revealed that he'd have to smoke some cigarettes, and sip a beer, in order to cement his membership in the Krew.

He smiled. *Patience.* A little monkey business wouldn't kill him. If he started working in the morning, everything would go all right. The mask had promised him so.

Brad rubbed his gritty forehead. "We still got a couple days before Halloween, maybe by tomorrow night we could be up and running …."

Alan smirked. "Nice shoes, fuzznuts."

Brad's headache ratcheted a little tighter. The daylong struggle to get these lazy slugs to do anything at all made the

Secret Four's stifling of his creativity seem like nothing.

He kept his cool, despite the snickers of the others, until his gaze whisked across Lucy's intense blue eyes. He blushed and looked away, her tanned blondeness blurring in the corner of his eye. The protest that he didn't want to scuff up his good kicks while working died halfway up his throat. The Krew didn't worry about crap like that, especially Lucy, whose gigantic boobs were rumored to be fake, and whose parents bought the Bartlet Estate and let Lucy do whatever she wanted with this cottage, the former servants' quarters.

"I," said Lucy, "am *so* over haunted houses."

Brad winced. This wasn't going like the mask showed him. He must've taken a wrong turn somewhere ....

"Fuzznuts is wearing his dancing shoes," Alan said. "Somebody put on some music so fuzznuts can bust a move!"

They laughed at Brad. He fought back hot tears. He edged towards the door. The sun setting, he realized that he'd been gone all day. The Secret Four were probably still cleaning up the remnants of the Spooktacular. He needed to stall until full dark if he wanted to sneak home and avoid the nasty looks of Rusty, and of his sister, and of all the rest of them.

Chester charged through the door. Brad hopped away from him. Chester panted, then said, "They're open!" He spewed a rambling, gasping report, the upshot being that the Spooktacular was not only open for business, but also more crowded than ever. He launched into a description of the new attraction.

Lucy *snkked*, then said, "That sounds stupid."

Brad didn't think so. He felt sick to his stomach. He remembered talking to Ron, his mother's boyfriend, about the feasibility of a giant, swiveling teeter-totter, with Ron's old van serving as the platform, its roof reinforced and supporting the ride's base.

"There's a line going down the block!" Chester said.

Brad bowed his head and closed his eyes. He saw himself sitting in the tiny chair before the Secret Four, oh, their stupid hoods and their stupid, veiled faces. He cringed, seeing himself begging them to take him back.

"Everybody's over there," Chester said.

Lucy whined, "Everybody's against me."

"What we need," Alan said, "is somebody like Joe Cross."

The others murmured their reverent agreement. Joe Cross stole the cherries off the cop car while Charlie the cop was napping in the front seat. Joe Cross spray-painted a giant penis on the water tower. Brad lifted his chin. Joe Cross was dirt poor, still was, still lived at home even though he quit school three or four years ago.

Brad stepped back against the darkish wall. The image of begging the Secret Four loomed clear and large in his mind's eye while he groped for a Joe Cross-worthy stunt. He needed help to figure it out.

Brad shifted the mask and peered into the tub. He understood now that he'd gazed into the wrong water. A rivers flows, changes.

He yanked the chain and the drain's plug popped free. Kneeling on the tiles, leaning his chest against the tub's porcelain rim, he felt the churn of the swirling water in his bones. The shrieks of delighted children penetrated the bathroom's walls. The Spooktacular thronged just a few yards away. Yeah, this was the right water.

He let his eyes go out of focus. The mask's reflection distorted into a wavy, orange-streaked black blob. The orange streaks morphed into raging flames, the black into charred wood.

Burn it down.

He nodded his head, and the vision disintegrated. Strobing red light, no, *lights*, the cherries, fire trucks and cop cars, lots of them.

Like Joe Cross on steriods. Exponentially greater.

He nodded again. He got it. This stunt would be bigger than a hundred Joe Cross stunts. The Krew would forget all about Joe Cross. Everybody would.

A white slash against a brown background. Brad frowned, the narrowing of his eyes causing the vision to fade. He relaxed his brow, unfocused, and the vision returned, this time bringing several small white slashes with it, albino, upside-down rainbows ....

Smiles.

The big one, Lucy. Smiling at him, smiling up at him, and the others, smaller, smiling up at him like courtiers smiling up at their king.

A sucking gurgle snapped him out of his trance. The last of the water circled the drain, then disappeared. That was fine.

He'd seen all he needed to see.

∗

The boards of the rickety front porch squeaked under Brad's butt. He yawned. The Spooktacular's noise had kept him from drifting off, and the night's unseasonable heat had driven him out of the house. They'd finally shut down. Pretty soon they'd be done cleaning up back there.

He gripped the crumpled, rolled-up mouth of the over-sized paper bag. He didn't dare leave the mask unattended. He rocked backwards in preparation of levering himself to his feet.

Footsteps *scritched* through the grass along the side of the house. Brad resettled and placed the bag in his lap. He had to seem chilled out, innocent. Skulking inside now might make him look like he was up to something.

Rusty stepped into view and both looked away. Rusty said, "W'sup?"

"Nada." Brad hoped that was it, that Rusty would keep on keeping-on.

Rusty stopped and leaned against the porch's banister. "What's in the bag?"

Brad sat still while thrashing for something to say. *Tell the exact truth.* His voice came out calm when he said, "Halloween costume."

Rusty sighed. "Tell ya the truth, I'll be glad when Halloween's over."

Brad's grip on the bag tightened. Somewhere on the edge

of town, a car coughed to life. Rusty performed a lazy swing of his leg, the soles of his sneaker skimming tips of grass. He said, "I can talk to them. Getcha back in."

Brad twitched. He almost blurted out that Halloween was tomorrow, that there was only one night left. *Be cool. It'll throw them off.* He stared at the bag. The mask was fragile. He could mash his hands together, pulverize it, right now.

"We could use ya," Rusty said, while looking at the deserted street. "The thing with the zip line would'a never happened."

Brad caught himself nodding. "Whatever." He held his breath. That wasn't what he meant to say.

"Cool." Rusty pushed himself off the porch and cut across the neighbor's front yard.

Brad exhaled. He knew his mom had been on their asses to let him back in. Rusty would probably threaten to quit if they didn't. The Secret Four would give in. They wouldn't risk anything going wrong on Halloween. *The Thing under the Blanket.*

He shuddered.

The King of the Krew.

Brad sat on high. Red lights revolved and reflected off windows across the street. They'd put the fire out, but char still tainted the air, the red glow still showed tendrils of smoke rising from the rear of the house.

The alarm seemed to attract the whole town. Folks milled on the sidewalks on both sides of the street, and in both neighbor's yards, outside the yellow caution tape. No question, the fire destroyed the Spooktacular. But stray embers had ignited the back porch.

The paper bag rested on the pickup's bed between Brad's feet. So did his backpack, stuffed with his schoolbooks and a couple changes of clothes. His sister sat in the beater's cab, and kept glancing at him over her shoulder, shooting him dirty looks. She knew. The rest of the Secret Four, including Rusty, mingling with the rubberneckers on the sidewalk, wouldn't look at him, even though he perched atop the bed's side panel.

He spotted Krew members. He slid all the way down into the bed and hunched below the top of the side panel. It wasn't supposed to go like this. The back of the house wasn't even burned that bad, but Charlie, serving as both the chief of police and the fire marshal, wouldn't let them go back inside until a thorough inspection could be completed, which might take weeks. In the interim, they'd be staying with Gertie, his mom's best friend, who had three kids of her own, and who was just as poor as they were. Their landlord would seize this opportunity to kick them out for good. His mother was already talking about a trailer as their only option. He winced. *Trailer trash.*

He peeked over the side panel. The Krew's ranks had swollen, with Lucy at the center. Chester spied him, shouted, and pointed, and they all *laaaaughed*. Brad ducked down to the grimy bed. Everything the mask had showed him had come true.

He placed a palm against each side of the bag. He could clap them together, like smashing cymbals together, and annihilate the damned thing.

He blinked. He exhaled a shaky breath. He removed his damp palms and rubbed them against his blue-jeaned thighs. He slitted his eyes. He needed the mask, to show him how to get out of this mess, and how to get even with the Krew. Orange embers floated in the night air. His nostrils flared. His mouth twisted into a cruel sneer. He'd make them all trailer trash.

Bumps in the Night

Jovan Jones

The pitter-patter of the rain tapping on the windows provided the back drop for the leaky faucet in the kitchen sink. The refrigerator hummed steadily while a teapot hissed on the stove. Sinclair Wheaton sat in her dingy recliner reading the local section of *The Charlotte Observer*. The headline read:

Costume Store Owner Murdered: In an apparent robbery, costume store owner, Julius Vincent, was bludgeoned to death by an unknown object just minutes before closing his store, Comedy and Tragedy. Investigators have no leads at this time and are . . . .

A comforting thought entered Sinclair's mind. *Wow. There's a psycho walking around with a costume looking to bash some heads on Halloween. Thank God for that .38 under the sink.*

It was six o'clock P.M. The neighborhood kids would start knocking on the door any minute. Sinclair arose from her seat and stretched. In the middle of her yawn, there was an obstreperous knock on the front door. The loud rap discombobulated her.

"Hold on! I'm coming!" she said.

Sinclair hurried to the door and scooped a handful of candy from a large wooden salad bowl propped on a wicker end table. She slipped her vampire fangs in her mouth and opened the door, "Happy Halloween!" she exclaimed. Nobody was there. She looked around, and didn't notice anyone walking the streets either. "I must be . . . ." *Doon, doon, doon, doon!* The sound was coming from the service porch.

Sinclair whipped around and clutched her heart. The palpitations in her chest traveled to her throat, blocking her ability to scream. She froze like a skinny dipper in Lake Michigan in January. "Who's there?" Her contralto voice phonated to soprano. The washing machine buzzer sounded off. Sinclair calmed down. *Of course! The washer must've been off balance.* She had forgotten about the load of clothes in the washer. She took a deep breath and then laughed at her over-reaction.

Sinclair smiled, reminiscing about past Halloweens. She thought about trick-or-treating, the haunted houses, and her favorite scary movies from the eighties. Her reverie was interrupted by a real knock at the front door. Sinclair jumped and stared at the door like a foreign object before collecting her nerve to answer it.

"Trick or treat!" There were three little kids with their treat bag ready for teeth rotting goodness. One girl was about seven or eight. She was heavily made up like a circus clown with the red clown shoes; yellow and white polka-dot suit, and that creepy black and white clown smile. Another little girl had fairy wings, an iridescent wand, and a tiara bejeweled with different colored plastic Dora's all around it. Sinclair looked upon the third kid with confusion. The boy was about six or seven with a NY Yankees uniform with fake syringes taped all around his arms. *Boys like sports and zombies so . . . .*

"Come on, A-Rod. The nice lady already gave you a hand full of candy," the kids' father said as he waved to the kids to come. Sinclair covered her mouth in surprise to the revelation and laughed hard at the satiric costume. The streets were now vibrant with children looking cute and demonic with their parents in tow, waiting to taste a few treats of their own, like candy pimps.

She extinguished the porch light once the candy ran out. It was time to relax, and enjoy a flick on the tube. Sinclair leaned back in her recliner and grabbed the remote to her twenty-seven inch Mitsubishi tube television. The red numbers on the cable box resembled predatory eyes lurking in the shadows. *Poltergeist 2* was on AMC.

I'm your friend, and I know what you are thinking.

How?

Now, let me in. Let's talk about it. Let me in.

You're my friend.

Let me in.

Daddy!

Now! Before it's too late!

No.

You're gonna die in there, all of you, you're gonna diiieee!

The television's blue light danced like demons around a bonfire on the naked flesh colored wall of her living room.

Sinclair's eyelids grew heavy staring at the T.V. She sank into the cushioned recliner and nodded off.

Psychic spies from China try to steal your mind's elation . . . . Little girls from Sweden dream of silver screen quotations and if you want these kind of dreams it's Californiacation . . . .

The loud music blaring from her neighbor, Ryan's black seventy-six Camarro jolted her awake. Sinclair stood and shuffled to the window. She peeped through the blinds. A brown skin beauty with long flowing hair emerged from the passenger side. She strutted to the front porch as Ryan's eyes stayed glued to the basketballs concealed under her skintight dress. *What a creep!* Sinclair used to be attracted to Ryan, until one day she saw him high out of his mind, and realized he resembled the image of Jesus on the cross. Her cell phone rang.

"Hello."

"Hey baby, it's me." Ryan's raspy Wolfman Jack voice was slurred.

"Don't you have company?" Sinclair asked.

"Do I ever! Wow! They say once you go black you never go back, but I'd come back for you, baby."

"What do you want, Ryan?" She tried to conceal the fact that he'd made her smile.

"Seriously, I wanted to let you know that I saw some dude walking through your yard, but I don't see him now. I'm making sure you're cool."

She shuddered at the thought of some weirdo scoping her pad. The hairs on the back of her neck stood up. "Hold on," Sinclair jogged to the service porch and looked out of the screen door. She didn't see anyone, "I'm cool. Thanks for looking out."

"Right on, baby," he hung up, leaving Sinclair a little on edge.

She went back to her recliner to finish the movie and fell asleep again. A faint clink jarred her from her slumber. She got up to put her clothes in the dryer.

"Don't tell me the washer is leaking," Sinclair flipped the light switch and saw a big red puddle. "Oh, God," she stumbled back into the door gripping the door jamb. A low clicking noise tapped on the door. The latch on the door was dangling. She always secured that latch. Her body tensed. Sinclair honed in on the sounds of her environment.

The rain plopped audibly on the roof. The sound likened to a phalanx of rats scurrying atop a hardwood floor. The kitchen faucet's drip had become sonorous. The wind whistled its cold breath through the poorly insulated windows. The house creaked like an old man's knees. Sinclair's eyes widened with vigilance. She loosed her grip of the doorjamb, and maneuvered around the puddle. Red liquid was splattered on the washing machine, too. The frightened woman cautiously approached it. The perversion of curiosity intrigued her like a rakish lover. *What if the man Ryan saw was still outside? What if he's in the house?* The sound of shattering glass jarred Sinclair from her contemplation.

She desperately tried to find her coordination as she fumbled with the locks. Heavy footsteps pounded the hardwood floor. She glanced over her shoulder. A man's work boot poked out from behind the wall of the washroom. Sinclair shot through the back door. Her backyard connected to a stretch of woods that lead to a soccer field at the YMCA. With the agility of a thirty-seven year old human resource manager, and the fright of a rabbit being chased by a hawk's shadow she staggered and bumped painfully through the woods. Sinclair tripped and came eye to eye with a couple of hissing, pale-faced possums. She yelped and they scurried into some bushes.

"Hey! Hey!" The man pursued her. His voice provoked her to rise on all fours and get upright. The vegetation was dense. Sinclair hoped it would be difficult for her pursuer to locate her through the thicket. Surveying the woods, she saw the silhouette of a thick bodied man nearby. His face was shadowed.

Remnants of light from the street lamps weakened as they ventured farther into the woods. Ominous rain clouds blocked the moon light, as they cried from Heaven. Sinclair executed her steps with exaggerated deliberation, making sure she didn't lose her footing again. Her senses heightened. Anxiety colluded with the fall air to induce a vexing chill through her flesh. The wet leaves were slick on the sodden ground. Dead branches resembled amputated limbs tossed about her feet. The stadium lights from the soccer field barely penetrated the coppice of dogwood trees, loblolly pines, and several other piedmont region shrubs.

Sinclair lost sight of her pursuer. He was sure to hear her fighting through the bushes. She would have to find another way through. *You can do this Sinclair.* Her attempt at reassurance faltered when the man reappeared about fifty feet away with a flashlight scanning the woods. He had a determined march as his heavy boots mashed the forest ground littered with those amputated limbs of birch. "Clair! Woman, have you lost your marbles?" The sound of her name repressed her flight mode. How could Jason Voorhees know her name? "I know things have been rocky . . . ."

"Jeremy?" Jeremy was Sinclair's on and off again boyfriend for the last three years.

"Don't run from me, babe. I just want to talk, about us."

Sinclair paused, before erupting into a guffaw. Jeremy followed her raucous laughter and came to her. "I love you, but we're going to have to buy you some more marbles," his tanned skin had become pale in the cold rain, and his Carolina blue eyes were weary. Sinclair felt comfort gazing into them, the laughter easing her tension. Jeremy shook his head in amazement. He wrapped his arms around her and kissed her giggling lips. "Let's get out of these clothes," he stroked her chin, and then led Sinclair back to the house with her hand in his fist. The image of the red puddle on the floor rekindled her terror.

"What did you do Jeremy? Oh, my God, what did you do?"

"Wha . . .," his face contorted like he'd sucked a lemon.

"*What* did you do?"

His mouth opened, but only the smell of garlic and Michelob came out.

"The blood, Jeremy! What's the story behind all that blood?"

He smiled devilishly, "It isn't blood. I spilled sangria on my clothes on my way over from work. I wanted to surprise you, and maybe have some drinks, ya know. It's been a while since we've just chilled out together."

They'd split up again due to a late night text from a woman named Candice saying what a good time she had with Jeremy, and next time hopefully they wouldn't have to rush. When Sinclair confronted him about it he denied doing anything with her, but the denial was a contradiction of the evidence at hand. After the evil rumination of worrisome thoughts, she felt it best to break the relationship off again. That was two weeks ago. She figured he must've come because he was horny and needed some relief. If that was the case, they were in the same boat. That's why she never took back the key. She didn't know if it was love or a perverted infatuation with a gorgeous jerk, but whatever it was, like Diana Ross said, "She didn't need no cure."

This may come as some surprise, but I miss you. I can see through all of your lies, but still, I miss you. Sinclair cuddled with Jeremy in bed after making love. Sade's sensual lyrics spoke to her as if her old component stereo were a medium for her soul. The night's tension was gone. The spirit of Halloween had truly set her ablaze, she reasoned. Sinclair's mind played tricks on her the entire night. First, she mistook the unbalanced load of clothes knocking around in the washer as someone pounding on the door. Then Sinclair thought the sangria was blood. The glass she heard shatter in the kitchen was her water pitcher, Jeremy explained. She rested her head on his hairy chest. *He needs to clip those nose hairs.* From her angle, it looked like the boogers in his nose were growing beards. She sat up and started out of the bed to grab her nose trimmers when the disturbing image of the back door's latch dangling popped into her head.

"Wake up, Jeremy!" She nudged him to no avail, but then pulled the hairs around his nipple.

"What . . . what are you . . .," he ceased his attempt at getting an explanation, and focused his eyes on her voluptuous porcelain hued breast. He moved toward them with his mouth open. *Smack!*

Sinclair slapped the back of his neck. "What are you doing?" He asked.

"Why did you leave the latch on the back door hanging?"

"Woman, if I didn't love you, to the moon!" Jeremy impersonated Ralph Kramden, "I never opened the back door. I came through the front. You were asleep. I didn't want to wake you, so I took my clothes to the service porch."

"Well, how is it that you got sangria all over there, but not in the rest of the house?"

"I had them in a plastic shopping bag. It must've leaked once I set it down. Sorry babe. Did you want me to clean it up?"

"What are you handicapped? Of course, clean it up. Wait a sec. How could you not know you left scary juice all over the floor? You didn't notice it dripping all over the washing machine?" Sinclair was getting aggravated just thinking about Jeremy's inconsideration.

"What are you talking about?" He rolled over and sighed.

"Did you at least turn on the dryer when you put my clothes in, or did you just toss them on top of the dryer?" Sinclair asked.

"Claire, babe, listen to me, please. I never put my clothes in the washer. Therefore I did not take yours out. I was trying to be as quiet as possible seeing that you were snoring like a bear in hibernation. Look, I didn't even know the stuff was on the floor until you went running through the woods like a lunatic, and I went after you like a mental asylum orderly. Now stop abusing me and go back to sleep. Your psychosomatic rage has drained me. Love you. Goodnight," he turned around, farted on her leg and went back to sleep. Once the putrid smell of deep fried chitterlings and spoiled milk subsided, Sinclair disregarded her paranoid inhibition about someone having been in her house, and attributed it to her over active imagination. She shook her head and drifted to sleep.

Sinclair awoke to the sound of water splashing into the toilet bowl. *I hope while he's up, he takes the initiative to clean up his mess.* She stretched and felt cold feet. Somebody was pissing in the toilet, but it wasn't Jeremy. The hallway floor creaked. The intruder was coming toward the bedroom. The curtains were drawn and the lights out. She reached over to turn on the lamp atop the nightstand. *Click, click, click!* The power had been cut. She nudged her slumbering boyfriend to wake him. He did not respond. She twisted his nipples and slapped his face. Right as she fixed her mouth to scream his name . . . *Flick.* A tiny flame illuminated a dark chiseled face. The stranger stood in the doorway, lighting a cigarette.

Sinclair froze. In the second it took to light the cigarette, she saw his dark eyes. The flame reflected off of them like the last candle in Tenebrae Service.

"Sweet, Sinclair Wheaton, you are definitely a work of art," his voice traveled through the black room with the depth of a minor g chord on the cello.

"Get up, baby," she pulled, tugged, and slapped until she felt warm wetness on his chest.

"Ha, ha, ha," the stranger's nefarious laugh almost incited Sinclair to have a bile movement. "You need a man who can take care of you, you know, like you deserve," the cherry hanging from the cigarette extended as he sucked in the smoke.

Sinclair's stomach wrenched as she dry heaved. She asked, "What did you do?" The question was meant to be a thought, but escaped her mouth. Sinclair's eyes adjusted to the dark. She saw Jeremy's silhouette lying next to her. Horrible images of his neck sliced caused her to wrench again only this time sour bile accompanied it. "Why?" Lying next to her dead boyfriend, and completely naked while a strange man played psycho games with her in the dark was annoying her to the point of madness.

"Coward," she whipped out of the bed knocking over the lamp. The sound of the shattering light bulb somehow gave her a surge of courage, like the bell for a fighter in a boxing match. The amber light of the cancer stick fell to the ground and the dark figure in the doorway stomped it out. Steps thundered toward her. The air in the room was thick. An indistinguishable musk deodorant invaded her nostrils. Sinclair's newfound courage betrayed her, and she made a dash in the direction of the bathroom. Her legs felt like marble pillars weighing her down. She stubbed her middle right toe on the corner of the door, fell into the john and landed hard on her left shoulder. She kicked the door shut. Sinclair got to her knees and locked the door.

"Don't be frightened, sweetheart. I'm not going to hurt

you. I want to make you feel good," his voice trebled through the door, like they were occupying the same room. Her thoughts raced with a nerve-racking pace. She was lathered in rank, nervous sweat. The sickly smell permeating her pores made her nauseous all over again. A hard thud emanated from the door and knocked her back. Another violent thud came this time accompanied by the jiggling of the doorknob.

"No," she held the knob tight to keep it from being opened. She wept, while he grunted, ramming his shoulder into the door. The crackling sound of wood splitting broke her down. "Why are you doing this?" Sinclair folded into a fetal position conceding her strength to make her soul right with God. In an eerie suddenness, the pounding on the door ceased, as did the jiggling of the doorknob. The peach colored vanity lights illuminated the room. The relief from the darkness felt as if she had been freed from a body bag.

Her bathrobe hung over her head. She put it on. It was comforting. She didn't feel as vulnerable. Sure, the murdering mystery man was probably still out there, but at least she could see, which increased her odds to survive. With that in mind her nerves settled a bit. An empowering piece of information sparked her memory.

If someone breaks in, run to the bathroom. Lock yourself in, cock the gun and call the police. Her father had instructed after buying her a .38 Ruger and putting it under her bathroom sink. *Crooks usually look for guns in drawers, under beds, closets, but they don't bother with the john too quick.* Sinclair pursed her lips, pulled her hair back on her sweaty head and retrieved the gun from under the sink.

The anger, fear, and vulnerability all mixed with the unreasonable insecurity of being concerned about how she looked naked. It shouldn't have mattered to her, but it did, and for that illogical insecurity she felt a rage stimulating her vengeful ambition. She turned the handle slowly, and eased the door open. Her hands were shaking. Sinclair clutched the pistol in firing position. Her heart pounded in her ears like Sheila E on the drums. She peeped around the corner. An ominous looking skin headed black man was hovering over Jeremy with a bloody knife and cynical grin on his mug.

In a flash, Sinclair pivoted on her back foot like she was going to throw a punch. She sized the man up and fired. He threw his hands up, but she squeezed the trigger, delivering the bullet to his heart.

"Jesus Christ," Jeremy's muffled cry seeped through the ringing in her ears. Sinclair stood wide eyed and perplexed. In her confusion, she dropped the gun, and it fired. Jeremy slid his bridges on and checked the fallen intruder's pulse. "I think he's dead," Sinclair read his lips. She couldn't hear anything but the high pitched ringing from the shot. His frantic disposition shifted to a solemn slump. "What have you done, Claire?" He interlocked his fingers on top of his head, let his arms drop back to his side, and then punched the wall in frustration. His actions were contradictive to the current situation. They were the victims. He had blood all over his neck, face, and chest. *You're lucky to be alive, yet you . . . I . . . .*

"It was a Halloween prank, Clair," his eyes were filling with tears as his voice cracked. "Harold was my friend. We went to the army together. We . . . ."

"Stupid! Stupid idiot! Who pulls a prank like this?" Unconsciously, she snatched the gun off the floor. She didn't realize it, but she was pointing the gun at Jeremy while she spit an array of expletives, and deprecation from her throat.

"Hey, hey, hey! Calm down, please," his palms were waist high and down in a calming gesture.

Sinclair closed her eyes and welcomed the calming effect of the darkness behind her eyelids. When she opened her eyes the room looked like a Broadway stage set. Blood oozed from Harold's chest onto the flowered throw rug beside the bed.

Sangria. "Call 911," Sinclair said.

Jeremy saw her crazed face. She was laughing uncontrollably. She had lost her mind.

Lead detective Rondale Pearson sat in the recliner, questioning Sinclair and Jeremy. His stoic, swarthy face with leathery jaw from shaving practically every day for almost forty years was intimidating. He preferred it that way. They could've gone outside or to the police station. It was policy to do so. Detective Pearson learned early in life that following the rules all the time could make you stagnate. Jeremy's explanation about his intended prank to have Harold stalk Sinclair and act like he murdered him was so stupid that Pearson couldn't help but to think it true.

"Ronnie, check this out man," a slim, bird faced man with a New England accent requested Detective Pearson's presence on the service porch.

Jeremy addressed Sinclair when Pearson left the room, "You think he thinks we set him up to be killed, don't you?" He put forth no effort to whisper.

"Do you think we should be talking right now?" Sinclair questioned with sarcasm while shaking her head no. "You're an idiot, Jeremy. Shut up," she did whisper, but her eyes were screaming.

"You two come here, please," Pearson called from the service porch.

They complied. Pearson's peepers burned holes through them. Sinclair would've been upset about his accusatory glare if it wasn't so debilitating. She wondered how a culpable person might hold up under his gaze.

"What happened here, Jeremy?" He asked. His gaze was steady on Sinclair.

Jeremy tittered, "I spilled sangria all over myself. I . . ."

"Yeah, we know that ain't blood," the detective pointed at the bag of clothes. "What's this?" He nodded at the washing machine. Sinclair hadn't noticed before, but the shade of red was different, so was the texture. The stuff on the washer was deep red, almost burgundy, and thicker. The stuff on the floor was more like fruit punch. Pearson opened the top of the machine with his gloved hand. It smelled like strong brie cheese and rotten eggs. Jeremy jumped back into the wall. Sinclair inched toward Detective Pearson. She looked at him, preparing for that predatory stare, but he was grinning with the slim forensic investigator. Sinclair gaped in horror.

The severed head of her next door neighbor, Ryan had

been shoved in the washing machine. His long black hair was stuck to the tub. It looked like ruffles in a coffin. One eye was half opened and the other was hanging out of the socket. Chunks of pink flesh were scattered throughout, and part of his bottom lip had been torn off, exposing his jaw that housed nicotine stained teeth. Sinclair lifted her head slowly and met the detective's eyes, "Questions?"

"You better know it."

The man watched from the woods. His hands dirty with Ryan's blood. He watched the scene unfold. There were a few hours until dawn, but Halloween was officially over. The voices pleading for blood in his mind were acquiesced. The costume shop owner never suspected a man with a cane would murder him, let alone with such brutality. He relished the memory. Deception was so easy in a world where people forget they're still animals. He wanted to witness the look on the woman's face when she opened the washing machine, but a big black guy beat him to the punch. Right when he closed the lid on the washer, the black man slipped through a window in the living room. *Maybe that man was shot. Hmmm . . . better him then me.*

The watcher pulled the large bamboo earrings out of his pocket and dangled them in front of his eyes like chimes above a baby's crib. He pictured the look on her face when she awoke to her boyfriend's head severed from his body. The woman screamed so loud she gave him a headache. He walked through the woods and came out the other side to the YMCA's soccer field where his old F-150 idled with Ryan's girlfriend gagged and bound in the passenger seat.

"You are really pretty. You already know that though, don't you?" He slid his fingertips up her thighs. "Too bad I'm married, because you are something else. I mean it," he pulled out a jagged tooth hunting knife, and stared at it as if it were a Van Goethe masterpiece. His thunderstorm grey eyes were glazed and vicious, but his tone of voice was cheerful. He set down the knife, started the truck, and headed toward the highway singing along to Michael Jackson's "Thriller." His mind conceived many creatively cruel ways of torturing the brown bombshell begging for mercy with her pathetic eyes.

A Night Behind Bars

DJ Tyrer

The great concrete edifice was as intimidating in the dying sunlight as might be expected for a prison. I was glad I was there for a Hallowe'en party and not to serve a sentence. A friend of a friend had arranged for it to be opened for one night only for fun; it had been shut down three decades earlier.

Stepping through the gloomy entrance, I realised I had to be one of the first to arrive. Nobody was in the lobby, unless dangling plastic skeletons or a manikin clad in an arrowed convict uniform counted. I was glad the invitation said 'costume optional.'

"Hello?" There was no reply.

It was ironic that Neal had managed to find such a perfect place to hold a Hallowe'en party only to go and spoil it all by decorating it in such a tasteless fashion with the fake cobwebs, rubber spiders and plastic pumpkins that became synonymous with the date. The long reception desk that dominated one side of the lobby was arrayed with trays of nibbles and bottles of drink that further undercut the stark horror of the penitentiary.

"Hello?" There was still no reply, so I decided to help myself to a bottle of beer before going to take a look around the place. There was only one way out of the lobby, a large archway—barred gates rolled aside—that led into the prison proper. Unfortunately, the enormous hall that lay beyond was not so limited in options and I found myself scratching my chin as I tried to decide which door to choose.

I reasoned that as Neal was in charge of things, he'd probably decided to set himself up in the Governor's Office. It looked as if he had—there was a bank of monitors and a huge leather chair—but he wasn't in situ. I wondered if there was some way of contacting him, but I didn't fancy messing with the equipment. I stepped back into the hall instead.

"Hello!" I shouted out as loudly as I could. "Hell-looo! Anybody there? Knock once for yes." I laughed at my feeble joke. "Screw this," I muttered and decided to pass the time looking about. The invitation had described how some of the cells were supposed to be haunted, and I thought it might be interesting to take a look around to experience the atmosphere.

Swinging open a heavy wooden door marked, "Cell Wing A," I strolled along the wide, concrete passageway that led to a barred gateway, which swung open at the lightest touch. The cellblock had three levels of cells either side of a central passage. The shadowy interior gave a sense of despair and perhaps a little menace, as if the emotions of a half-century's worth of prisoners had imprinted themselves upon the cells that had held them.

I gave a little chuckle at the morbid thought. I wasn't sure whether to be glad that Neal and his decorators had resisted the urge to fill the cells with further convict-styled manikins or whether a spot of tackiness might have made the place a little more bearable. Still, I wasn't going to let my mind run away.

It was either stay where I was or go back and wait for someone else to arrive. As I was here, I decided to take a look in one of the cells. They had the sort of door with a flap in it rather than a barred gate.

Opening the door, which was unlocked, I stepped inside. The cell was small and grey with two raised slabs of concrete to serve as beds and no toilet or sink. There was just a small barred window. It must have been horrendous to be locked up for hours on end in such a place.

I heard a clang and a click. The door slammed and locked.

I span around, dropping my beer, and shouted, but no amount of harsh language broke down the door. I heaved against it and it wouldn't budge. What did I expect of a cell door? They were built to keep people in.

Hammering on the door, I shouted for help. It seemed rather hopeless, unless ghost hunters came. Whoever had locked me in wasn't about to let me out. Even if there was anyone about, I doubted whether my shouts would reach anywhere else in the prison. But, I was in luck. I heard footsteps, then the door unlocked and swung open.

"What happened?" It was Neal. Although I didn't know him personally, I'd seen his photos online. I wondered if he locked me in, only he seemed genuinely bemused to see me. "I saw you on the monitors wandering in here and thought I'd come say 'hi', then heard you shouting and, well, here we are…."

"Someone locked me in…."

"There's nobody in here but you and me."

"But…." I didn't want to accuse him, especially as he seemed genuinely perplexed.

He shrugged. "Guess it must've swung shut behind you."

"I guess."

"Well, I see you found the beer," he nodded towards the broken glass on the floor. "How about another brewski, eh?"

"Yeah, sure." I was feeling a bit embarrassed about the whole thing and about having felt so scared. "Um, sorry about being a nuisance."

"No worries, uh?"

"Will. I'm a friend of Marcus, Marcus Van Camp."

"Oh, yeah, Marcus—great guy! Will? Not Marcus' mate, Will the writer?"

I nodded. "Guilty as charged." I was feeling embarrassed again, hating to be the centre of attention.

"Yeah, I've read some of your blog—great stuff! Pleased to meet you. I'm Neal, of course, but I bet you guessed that already!" We were back in the hallway. "Right, well, let me get you that beer. Aha! Looks like some more of my guests have arrived! Welcome, welcome!"

Just as we'd entered the lobby, two men and two women had come in through the entrance. They were dressed in costumes: an old-time cop and—oh, yes—a convict with arrows on his outfit, and a sexily-dressed policewoman and what I assumed was meant to be a gangster's moll with a long feather boa.

Names were exchanged, although they didn't stick, and beers handed out. Neal's staff for the evening, dressed in immaculate, old-style prison warder uniforms, appeared from wherever they'd been and began to oversee the buffet.

As more guests arrived and the lobby began to fill, I positioned near the entrance, hoping to see Marcus or anyone else I knew. I'd never been much of a party person and always felt a little out of my depth, never quite sure how to interact with others, how to fit in: perpetually embarrassed.

At last, I spotted Marcus. He strolled in wearing a smart suit: that was typical Marcus, stylish and happy to flash the greenbacks. Steve and Marian were with him and a couple of women I didn't know. Steve was Marcus' brother, a slightly younger, less assured version of him. Marian was Steve's on-again/off-again girlfriend and was in a slinky, little black dress that really looked smoking hot. The other two women were dressed in even skimpier dresses, red ones, with far too much makeup and were clinging to Marcus as if they couldn't stand alone.

"Hey, Will! Glad you made it!"

"Hi, Marcus! Hi, Steve, Marian!"

"Met these two miscreants on the way in," Marcus nodded at Steve and Marian who greeted me. "And, these are, uh, Nina and Wanda."

"Juanita!"

"Yeah, Juanita. Girls, this is Will."

"Hi." I didn't give them much consideration. Marcus was

always draped with women. I didn't know if it was because he's so smooth or if he rents escorts, but women constantly surrounded him. I did not think he could function if he were unaccompanied!

"How're things, Will? How's the blog going?"

We exchanged pleasantries and the usual small talk for a few moments, then Neal spotted Marcus and came over to offer effusive greetings and direct them to the reception desk-cum-bar for drinks and snacks. He and Marcus were like a mutual appreciation society—very annoying!

Finally, they drifted over to the bar and I went with them, helped myself to some roasted peanuts and another beer.

More people had arrived and Neal had produced a loudhailer from somewhere, which he used to address us, silencing the hubbub of the conversation.

"Welcome, everybody! Thank you for coming to my little soiree!"

There was a ripple of laughter at that. I couldn't say I found it that funny.

"Help yourselves to the goodies on the bar. There's a disco in the dining hall and you are free to wander about the place, explore. But, be warned, do not tread lightly—this prison is haunted!"

There were a few snickers at the theatrical way in which he announced that, a couple of gasps, and a general perking up of interest. I suddenly wondered if that meant he was responsible for locking me into the cell, hoping I'd spread a little fear amongst my fellow revellers.

"Now, if you're interested in searching for ghosts, you can

poke about yourselves or join me on a little ghost hunt. The main hauntings are a cell on the second floor of B Wing where a prisoner committed suicide, a solitary-confinement cell below the Punishment Block and the infamous Gas Chamber where over two-dozen men and women were put to death for their terrible crimes.... Please, avoid those locations if you have a weak heart...."

Funny!

"I trust that, unlike the convicts who were imprisoned here, you'll have fun and enjoy your stay here! The ghost tour starts in fifteen minutes from outside the door to the Governor's Office—through there. So, party!"

There was a cheer and the room began to clear: doubtless most were off to the disco.

"Coming on the tour?" Steve asked me.

I shrugged, hoping I seemed disinterested. "Maybe, although Neal already set me up for one ghostly encounter already tonight...." I quickly described what had happened, downplaying my panic.

Marcus laughed. "Oh, he's probably got some more great scares lined up. Should be fun. Think I'll take the girls. You've got to come, prove you're not scared."

I shrugged again. "Whatever. Guess I will."

We slowly strolled through to the hallway and lingered by the office door, waiting for Neal to finish mingling with his guests. I just hoped he wouldn't aim any scares at me—playing the patsy once a night was enough for me.

Finally, having returned to the office, Neal exited it, saying, "Everything's ready." He was followed by an overweight man in jeans and a t-shirt printed with 'Bite Me' and a set of vampire fangs.

Other guests had drifted over and beside myself and Marcus' party, there was a couple dressed as a cowboy and saloon girl, a skinny bearded guy who'd come as a Jedi, and an obese, wheezing man in a two-piece outfit printed with a skeleton.

"Hi, everybody! So, you're ready to brave the true terrors of this fearful place?" One of Marcus' pieces of arm candy squeaked in fear and Neal laughed. "It's not too late to leave!"

"Don't be a killjoy, baby," said Marcus.

"Whatever."

"Good." Neal beamed. "Right, this is my assistant, Al, and he has some ghost hunting gear for anyone who'd like some."

A Dictaphone was passed to Marcus, a digital thermometer to the cowboy, a device for detecting electrical fields to the Jedi and a magnetometer to the obese man. He also handed out a couple of flashlights. We were quite the ragbag band of investigators into the unknown.

"Right, if we're all ready, let's get this investigation into the afterlife underway!"

Leading the way, Neal chattered away happily about the brutal regime that had kept the prisoners in line, the punishments, the deaths in the Gas Chamber and the riots that broke out. The general consensus of the group was that this was all quite entertaining, even amusing, with little dissent. I suspected he made it up—or, at least, embellished—most of it.

After a few minutes, we found ourselves in B Wing and clattered our way up a steel stairway to the second floor and the cell that was supposedly one of the most haunted places in the prison. The cell itself was no different to the one into which I'd ventured earlier, except there was a video camera on a tripod in one corner.

"The camera's hooked up to the monitors to record any spooky stuff that happens," Neal informed us.

"Nothing so far," muttered Al.

"There are a few too many for all of us to fit inside, so if those of you who are a little more nervous would like to stay out here with Al and me, that way we can make sure the door stays safely open. The rest of you get in there with those instruments and see whether you can detect the ghost."

Marcus, the cowboy, Jedi and obese man went inside obediently, and I decided to follow them in lest I be thought a coward. Marian gave Steve a nudge and he joined us. He didn't look too keen.

The others set their equipment.

"There's a definite chill here in this corner," said the cowboy.

"This magnetometer is jumping a bit," said the fat guy, "does that mean anything?"

"Maybe," said Al.

The Jedi had nothing to report.

Just then, Steve exclaimed a startled, "I think I heard something!"

"Try the Dictaphone, Marcus," urged Neal. "Play it back, see if you caught anything."

He did as he was asked; playing back from the moment we entered the cell and everything everybody said. There was the faintest whisper of something before Steve's exclamation.

"There!"   I was caught up in the moment despite my doubts.

"Go back a few seconds," his brother told him.

He played it again. It was difficult to hear. It took several goes adjusting the settings to make it understandable.

"Kill you!" At least, that's what we agreed it probably was saying. Assuming it was anything other than random static.

"Nice," muttered the saloon girl.

With just a little dim moonlight coming in through the window and the beams of flashlights to hold back the shadows, it was spooky to listen to. It was easy to imagine the unseen ghost of some homicidal maniac wanting to do us all harm!

Finally, having ascertained nothing certain, we left.

"The Punishment Block and the Gas Chamber are separate from the main building," Neal told us as he led us back down the stairs and through to the Governor's Office so that he could check whether the footage had caught anything. It hadn't, unless you were interested in close-ups of Jedi cloaks. Even if it had been capable, there were just too many of us in the cell to allow it to record any ghost that may have been present. Not that there were any ghosts. I thought that it was all just part of the entertainment or our wishful thinking. How wrong I was!

Having checked the footage, Neal took us out across the exercise yard and through a gate from which a path led to a low concrete building he identified as the Gas Chamber.

Gesturing at the sparse grass either side, he commented, "The bodies of all those executed here are buried on either side of this path."

"Eww!" exclaimed Marian.

"Gross!" exclaimed shrieked one of Marcus' escorts.

It was amusing to see everyone glancing nervously about. People could be a bit odd when it came to graves.

Neal pushed open a heavy steel door to the building and we went inside. The building was not very large, just a single large room within which was the iron body of the Gas Chamber itself with a glass window in its side opposite a series of raised benches where a small audience could sit to watch an execution.

"Take a seat, if you like—those of you who're feeling brave can step inside...."

There was only room for four people inside the chamber, so the lucky guys who'd accepted the equipment went inside. I didn't envy them! I might have thought everyone was being a bit silly about the graves, but I wouldn't have liked to stand inside a place where so many people had been killed. I certainly wouldn't have sat in a chair like Marcus dared.

"People have seen a shadowy figure within the chamber," Neal told us. Just like the cell, I couldn't see the chamber retaining enough free space for anything to appear. Nobody reported any unusual readings.

Suddenly, the fat guy in the skeleton suit began gasping and staggered out of the chamber before falling to his knees.

The escorts and saloon girl screamed and there was swearing as Neal and Al ran to the man's side.

"Gas!" Marian shrieked.

I was too shocked to say or do anything.

Then, the man produced an inhaler and sucked on it.

Asthma! The guy was asthmatic! Whether it was a fluke, or the fear, or the cramped conditions, something had set off an attack. Nothing weird or supernatural or anything like that. I felt a little guilty that we laughed. We weren't laughing at him. The laugh released tension, the realisation that there was actually nothing to be scared of. For a moment, we really had thought he was experiencing one of the deaths that had occurred there. I thought we were all a little sheepish as we left the building and headed for the Punishment Block where underground solitary confinement cells existed in perpetual darkness.

With only the light of the torch beams, the darkness was intense. The musty air chilled the skin. The area was terrifying without any elaboration.

"The souls of prisoners who died here after years without human contact are said to remain here in torment."

"The temperature is low," the cowboy told us, unnecessarily.

There were no electrical or magnetic anomalies.

"Please, turn the flashlights out so we can experience the awful blackness that was their constant companion. Perhaps we'll hear some of their torment...."

We were plunged into absolute darkness. It was almost as if everything had ceased to exist. I found myself expecting something horrible to happen—but it didn't.

"Back on!"

Light flared. The beams seemed amazingly bright. We all stood blinking for a moment. Then, the saloon girl screamed.

The cowboy ran over to her and hugged her. "What's wrong?"

She was almost hysterical, but managed to stutter out what had happened.

"I—I—I—th-thought you were h-holding m-my h-hand...." He hadn't been. In fact, she had been standing a little way off on her own. I couldn't blame her for screaming. I think I would've in her place.

Spooked, we didn't remain there a moment longer. The sheer terror on her face and in her voice really freaked us out and we were glad to get outside. The girl was still sobbing and her boyfriend was hugging her as we went. After the pitch-blackness, the shadowy moonlight was no longer scary at all.

Although whatever had happened to her had given us all a chill, it wasn't the positive proof to convince me ghosts were real.

We headed back to the main prison building and spent some time in the lobby, drinking and chatting before heading off for the dance floor where I actually managed to hit it off with a cute pre-med who gave me her number.

Finally, in the early hours of the morning, the guests began to drift out to their cars and head home.

I strolled outside with Marcus and the others.

"Excellent party, hey?" laughed Marcus.

"Certainly unique!" I told him.

One of his dates shivered and said, "I don't think I'll ever sleep with the light off ever again!"

Her friend concurred.

Secretly, I sort of agreed. I doubted the poor saloon girl ever would.

"Well, night," I said, heading for my car, and waving to the others as they got into their vehicles: Marcus in his gorgeous sports car and Steve in his knackered old station wagon, which was a real money sink, always in need of repairs.

I was about halfway home when my cell rang. Answering it, I was surprised to hear Marcus' voice. He sounded shaken.

"What's wrong?" I asked.

"I just arrived home to find a cop waiting for me...."

"Oh? Problem?"

"Yeah.... It's...." He sobbed. Marcus never sobbed.

"What?" I was starting to feel a little freaked. It was still dark and there was an early-morning mist.

"It's Steve and—and Marian.... They crashed, man... they're dead...."

"Oh, man...."

"Brakes failed..."

That didn't surprise me. He should've got a new car. Marcus had often offered to buy him one, but Steve was too proud to accept. I guessed he was wishing he'd insisted.

"I'm so sorry, bro...."

He mumbled something.

"Sorry?"

"Will—they crashed on their way *to* the prison."

"Sorry?"

"They never reached the prison, man. They died early evening...."

I later read the report, which confirmed the time of their accident, and Marcus saw their bodies in the morgue. There was no doubt as to what had happened. They never arrived.

We checked with Neal. He still had the recording from the prison cell: a hiss of static that seemed to say, "Kill you!" then, clear as crystal, Steve's voice exclaiming, "I think I heard something!" We hadn't imagined them... and it seemed we'd recorded the voice of a ghost.

That was when I knew ghosts existed.

When the Wine Begins to Sour

Matt Kolbet

"There are two types of wine drinkers, and you need to be able to tell which is which," Jackie said. Her theory was neither new nor particularly convincing.

"Okay." Suzanne waited. She had moved to Oregon because it was an easy escape from California and her ex-husband—six years wasted, trapped—but she had hated everything that first month until the job at the winery appeared and she became enamored with the land and what it produced. She knew enough already of Jackie that whatever Jackie wanted to say would come in its own time.

"There are people who don't want to waste any wine. They drink it all, never letting a drop go in the bucket. They figure they're paying for it, so they drink it even if they don't like it." Jackie looked at the bottle in her hand. Suzanne didn't want to ask if Dourmand had any wine that people would dislike.

"The other kind doesn't want to waste their taste buds. They've only got so many in a lifetime." Like breaths, thought Suzanne. You can hold your breath and try to keep death away. "If you sip a wine, you'll taste it. Understand?"

Suzanne nodded as Jackie went into the back. It was a quarter to eleven, when they would open. She had heard Jackie deliver the same speech, like a spell, the last three days, when the winery was closed and she learned the history of the soil, the winemaker and everything she would be pouring. Today was Saturday, and though it was March, it was still raining. The rain would not be enough to keep visitors away. Locals liked to escape from Portland to taste wine where it was made, and visitors wanted something that couldn't be replicated in another state. The earth and weather made wine something unique.

The clock made its steady approach to the hour. When it was five minutes to eleven, Jackie reappeared. "Better unlock the doors. Some people come early and we don't want to inadvertently turn them away." Suzanne wondered if this was a third type of person, one that altered the equation. She dutifully unlocked the door and gave the room a last look. It was no good sweeping when people could see you. Even the sight of a broom was unsightly, a reminder that the world could be messy. It was the same reason Suzanne had gotten the job. Her predecessor had gotten pregnant, and, as Jackie said, "People don't want to think about infants and wine at the same time. It's not sophisticated. If you want to get drunk and make a baby, you go to a bar. If you don't worry about your own kids drinking, they sip your beer at summer barbecues." The policy felt unfair, dishonest even, but Suzanne needed the job. The image the winery wanted to present was clean lines, a mixture of modern agriculture and industrial thinking. A few barrels sat in the corner, next to a small table with cheese on wooden blocks and gleaming knives. The dump bucket was polished steel, and two paintings of hills that rolled off the canvas contrasted with a large mirror where you could lose yourself in self-examination.

At precisely eleven, the door opened and a bell overhead tinkled. Three women stepped across the threshold. They were, thought, Suzanne, a comic sight, but she only smiled more broadly, knowing this was her first test. If she failed, Jackie would sigh and fire her, saving the complaints for Suzanne's replacement.

"Welcome to *Dourmand*," said Suzanne. The word could have sounded gloomy except for its French pronunciation. You could practically hear it being italicized. The three women returned her pleasant expression. They seemed to be in the midst of a conversation, but let the words drop away as they followed Suzanne to the wine counter.

One of the women was tall, noticeably tall. She probably got the same kind of questions all the time, about her parents or her proclivities. The next woman was unremarkable, except for the severity of her expression, which altered only slightly when she grinned. The last woman was short. She did not have features that seemed out of place or disproportional, but her height, or lack of it, could not pass without remark. If she had been alone, Suzanne might have asked for her driver's license and subsequently made a joke of it. Taken together, they were a statistician's dream.

"Hello, Ladies," Suzanne said, mentally reviewing the openings Jackie and had recommended, and altering them to make it sound natural. "I'm sorry our spring hasn't arrived yet. Fortunately, we have some wonderful flights to taste. They'll warm your mouths and hearts while we wait for the sun to put in an appearance."

The three women nodded politely and handed three ten-dollar bills to Suzanne, who made them vanish as though they were not worth her attention and need not be mentioned again. She poured the signature Pinot Noir and set three embossed wine glasses on the counter. This was part of her training— "part of the experience," said Jackie. Customers, connoisseurs in training, averred Jackie, should lift the glass, noticing the colors swirl in the light, activating their sight before they tasted the wine.

"If they lift it on their own, they take their time. They smell the wine and enjoy it more."

Suzanne waited. Part of her wanted to reach over the counter and hand the glass to the short woman, but that was ridiculous. The woman was merely short, not a child. The whole situation was fraught with embarrassment.

All three women sipped at once, their unity evidently a product of practice.

"It's like the blood of Mother Earth," said the middle woman and her companions laughed. The short woman practically squeaked, but more like a cat than something it would deign to chase. The tall woman chortled round noises, but the woman who had spoken did not color at the others' risibility.

"No one speaks like that anymore. They haven't for years," said the short woman.

Suzanne, fascinated by their play, forgot herself and spoke up. "Oh, but I know what you mean!" She blushed as soon as she spoke. Thank god Jackie was elsewhere.

"You do?" asked the tall woman.

"Well, I'm sorry to interrupt. But, I think I do. The grapes change. It's not up to us, or even the soil. We do our best to keep everything hydrated, of course." She had forgotten herself again, but no longer minded. Her skin remained pale and her pulse ticked evenly. "But it's all the weather, really. If it gets too hot, or we have a late freeze, the grapes change. We can only try to recover, to aim for something we want. Once," she grasped for the year Jackie had told her and gave up on it, "there was a fire over the next hill, and the wines that year tasted almost peppery. And sometimes there are summer storms."

"Yes," said the tall woman, stroking her chin, "thunder, lightning…." she smiled and sipped again, "and you know the rest." Her companions smiled. They looked again at Suzanne shrewdly, apparently not upset at her intrusion. Still, they moved a few feet away from the counter and slowly swallowed gulps of their first pour, speaking in whispers. No one else came in for a few minutes and Suzanne studied the women, hoping to catch and eye and offer an apologetic look, or smile invitingly, ready to assuage any ill thoughts with another drink.

While she gazed, Suzanne noticed none of the women

moved their wrists. Yet the wine in each glass swirled expertly. She saw then, that the middle woman was moving her the index finger on her free hand in small circles. Immediately she looked at the hands of the other two women, but they were still, or reaching for a bit of cheese from the food table. Only the one finger moved, yet all the wine swirled.

Unsure what she was truly seeing, Suzanne did not noticed a middle-aged man who came and stood before the counter. He placed himself there like a soldier awaiting orders. His wife, out of breath, followed at his heels. Blinking, Suzanne realized she had not even heard the bell at the door ring to announce them.

"It's our anniversary!" the woman exclaimed. Suzanne nodded noncommittally. She had lost sight of the witches, as she now thought of them. The tasting room was small, yet she could not seem them for this bloated couple. "He said we could do anything I wanted, so I thought, why not go wine tasting?"

"Why not, indeed?" said Suzanne. Where had the witches gone? She had recovered herself enough to put a little false enthusiasm in her voice, and the woman at least—her husband looked bored—had ebullience enough for both of them. "It's a good day for it." None of this was in the script Jackie made her memorize. It was too flat, and she knew if Jackie heard her she would be disappointed.

"Yes, it is a lovely day. I thought the very thing this morning. So here we are!"

Suzanne ran through the wines Dourmand had, told them where they would begin their journey—that was more in the neighborhood of the script—and poured a glass each for the couple.

"Some people like to swirl it around, to catch the colors before they taste it," suggested Suzanne.

"Yes, they do," said a deep-toned voice. It was the tallest witch. The couple noticed the three women and seemed about to comment on the oddness of their collective appearance when the shortest witch moved a finger and the excited wife began coughing. She handed her glass to her husband and walked to the deck at the back of the winery. He followed her dutifully.

Suzanne poured the second glass, a Cabernet. After it splashed in the glasses, it seemed darker than Suzanne remembered. The woman drank it quickly. They did not speak to Suzanne, who decided not to press them with questions. Nor did they address each other, but seemed to enjoy the quiet of the tasting room. Suzanne felt she could hear the clouds moving. She had no idea where Jackie had gotten to, but told herself this, too, was part of the test. After all, she only needed to pour when asked. As the three women finished the second glass, the middle-aged man returned with his wife in tow, shattering the silence of the room. He was huffing a bit and Suzanne thought he looked different, perhaps fatter, or older. It had been ten minutes since she had seen him. She wondered if the weather had turned worse, or if his appearance suffered from the artificial light of the tasting room. She could not free herself to go watch the winds from the deck. The witches, by contrast, looked flush and healthy. They asked for their third tasting before the man or his wife could commandeer Suzanne's attention or space at the counter. Glasses filled now with a

Malbec, also closer to black than purple, the witches withdrew.

The fat man leaned on the counter, toppling a stack of coasters that doubled as business cards for the winery. If customers didn't want to buy glassware, they had a free souvenir, a reminder of what might have been.

"This stuff is powerful," he said, holding up his empty glass. Suzanne cocked an eyebrow. The couple were just finished with their first tasting, and she doubted such a small sample would affect such earthy people so much or so quickly. Perhaps they had been to another winery already. She tried to think if any places opened before eleven. Or, more likely, they had been drinking at home. Mimosas with breakfast, then out to make a day of their debauchery.

When she had both glasses, Suzanne gave them their next pour and slid them expertly across the counter.

"I don't usually feel like this. The wine tasted good, though. I'm not complaining. Sometimes, it even seemed salty. It's just a different experience."

"Yes, I've never had anything like it," agreed the wife ambiguously. They smiled at each other and retreated to the balcony again. For a moment, Suzanne wished she could follow them. Seeing the witches near the food table, picking at a bit of chocolate while dark liquid swirled effortlessly in their immobile glasses, she recanted.

The witches were another type of drinker, she thought. There went Jackie's theory. Suzanne imagined they could drink all afternoon and show no ill effects. But they wouldn't. They were not greedy. In fact, Suzanne sensed a kind of justice about them. They saw others headed toward a precipice and helped dissuade them from going over. The fat couple were loud to a stereotype. Worse, they were unhealthy, a nuisance to the whole experience people craved at wineries. They could have stayed home drinking PBRs and guffawing on the couch. Suzanne suspected they would be leaving soon, without finishing the flight of wines.

She did not know exactly how the witches did it. Blood. How their glasses came to hold some of the man and woman's blood, a marriage of wine and essence, she did not know, but she suddenly understood. That would account for the hue Suzanne noticed as well as the couple's exhaustion.

Less than five minutes later the woman returned, a look of terror neatly written across her face. "Oh, we have to go," she said, shaking her head. Her husband trod in slowly behind her. "Merle's having chest pains."

"Do you need me to call..." Suzanne stopped. She didn't want to alarm already-worried woman.

"No, dear. I don't think it's a heart attack, though the doctor has warned him. I thought wine was supposed to be good for the heart anyway." She looked accusingly at Suzanne for a moment before returning her eyes to her distended feet. Suzanne recognized the look—a woman insulated by her life, but finding it was beginning to scratch. "Oh, and we've left our glasses out there. We were only mid-way through the tasting—"

"Here," said Suzanne, handing her two small cards. "These are for a free tasting. Whenever you want to come back, we'd be happy to see you." The lie was easy on her lips. "And don't worry about the glasses. I'll collect them."

"Oh, thank you, dear. Merle did have his heart set on something special for our day." She threw a glance back to her husband and began to walk out. They left without even touching hands.

Jackie emerged from the back where she must have been doing inventory. She was smiling, for after the couple left, three larger groups arrived. They were talking boisterously with each other, but did not seem rushed. Two of them looked like they might be bachelorette parties and the third was a handful of guys who had either followed the limousine or were just now realizing their good luck. The glasses left by Merle and his wife would have to wait.

Before any of the groups approached, the witches appeared in front of the counter and set their glasses down. "Delicious, all of it," said the tallest of them.

"Do you want to move on to the whites?" Suzanne asked. She noticed Jackie setting up to pour at the other end of the counter.

"No," said the tall witch. "We prefer reds, and we've have enough for one day."

"Thank you for coming in," said Suzanne. She hoped she did not sound brusque.

"It was our pleasure."

Jackie took their glasses and put two of them away to be washed later. She wondered if she would need to rinse them twice. The third glass she left out. The party of young men had accosted one of the bachelorette parties, so Suzanne still had a moment to herself. She examined the glass. It did not look unusual now that its owner had abandoned it. She raised a hand and spun one of her fingers in a circle while she stared at the glass. The small puddle of wine dredged at the bottom of the glass did not move. Without thinking, Suzanne picked up the bottle of Malbec. There was very little left, certainly less than a pour. Suzanne emptied the bottle into the glass. The liquid was beautiful and alluring. She lifted the glass and moved the liquid first clockwise then counter-clockwise.

Oh well, she thought, we can't all be so lucky. She set the glass to her lips and sipped. As part of her training she had had the opportunity to taste the full range of Dourmand's offerings, and the wine tasted as it always had: soft, rounded, and fruit forward.

Suzanne set the glass down, ready to welcome the first of the two remaining groups. They settled after a moment of innocuous banter; it was clear they were more interested in each other than the wine, so Suzanne kept the summaries of expectations short. Once everyone had a glass, they stepped away from the counter, though no one else was pressing for service and the sight of so many people was likely to drive away potential tasters. Even the limos in the lot would do that.

Jackie was in a hiatus as well, but rather than returning to the back or restocking the bottles they kept in the front, she strode to Suzanne's pouring station. When she arrived, she put a hand down and traced her finger through invisible dust, looking for another reason to scold Suzanne.

"When you're done with this bunch, you're fired!" she hissed. Suzanne was surprised. She didn't think the witches had anything to do with it, but she felt Jackie had the order of things wrong. Before she could ask why, Jackie went on: "I saw you drinking." She did not seem bothered that it was a winery. "I know the signs of people backsliding. You sip a little, but that soon becomes a lot."

"I see," said Suzanne. She looked at the clock. It was not yet noon. Why would I stay to serve anyone else, she thought. If I'm fired, shouldn't I just leave? But all she said was: "See you, then."

Jackie blanched, but did not sputter. She eyed Suzanne for a few seconds and then, keeping her voice low, growled, "I won't give you a recommendation." Suzanne nodded. She was reminded of her ex-husband and how he used to say things that sounded powerful, but were ultimately meaningless, like his threats to keep her indoors. No chains would be adequate. Or his intimations that he would change the locks, when volcanoes wouldn't keep her away. If Suzanne became *persona non grata* at Dourmand, it made no difference. There were scores of wineries in this region of Oregon. This seemed like an invitation to explore. She had worked at the winery less than a week, and the absence in her resume would not draw attention or ire when she went for her next job. And if she explained how she had just moved and needed to get settled, the week would disappear. Time itself might be subject to such vanishing.

Though she considered pouring herself another glass, or absconding with a bottle, one for the road could turn the merely inconvenient into something criminal. Instead, she smirked. "I guess I can live with that," she told Jackie. She began moving toward the door.

At the moment, both bachelorette parties and the men hunting exhausted their conversation and came to the counter for their next taste.

"Wait!" Jackie said. She held up a finger to excuse herself to the customers for a breath. Suzanne had turned back, thinking there was more than fortuity in the timing. "It's fine," said Jackie. "Really, it's fine. I take it back." Her eyes pleaded.

You say that now, Suzanne thought. *What will you say at four o'clock?* Besides, she knew it was not fine. Suzanne shook her head and walked on. She understood that some spells and scripts could not be re-worked. That wasn't Jackie's strength anyway. As she walked out, she knew that the winery would soon be uncomfortably loud and frustrated. It was no way to work, nor a way to live.

In the parking lot, Suzanne saw the three witches waiting for her. Somehow, she had known they would be.

"That didn't take long," said the middle witch.

"No," Suzanne agreed. She wondered if it mattered which witch spoke, but did not know how to ask.

"When you've worked together as long as we have, you come to understand one another," said the tall witch. She looked back at the doors of Dourmand; they barely contained the impatience inside. "You and she wouldn't have found it, even if you stayed for years."

Suzanne thought again of her ex-husband. They had never been able to understand each other, even when they said *I do*. Their rhythm had always been off. She saw the witches nodding, but it was not merely sympathy. They did not pity her.

"You can always find another job. You can even get married again if you want to." Suzanne did not know which of the three had spoken, but it did not matter. "What do you want to do right now?"

Suzanne had no thought of going back into Dourmand as a customer. Not even to bring the witches with her and have them a drink a toast to Jackie. That was done. She knew, too, that she could learn from the witches. And if the cadence was right, she would see where it led her. She had visions of going further North, but, for now, she planned only to discover, to keep going out and to return home when she wanted. To invite friends.

"Can you show me some places you know?"

They nodded as one.

"Good," said Suzanne. "Tell me one more thing."

"Anything."

"How many types of witches are there?" It was the first time she had called them that aloud.

All three women laughed. "More than us, if that's what you're worried about. More than you could imagine. We come in all flavors."

The Hearth

Kevin Hayman

Robert Clayton's eyelids felt heavy and stiff. He tried to open them. Hell, were they stitched together? Then they sprang open to a blaze of light, so overwhelmingly bright that he instinctively covered his face with his hands and screamed. His loud yell echoed off the cold room's walls as he lay in the shelter of his palms, grimacing.

As the throbbing pain settled he became aware of a continuous beep emanating from his right, and from afar, he could hear the mumbled sound of distant voices. At least it meant he wasn't alone.

But, Jesus, what was that smell? Disinfectant? Urine? It reminded him of the last few days of his mother's life, as she lay helplessly fighting Leukemia in a hospital ward—it wasn't a memory he was fond of.

Slowly, he removed his hands from his face and opened his eyes; no resistance this time, just a dull pain that quickly eased.

The first thing he was able to focus on was a tall metallic stand that stood beside the bed. There was a bag at the top that seemed to be administering a liquid in to a vein in his right arm. Behind the stand on a wooden chair were a pile of folded clothes and an iPhone. To his left was a banal plastic-coated cabinet, which supported a black leather book—possibly a Gideon's bible—and a glass vase with a single protruding rose. The repetitive beep sound continued like a ticking clock. *Beep, beep, beep.* Only as he looked closely did he realise the source— a machine—a small light flickering across a screen in time with his heartbeat. *Well, I'm alive at least*, he mused.

Beyond the bed were four cream-coloured walls and a door painted in duck-egg blue, which had been left slightly ajar. The room was small and unflattering, not too dissimilar from the one his mother had recently passed in. Robert lay back into the pillow, curiously watching the rose. How in God's name did he get here?

Footsteps grew louder. A sumptuous young nurse, with strawberry blonde hair tucked neatly under a cap, appeared and took a clipboard hanging from the bed frame. Almost hypnotically, she pulled a pen from her lapel pocket, trawled through it, made a quick scribble and returned it to the bed frame, without even glancing in Robert's direction.

"Where am I?" Robert said feebly.

The nurse jerked back and put her hand to her chest, as if

to stop her heart from beating out. When she had regained control of herself, she seemed to find the humour in it.

"I'm sorry," she said, giggling a little. "I didn't realise you were awake yet. You startled me."

"Sorry," Robert said sincerely.

"No, really, it's my fault. I should have been more observant when I came in. We get through so many of these checkups and," she took a deep breath and composed herself, "I guess I just thought you were sleeping."

Robert looked up at the hanging drip and joked, "Negligence is not something I can lecture on, believe me."

The nurse smiled.

"My name's Sophie," she said politely. "I'm a practising Nurse here at Guy's Hospital. You took quite a fall some weeks back and we've been nursing you best we can back to full health. How you feeling?"

"*Fall?* How many weeks back?"

"I'm not sure exactly. You were transferred here from the Blagdon Heath Clinic two weeks ago. Doctor Reynolds will have all your papers. I'll call him just as soon as I know how you're feeling?"

"I'm fine, a little thirsty maybe."

"I'll fetch you some water. You're sure that's all? No dizziness, headaches, chest pains, sickness?"

"Well, my back hurts a little. And the lights in here are killing me."

"Your eyes will take some time to adjust, I'm afraid. As for your back, I can prescribe some stronger painkillers if you feel you need them."

"I'll see how I get on without them for now."

"Just the water and the doctor it is then. In the meantime, you may want to read that book on your bedside cabinet."

Robert glanced over at the book he had mistaken for the Gideon's Bible.

"Your wife fills that book in every visiting hour," she said, approaching the door. "You're very lucky, sir."

Yes—of course, *Marie!* How could he forget his lovely Marie? A picture instantly emerged of his wife presenting him with a rose she had clipped. "I just love these roses," she said, whilst inhaling its exquisite scent. "Here, smell it. So fresh." Her expansive eyes beamed with elation.

Robert reached for the book. "Jesus," he said as he twisted his back awkwardly toward the cupboard. *Should have opted for those stronger painkillers.*

The black leather book had no text on the front cover, but inside Robert recognised Marie's handwriting immediately and felt a warm tingle ease his aching back. It wasn't just her handwriting or the smell of her Chanel Coco perfume from the pages that reawakened his memory of her. It was the blue ink from her fountain pen, which dressed her in a blue summery maxi-dress, and the swirl of ink on her G's and S's, which majestically blew her auburn curls about in his mind. By writing in the book, she had returned herself firmly back in Robert's consciousness. He started to read.

17th May

Robbie,

I've decided to write in this book every time I visit. This way, when you get out of hospital, we can read it together and maybe even laugh a little. I guess it makes sense to start from the very beginning. Dr. Reynolds wasn't sure how much you'd remember when you came round, so perhaps this book can serve as a sort of memory-jogger for you. He-he!

Robert stifled a smile into his hand, momentarily forgetting that he was alone in the room.

On the 19th of February, we bought the house of our dreams. You said that ever since you laid eyes on it, you fell in love with it. I did, too. Hopefully, we are reading this together now in the living room, but if we're not, if we're still at the hospital, then let me remind you: It's the old nunnery in Blagdon Heath called Greenbank—a big, redbrick building that was erected as far back as 1771 I think, surrounded in woodland (with a big rose bush in the garden!!). It has big, iron-cast gates outside and a main entrance with stairs leading up to eight bedrooms. There's even a small chapel on the land, but is well in need of a hammer and some nails! The place had pretty much been neglected for the last hundred years or so and when you mention to a local how interested you were in purchasing the property, he gave you some cock and bull story about it being haunted, ha! As if! Anyway, despite our jealous friend's advice, after receiving your mother's inheritance, we finally had enough money to buy and renovate it. We moved in on the 19th of March and started the restoration.

"Mr. Clayton," said a stern voice from beside the bed. He hadn't noticed anyone enter the room.

"Sorry, Yes?"

"It's nice to finally have the pleasure. I'm—"

"Dr. Reynolds, I presume?" Robert said.

"I *am*, yes. How did you know?"

Robert tapped the book. "My wife's been keeping a journal."

"Ah, yes. I've seen her here with you. She's a very devoted woman, Mr. Clayton. You're a very lucky man."

"Thank you."

Dr. Reynolds smiled and glanced back at his notes. He was a tall man of more than six foot. He wore a white coat with a number of pens in his upper pocket. His hair was a light grey with a few surviving black strands, but like the nurse, he seemed somehow youthful in appearance. He began nodding at his notes, before returning the clipboard to his side. "Well, let me see now. Do you know what day it is, Mr. Clayton?"

"No, Doctor, I *can* remember who I am, my wife, my birthday, stuff like that. But the last couple of weeks are just sort of blank."

Dr. Reynolds nodded. "That's not uncommon in coma patients." He crouched beside Robert and shone a small torch into his eyes, one at a time. "Good, no unusual pupil activity." He brought the torch down and placed his hands together on the clipboard.

"Well, Mr. Clayton, its eight o'clock on Wednesday, 29th of May. You've been here at Guy's Hospital for nearly two weeks now."

"*Two weeks?*"

"Uh-huh. According to your wife, you fell from a stepladder trying to paint a dado rail in your bedroom. Do you recollect any of that?"

Robert shook his head.

"No. Okay," said the doctor. "Could you tell me your full name and date of birth?"

"Sure, eh, Robert Clayton, 29th of August 1975."

"Good, and tell me Robert, what's your favourite drink?"

Robert paused for a moment. What was his favourite drink? Beer? Whisky? Then it came to him. "You know, I quite like a cup of tea with Marie, just before bed."

"You remember Marie?"

"I didn't at first. Then, I started reading the journal she's been keeping for me and it all came flooding back. Well, some. Maybe I'll remember more as I read on?"

"Maybe," Dr. Reynolds said. "Sometimes, it just takes a few things to jog the memory. Other times, unfortunately, it's gone for good. And of course, you should prepare yourself for the possibility that you may have a problem with your short-term memory in the future. But the early signs are good." The doctor stood and placed the torch into his pocket. "We took a CT scan a few days after you were brought in and I'm pleased to confirm that there was nothing uncommon to report, no swelling or bleeding."

"Great."

"Yes indeed, though I'd like to keep you in for at least another week for observation and to get your levels back up. You'll be extremely weak with only the drip to support you over the last couple of weeks. It would be good to get you back onto solid foods again."

"Certainly, Doctor."

"Good. The nurses will take good care of you and if you need anything, just pull the cord."

"Just one more question before you go, Doctor, when are the visiting times?"

"An hour every day at two and seven."

"Oh," said Robert. Neither hour seemed near enough.

"You took a pretty big blow to the head, Mr. Clayton, so try and take it easy. I'll be back again to examine your progress."

As the doctor left the room, Nurse Sophie immediately came in with his glass of water. Robert gulped it down in one, and returned to reading his wife's journal. The nurse took the empty glass away.

> *Yesterday, while trying to paint our bedroom, you had a fall and banged your head. I had the scare of my life when I came in from the shops to find you lying unconscious in a puddle of blood. That image will haunt me for the rest of my life, Robert Clayton! Boy, are you clumsy? Still, I guess it was a blessing the carpet fitter hadn't laid the new carpets yet, hey? LOL*

Robert smirked, laid his head back and slowly began to doze. He dreamed he was in a field during summertime.

Bright rays of saffron light sprayed out from the vibrant sun like a child's painting caressing the emerald green fields he found himself walking through. There was a fresh smell of roses in the air and birds were twittering. In the distance was a familiar redbrick mansion with a dilapidated chapel off to the left; it was *Greenbank*.

He approached the building with a tin of gloss paint in

each hand. He passed through the large, English Oak doors, mounted the grand staircase and entered the main bedroom on the second floor. As he laid out the tins on an old towel sprawled across the wooden floorboards, Marie called up to him: "Robert, I'm off to the shops," she explained, "do you want anything?"

"No, I'm good," he replied, opening the first paint tin. He erected and climbed a three-tier stepladder as the front door closed downstairs. To his left, the smell of roses and cut grass passed through an open grand casement window, providing the room with a welcome relief from the paint fumes. He reached beyond a hanging mirror, to where newly laid wallpaper met the bottom of a dado rail, and began to mask it with tape. Outside a breeze picked up and started to whistle through the small gap in the window. At first, it had a charming quality about it as it was carried along on a chorus of birdsong in its briskness, but it quickly grew denser and stronger and forced the sound into a loud menacing screech: *hearthhh....* The unsettling noise entered the room on a draft that rode a chill up Robert's spine like a cold hand. He shivered.

The window snatched open with a bang. He slipped and threw his palms to the wall for support. Cold wind swooped into the room. The window then started to batter against its frame riding each howling gust of wind.

He steadied himself, climbed down the steps—heart thumping in the back of his throat—and closed the window. He wiped the sweat away from his glazed forehead with his trembling hands and drew in a deep breath. The room was quiet.

When his racing pulse had returned to something like its normal speed, he mounted the stepladder once again, determined to return to his painting. He dunked a brush deep into the paint and started spreading it over the dado rail whilst simultaneously shaking his head and laughing at being startled so cheaply. But the laugh grew louder, coarser and far more intense, until it was a deafening cackle. It dawned on him that the laugh was no longer a product of his own vocal chords.

A second blast of wind crashed into the room, smashing the windows wide open. Glass fragments shattered across the bare oak floorboards. The loud and disturbing *hearth* screech rang through the room like a warble. The tin of paint crashed to the floor, splashing gloss over the floorboards, the walls and his lower legs.

He grabbed the stepladder handrail for support, but it started to sway to and fro as if possessed. In the mirror in front of him appeared a face. An old, pale face of a woman with dull eyes and veil drooped over her hair. Her jaw was grossly misplaced, clutched over her front dentures just below the nose, as if it had been smashed into position by some heavy blow to the chin. Then her jaw drooped open in a kind of rictus and from it projected a deafening, harrowing scream, *"HEARTHHHHHHHHHH!!!!!"*

His feet gave way and he fell from the ladder, hitting his head on the hard flooring. Blood splatters overlaid the gloss paint. He lay still.

Robert awoke in the hospital bed flustered and shaken. He momentarily considered pulling the cord for the nurses to come in, but refrained himself. *Get a grip, Robert. Just a stupid dream.* Although he was thinking it, he didn't entirely believe it.

Something then hit like a bullet to the brain: it was the time he had gone to view Greenbank and a local passerby had tried to convince him that it was haunted. *He was right*, Robert thought morosely. *Local nut maybe, but he was right. Wasn't he?*

At the time, Robert had got lost following his Sat Nav across Blagdon, when he spotted the man walking up the narrow country path.

"Excuse me," Robert shouted, arched out of the car window as it slowed. The man casually turned to face Robert, who instantly noticed the long 'S' shaped scar running down the left side of his face. "I'm eh," Robert consciously tried to ignore the man's disfigurement, "I'm looking for Greenbank. It's around here somewhere, I believe."

"*Greenbank?*"

"Yes, it's an old red brick building—"

"I *know* the place. Used to be the nunnery."

"That's right, it *was,* so I believe."

"Just follow this here path right up 'til it ends, then take a left. Greenbank's right on the corner." Robert was about to thank the man for his directions when he said, "If you want my advice, you'll stay clear of it, though. Damn place is...."

"*Haunted?*" questioned Marie later when Robert told her about the man during supper.

"Oh, yes," Robert said, nodding in agreement. "So he said. More than likely been on one of those *Most Haunted* programs."

Together, they shared a skeptical laugh, though it was slightly contrived on Robert's part, because what Robert had failed to mention to Marie was that the man had seemed truly concerned, as if he had *known* it were haunted, rather than merely just believing it to be. The man was deadly serious. He hadn't sniggered whilst speaking, hadn't smiled. Hadn't cocked a wink in Robert's direction as he left. He meant what he said, and that 'S' shaped scar down the left side of his face only heightened the sincerity of his warning.

Robert reached for the iPhone and checked the time: 2:25. *Visiting time?* *"Your wife fills that book in every visiting hour,"* the nurse had told him. Where was she? She always kept her promises. *She's at home,* his mind told him, *alone with the nun in the mirror.* Robert's heart started to pound against his chest. *If you want my advice, you'll stay clear of it, though. Damn place is haunted.*

He grabbed the journal and began scanning through it.

18th May

You look so pale today, Robbie, but Dr. Reynolds assures me not to read anything into it. I've brought you a little rose for good luck and I'll place it in a glass of water by your bed. I hope you can smell it in your sleep. Tomorrow morning, you're going in for a CT scan. I'm keeping my fingers crossed for you, babe xx

19ᵗʰ May

Your CT scan went well according to Dr. Reynolds. I'm so relieved. I prayed for you last night. Can you believe that, Mister? You actually got me praying for you. Now get better and come home to me. COME HOME TO ME!! xx

Somehow, those words seemed more like a desperate plea for help than a goodwill gesture. And he wanted to be with her. With all the will in the world, he wanted to, but the predicament was he was miles away in a hospital bed, far too weak to even move.

He stopped reading the individual messages and skipped straight to the last passage in the book. It started with yesterday's date:

28ᵗʰ May

The nurses tell me your stable and doing well. I know it won't be long now until you're awake and on the mend. Then we can get this lovely house of ours back up together, like it deserves to be. On that note, I heard banging coming from the bedroom yesterday, but when I went to investigate no one was there? I assume it was the builders joshing about, taking advantage of a young lady, probably. Still, I wish you'd told me to expect them. You may be in a coma, Robert Clayton, but it doesn't excuse you giving a key out to builders without letting me know first! ☹

Robert had not booked any builders or given a key to anyone. Only the carpet fitter had been booked, but he wasn't due until mid-June. *It was the nun banging,* his mind was telling him. He could see her, clawing at the mirror, with those dead eyes and that crooked jaw screeching, *HEARTHHH!!!*

> *Tomorrow morning, I'm going up to the bedroom to start measuring up the windows for our curtains. I was thinking maybe yellow in there? xx*

Robert put the book down. Jesus, if it was possible to put him in a coma for two weeks, what would happen to Marie? A bulge of vomit swelled up in his belly and surged forcefully up his throat. He leant over the side of the bed and hurled onto the floor. She was in trouble. If not, surely she would have been at his bedside.

He reached for the iPhone and dialed Marie's number.

It rang. *Come on Marie, pick up.*

After ringing for what felt like a long time, the answer-phone finally kicked in. *Must be on silent mode. She hasn't heard it vibrating in her handbag, is all? Yes, that was it. Or, the nun has gotten to her.*

He grabbed the tube connected to his left arm and yanked it out. A small spit of blood tossed through the air. He took the pile of clothes on the chair and quickly dressed himself. He pocketed the iPhone, stuck the rose in his top pocket and staggered to the door when Nurse Sophie appeared and tried to stop him.

"Mr. Clayton," she hollered, "what are you doing? You should be resting."

"Sorry," he said, determined for the door, "I need to be somewhere."

The young nurse watched helplessly as Robert pushed his

way past with his left hand while simultaneously holding his back straight with his right. His head now felt more like double its normal weight and his vision was beginning to swim. In the distance, he could vaguely make out an exit sign, for which he headed. The cries of his young wife were ever-present in his mind: *COME HOME TO ME.*

A cab driver sat in a nearby bay as Robert fled the revolving hospital exit doors. The cabby spotted him struggling and came rushing out to his aid.

"Do you know Blagdon Heath?"

"Yes," said the cabby, supporting Robert's arm as he walked him to the cab. "I had a sister who moved down that way."

"Take me there."

As the cab sped away from the hospital grounds, Robert caught a glimpse of Dr. Reynolds in the wing mirror, trying to flag the car to stop. But if the cabby had noticed him, he paid no attention and stuck the pedal to the metal. He had a good fare to make out of this ride. Why would he stop?

In the taxi, with his heart pounding and back throbbing, Robert pulled out the iPhone and tried Marie's number again.

No answer.

Then he dialed 999.

"Which service do you require, please?" asked the voice at the other end.

"Police," said Robert, wiping sweat from his brow.

There was a quick sound of a buzz, then of the receiver being lifted.

"Police emergency," said a voice.

"Yes, I need to get a policeman to Greenback in Blagdon Heath immediately."

"What's the emergency, sir?"

"It's my wife, Marie," Robert explained, "she's in danger." But as the words were flowing from his mouth, he realised just how stupid he must have sounded.

"Let me get this straight," said the call operative when Robert had finished speaking. "You want me to get a policeman to your house in Blagdon, because you're afraid your wife may have been attacked *by a ghost?*"

"Look, I know this sounds crazy but you have to believe me. I've got a terrible feeling about this."

"Sir, I'm sorry, but we don't send out busy police officers on a whim."

Robert squeezed the phone to his forehead and scrunched his eyes shut. *Damn it!* The taxi driver was watching him via the rearview mirror with curious eyes.

"You got a problem back there?"

"No," said Robert, hanging up the phone. "There's no problem."

Though his signal was minimal, he was just able to key Greenbank Nunnery into a Google search. Strangely, it was the first time he had done this, and if it was some kind of peace of mind he was after, he wasn't about to find it. The results loaded. Robert clicked on the first weblink, which opened an article originally published in the 1900s.

> *The strange disappearance of a nun is thought to be the*
> *reason why the Greenbank Nunnery is finally closing down.*
> *Sources say the nun disappeared late on 29 May 1892. A*
> *new nunnery is due to be built in Castleford.*

The article was supported with a picture of the missing nun. It was the woman in the mirror.

Again, Robert felt nauseated, and the speed in which the taxi was flying down the motorway didn't help. But, this time he managed to control it. Lucky cab driver.

Robert gave the final directions to Greenbank as the car reached Blagdon. "Just follow this path right up until the end, then take a left." He was disgusted with how closely he sounded to the man with the 'S' shaped scar. *If you want my advice, you'll stay clear of it though. Damn place is haunted.*

"Holy crap," said the cab driver as he pulled up to the iron gates. "This place gives me the creeps."

"More than you'll ever know," Robert replied, dumping a heap of notes from his trouser pocket into the driver's palm.

"Wait a minute," he yelled as Robert started for the old gates. "There's more than—"

"Keep it," Robert said, jiggling the gates open. Slowly, he moved up the path to the main doors, his dragging left leg making a snake-like trail along the gravel as he went. It was just his adrenalin keeping him going. He drew in a deep breath between each step.

Finally, he reached the doors and opened them. "Marie?" he called. There was no reply, but he could hear the sound of wind blowing at the top of the stairs.

His back finally gave in as he hobbled to the spiral staircase. He fell with a heavy clout to the hard oak floorboards. He cupped his face in his hands for a moment and cringed. A little blood spilled from his top lip. It was almost as if something was trying to stop him. A banging noise came from upstairs. "Marie," he whispered, "I'm coming Marie."

He reached out his hand and started to claw his heavy body toward the stairs. Painstakingly, he managed to pull himself up each step by pushing off on his right leg and pulling himself up with his arms. Step by step. Slow progress. *I'm coming, Marie. I'm coming!*

At last, he reached the top and called again, "Marie, are you here?" And again, there was nothing, but that thumping sound and whistling wind.

He crawled through the hallway on his knees, feeling his way along the carpet with his bloodied hands. The thumping sound grew louder as he neared the bedroom. By the time he got to the door, he barely had the energy to push at it. From somewhere deep within, he summoned the strength.

As the door swung open, Robert felt the swift wind blow across his face, and what he saw made him want to scream, but he found himself muted with shock. A man was bludgeoning his lovely Marie's head into the fireplace, each blow making a horrifying *thud*.

MARIE!!!

The man turned to face Robert. He was, Robert saw, the man with the 'S' shaped scar.

"Noooooooooo!" Robert screamed. He reached out his helpless arms as the man dropped his wife's body to the floor. Her head hit against the hearth with an unpleasant thump. Blood quickly pooled up around her face.

"I tried to warn you about this place," said the man. "So help me, I tried."

Robert, paralyzed with terror, lay in the doorway, breathing heavily as the man headed towards the grand casement window. The setting evening sun shone through his translucent body with a red gleam.

"This place," he said, gazing out beyond the window, "it becomes you."

The sun broke out from behind a cloud and bleached the room with light. Robert shielded his eyes with his arms. When he brought them down again he found himself alone with Marie. She lay still, bleeding onto the hearth. Her jaw had been smashed over her top lip—like the nun in the mirror—and her eyes were looking vacantly out towards him.

When Robert eventually marshaled the strength, both physically and mentally, he staggered over to her and placed the rose by her side. "I'm here, Marie," he said softly. "I'm here."

He looked over at the mirror still hanging on the partially decorated wall. This time there was no image of a nun. No pale face or misshaped jaw. No dull eyes. Only his own reflection gazed back at him, and, as he looked closely, he saw the 'S' shaped scar running down the left side of his face. *This place, it becomes you.*

*

From the Blagdon Gazette, several months later:

Local man, Robert Clayton, was today sentenced to twenty years in prison for the brutal murder of his wife, Marie Clayton. Robert, believed to be confused from his own accident a few weeks earlier, had raced home from his hospital bed to kill his wife in cold blood. She was found by the fireplace in their 18th century home, Greenbank. Police were mystified when during the clean up they uncovered a one hundred year old mystery, when they found the remains of nun, Mary White, who had vanished in 1892. Experts are trying to determine the cause of death. Her remains were found under the same fireplace, buried beneath the hearth.

"Stingy Jack" and the Boys

Kevin Wetmore

for my father…

"I'm off to the cemetery. Extinguish the candles, put away your cassocks and cottas, and, Roger, I will not see you wear shoes that look like that to serve at a funeral again. Is that clear?" Nobody could glare like Father O'Malley.

"Sorry, Father." Roger felt his face burn. He kept his eyes on the floor as he removed his cassock. The other altar boy, the new kid, took the snuffer and walked back out into the church without saying a word.

"The very least we can do is show the deceased a final bit of respect as we entrust him into the Lord's hands."

"Yes, Father. Sorry, Father." Roger could not make eye contact. Finally, Father's voice softened a little.

"Well, the final prayers aren't going to say themselves. We must commit the body to the earth. As soon as you boys are finished here, head back over to St. Rita's. Don't dawdle. By my watch you should just be back in time for Sister Mary Ignatius's English class." He put his coat and hat on. It was a windy, overcast day—the last Thursday in October.

"Yes, Father."

"She'll tell me if you're late. Remember, leaving school to come here and serve as altar boys for funerals is a privilege. Don't dawdle," he repeated. And with that, he picked up his satchel and walked out to the street to climb into one of the cars headed to St. Mary's Cemetery to put Mr. McDonagh to his final rest.

The other boy returned. "Candles are out," he said in a lilt and began to disrobe. Now that they were alone, Roger could give him the once-over. The kid was new at St. Rita's. Roger knew his name was Tommy and he was from Ireland.

"Thanks for doing that. I'll clean the cruets."

"Cheers."

Roger held out his hand. "Roger Swanson."

Tommy finished pulling the cassock off over his clothes and returned the shake. "Tommy Maher."

"Where you from?"

"Ireland."

"Duh. Where in Ireland?"

"Howth. Heard of it?"

"Uh… no."

"Then 'Ireland' will do."

Roger wondered if the kid was making fun of him. "Why are you here?"

Tommy hung up the cassock and cotta. "Father O'Malley said I should start serving here, and since the funeral was the next thing that came up since I arrived...."

"No," said Roger. "Why are you here in North Hamden?"

"Oh." Tommy got a little sad, it seemed. "My folks died a month ago and my Gran was too old to take care of me. Me da's sister moved here after the war, married a Yank she met, so here I am, kipping with my uncle and aunt and learning the fear of the Lord at St. Rita's."

"Oh," said Roger, who couldn't think of anything else to say in response to that. They finished their duties in silence, put on their coats and walked out of Our Lady of Perpetual Sorrow to head back to class at the school across the street.

"So," began Roger. "How do you like North Hamden?"

"Well, it ain't home, but it ain't bad, y'know? The only folks I know is me uncle and aunt, and they don't know what to do with me."

"Well now you know me," said Roger. "Meet me by the flagpole after school and I'll introduce you to my gang."

"You have a gang?" Tommy's eyes got wide. "Are you Juvenile Delinquents or something?"

Roger laughed. "Not that kind of gang. It's just a bunch of kids that hang out together. We like the same stuff. There's me, Mikey, Kenny and Big Kenny."

"You've got two Kennys?"

"Yeah. Kenny Quinn has been my best friend forever. He lives down the street from me. We met Big Kenny and Mikey when we got to St. Rita's. Big Kenny stayed back a year, on account of he's not that smart, so he's bigger than everyone else. So, Big Kenny. Get it?"

"I guess," said Tommy.

They waited for the light so they could cross.

"What are you gonna be for Halloween?" Roger asked.

"Dunno. Didn't really think about it, I guess."

"You're kidding, right?"

"We don't have Halloween in Ireland."

"Well then thank God you're in America now. We're all going trick or treating. Kenny's scout troop also has us collecting for UNICEF, which is why my mom is letting me go. She thinks I might be a little old for trick or treating and that I should only go to the party at St. Rita's on Saturday. I mean, I know Halloween is on a school night this year, but you gotta go out, right? I'm dressing up like the Lone Ranger—it's my favorite show. Last year I was Davy Crockett. Maybe you could wear that outfit, I mean since you don't have a costume. If you want."

Tommy thought about it. "Sure. Why not?"

"Great, great. Meet me after school and you can come over and get the costume," and with that they entered the doors of the school.

✳

At two-thirty, as all the kids were getting out, Roger met up with the gang by the flagpole. They were all going to walk to his house to plan Halloween. This year was going to be the best one ever. Channel eight was showing the Universal horror movies over the weekend and Roger's mom said he could watch *Dracula* and *Frankenstein*. His family had a television, so the gang usually headed over to his house, although just as often Mrs. Swanson shooed them out of the house, telling them it was too nice a day to sit inside and stare at the Philco. But it was October and it got dark early and it was often cold and wet. One of the few advantages to living in Connecticut, Roger thought, was that it had a lot of what he thought of as "TV weather."

Mikey and Kenny were already waiting when Roger got there, and Big Kenny showed up a minute later. "Guys," Roger said, "I've invited the new kid to join us."

"Jeez, Rog," said Mikey, who was smaller than the others and made nervous by change. "Why?"

"Because he's OK. We served Mr. McDonagh's funeral mass today together and he's a good egg. He's from Ireland and his parents are dead and I don't think he's ever done Halloween before, so I figured we'd show him how we do it."

"He's never done Halloween before?" asked Big Kenny. "What's that got to do with his parents being dead?"

"Nothing," said Roger. "He's new, OK? And he doesn't have any friends. I figured we could teach him, you know? Here he comes. His name is Tommy."

Roger did introductions all around. "I'm sorry about your parents. Too bad they didn't do Halloween," said Big Kenny.

"Uh… thanks," said Tommy, and wisely left it at that.

The boys threw their book bags over their shoulders and began walking to Roger's house, six blocks away. They took the shortcut, which cut the route in half, but took them past Mr. McDonagh's house, just down the street from Roger's.

They laughed and told jokes and talked about their days and how mean Sister Mary Ignatius could be and Mikey showed his red knuckles where she had taken a ruler to them today. But then they fell silent as they approached the McDonagh house. It was dark. Even the lawn was forbidding. Crabgrass and dried patches made it look almost abandoned.

"I'm glad he's dead," muttered Kenny.

They all stopped for a second and Roger stared at him. Sister Mary Regina had told them it was a sin to hate someone and wish they were dead and when Eddie O'Connor has asked her "Even Hitler?" she told him that hating was a sin and angered God, so they were both impressed and scared that Kenny would say that. They were glad he was dead, too, but couldn't say it aloud.

"He was the meanest guy EVER," said Mikey. They all nodded in agreement. "McDonagh would keep any ball that flew into his yard," they told Tommy, and Mikey did a spot-on impression: "What lands in my yard is MINE!" It was too close to real for them to laugh.

"He kept a pellet gun to shoot at any dog that approached his lawn!" Big Kenny complained.

"Remember what he did to Todd's bike?" asked Roger. They all nodded again. "Mikey's brother Todd was riding his bike down their street and saw a baby bird had fallen out of a nest. He dropped his bike on the spot and ran to pick up the bird and help it. He was a little kid, just starting third grade and he loved animals. Mr. McDonagh was driving down the street and just ran over Todd's bike without even stopping. When Todd's father asked him why, he said, 'Bike shouldn'ta been in the street,' and slammed the door on them."

"I bet he's in Hell," said Roger, and the other boys nodded sagely.

"I don't think he is," Tommy sudden spoke up. "Hell wouldn't have him."

Big Kenny looked confused. This was not what the nuns taught. When he got confused, he got angry. "Whaddaya mean Hell wouldn't have him?"

Tommy looked at the house, looked back at the group. "Back where I come from, there's the legend of a guy named Jack. He tricked the Devil several times when he was alive, getting Ol' Scratch to sit in a chair he couldn't get out of. When Jack died, the Devil didn't need the competition, so he told Jack he couldn't enter Hell. Ol' Jack was stuck wandering forever, a candle stuck in a turnip his only light."

Big Kenny looked even more confused. "So he couldn't go to Hell, so the guy just wandered around with a turnip? That's the dumbest thing I ever heard."

"Could be," Tommy responded. Roger smiled. Tommy already seemed to know how to handle Big Kenny.

"And that's the origin of the Jack-o-Lantern, right?" Roger asked Tommy, who nodded.

"A Jack-o-Lantern is a pumpkin, not a turnip, you morons! You guys don't know anything!" Big Kenny was both smiling and ready to take a swing at anyone who might suggest he was stupid.

"It's a turnip in Ireland, Big Kenny. Over here, it's a pumpkin. They don't have pumpkins in Ireland, right, Tommy?" asked Roger, attempting to play peacekeeper.

"Oh, aye," Tommy concurred, mollifying Big Kenny.

All the boys quietly looked at the house.

"So what are you saying, Tommy?" asked Kenny.

Tommy looked at the group. "If this guy, Mr. McDonagh, is as bad as you said, the Devil might not want the competition. He might have to wander the earth with a candle."

They thought about that for a moment. "Naw," Kenny finally concluded. "I like it better if he's in Hell." The boys agreed with him.

"But think about it," asked Roger, "what would happen if he did show up with a candle. Halloween is next week. What happens if Mr. McDonagh walks up to us on Halloween?" The boys had not thought of that, but now as they considered it, they did not like the idea.

"I'll tell you what happens," said Kenny. "This." And he pulled out his knife that his father gave him when he joined the Boy Scouts two years earlier.

The boys all stared at it. Then Tommy said, "You're going to stab a ghost?" and they all laughed. Tommy didn't, but they chalked that up to him being foreign.

At Roger's house, they all went up to his room, rather than negotiate with Mrs. Swanson for television time. Roger grabbed the calendar off the wall on the way through the kitchen. "October 27, 1956," he solemnly intoned. "Two days from now. St. Rita's Halloween Carnival. Costumes and noisemakers and bobbing for apples."

"That's kid's stuff," snarled Mikey.

"I like bobbing for apples," said Big Kenny, who did.

"Yeah," said Kenny. "We'll go 'cause it will shut our moms up. Besides, it's over by four so Father can hear confessions and say evening mass."

"Exactly," said Roger. "We go, we play the stupid games, do the stupid costume contest, bob for apples," nodding at Big Kenny, who nodded back, "and then we come back here for *Dracula.*"

All the boys cheered.

"And this is what we do for Halloween?" asked Tommy.

"No," said Roger, with a laugh. "We're just warming up on Saturday. Halloween is the thirty-first. We'll go trick or treating up and down our blocks, getting lots of candy."

"I got something better," said Kenny, and they all turned and looked at him. What could be better than candy?

"After we get done trick or treating, we're gonna egg McDonagh's house!"

The boys gasped.

"He's dead," said Roger, thinking of what Father O'Malley said about respect for the deceased, even if it was mean, old Mr. McDonagh.

"Yeah," chimed Big Kenny, "so he can't hurt us or tell our parents. It will pay him back for all the mean stuff he did."

And so the boys reluctantly agreed to egg Mr. McDonagh's house after an evening of successful trick or treating. As they put on their coats to go to their own homes for supper, Roger suddenly exploded back up the stairs with an exclamation of, "I almost forgot."

He came back down with buckskins, a coonskin cap and a toy rifle, which he handed over to Tommy.

"There. Now you're Davy Crockett. Put this on and you'll look like a real American."

Tommy considered the clothes and then looked up with genuine appreciation. "Cheers, mate."

As usual, the boys were right about everything. The party at Saint Rita's was dumb, and dumb costumes won the prizes, because Sister Mary Ignatius was the judge and she didn't like anything fun. Big Kenny displayed his skill bobbing for apples and won a small biography of Saint Francis, which he gave to Mikey, because Mikey was a bookworm and Big Kenny did not like to read. Tommy was quiet, but looked good as Davy Crockett. Roger noticed some of the girls looking at him. He guessed Tommy even looked a little like Fess Parker and was a little jealous of him. Between the accent and his looks, girls noticed him in a way they never had Roger.

That night, Mrs. Swanson gave each of the boys a Mounds bar and a bottle of soda and they watched *Dracula*. Roger didn't want to tell anyone, but it kind of scared him. He did not like the idea of something climbing out of a coffin and seeking out victims. He kept seeing Mr. McDonagh's casket at the funeral and imagining him wearing a black cape inside it. He knew it made no sense, but he got the feeling Mr. McDonagh was waiting for him.

The first half of the week was the slowest time in Roger's life, ever. Each day dragged on. Every second in class was an eternity. It was as if God wanted Halloween to arrive as slowly as possible. Roger was going mad. But at night, when he fell asleep, he dreamt of Mr. McDonagh and his coffin. Roger would walk up to the McDonagh house to trick or treat (something which never happened in real life), the door would open and in the entryway would be the coffin. Mr. McDonagh would sit up in it. Roger would say, "Trick or Treat" and Mr. McDonagh would smile an impossibly wide smile (something else that also never happened in real life) and, in Bela Lugosi's voice would say, "What lands in my yard is MINE." He would then grab Roger, put him in the coffin and close it. Roger would yell and pound his fists on the coffin lid, and then he would hear shovelfuls of dirt raining down on the casket. He'd pound harder and no one would hear him. He'd then wake up with a start and took a long time to fall back to sleep.

✳

Finally, Wednesday arrived. The boys gathered at sundown at Roger's house. "Remember," his mother told him, "I want you back home in an hour. This is a school night. Your father and I are allowing you this treat. If you are late, you can forget any other treats any time soon, Mister. I mean it."

"Yes, Mom," Roger dutifully replied and the boys were out the door, scissors and elbows, carrying sacks to gather the candy this night promised. Roger was dressed like the Lone Ranger. Mikey was wearing a hobo outfit, made mostly from his father's clothing. Kenny wore his scout uniform, because he was also collecting for UNICEF. Big Kenny was dressed like a ghost, just wearing a big sheet with holes cut out for eyes. Tommy had arrived last, making the boys wonder if he would show after all. He was dressed as Davy Crockett again, but there was a new element to his costume. On his belt was a scabbard with a knife.

"Hey," said Big Kenny from under his sheet, "Davy Crockett has a bowie knife. What's that?"

"It was me Da's," replied Tommy. It was a black-handled knife and did not look like a bowie knife at all. There was no guard, the handle simply transformed into a straight, plain blade. The whole thing looked very old. "He got it from his da, and from his. I guess it's kinda something that reminds me of him. But it also will come in handy."

"That's right," said Kenny, pulling out his scout knife. "We're stabbing spooks tonight!" And the boys laughed.

"No," said Tommy quietly. "All Hallow's Eve is when the veil is the thinnest. My gran gave me this before I came to the states. The Irish know how to avoid spirits and beasties. 'A black-handled iron knife,' she said. 'Keep it for when the banshees come. Just in case.'"

"We're all Irish, dummy," said Kenny. "Quinn," pointing at himself. "O'Reilly," pointing at Big Kenny. "Bodie," pointing at Mikey.

"Shut up, you moron," Mikey shot back. "He's *from* Ireland. My grandparents were from Ireland, but I'm American and so are you and so are all of us."

"That doesn't mean his knife is better than mine," Kenny said, turning on Mikey.

"Nobody said it was. Now do you want to trick or treat or compare knife sizes?"

And the boys all guffawed and began to move to the first house.

They spent forty-five minutes going door to door, ringing bells and claiming candy. They ranged through the whole neighborhood and began to head home when Kenny stopped.

"C'mon, man," said Roger. "I gotta be home in fifteen minutes."

"This will only take five," said Kenny and reached into his scout rucksack and brought out a dozen eggs.

Big Kenny hooted and ran to grab some eggs. Mikey followed. Tommy and Roger hung back.

"I don't know, guys, it's late."

"What's the matter, Roger?" Mikey sneered. "You turning yellow on us?"

"Yeah," echoed Big Kenny, "You turning yellow?"

"No. I just don't know why we want to egg a dead guy's house. It won't bother him none. Whoever has to clean his house will just get sore."

"I already stole the eggs from my mom," said Kenny, "and he deserves it for being so mean. When people see his house with eggs on it, they'll laugh and think he deserved it and we'll have the last laugh on the mean coot. Unless you're yellow."

Roger sighed. He looked at Tommy. "You coming?"

Tommy looked down at his sack full of candy bars. He put his other hand on the knife handle and then walked over to join the others. It was decided.

Somehow the house was even darker at night. Mr. McDonagh always kept the curtains drawn, so his house had always looked dark, but now it looked even darker. Roger thought the house absorbed light.

The night, which had been cool, seemed colder now. A slight wind blew, threatening to make it colder still. They could hear the bare branches of the trees in his yard move and snap in the wind and the crab grass rustle. They could hear other kids trick or treating, but the night was winding down and no one would be coming near this house tonight. They had not come here any Halloween previously. Mr. McDonagh never gave out candy. In fact, one year he sat in the bushes by his house with the hose. If kids approached, he sprayed them with the hose, making them cold and wet. He'd then laugh and yell at them to stay off his property. In remembering, Roger was once again glad he was dead. Maybe throwing eggs at his house was the right thing to do.

The boys slowed down as they moved closer. They walked right up to the sidewalk and stood there for a minute, taking in the dark, foreboding contempt the house seemed to have for them. Even with its owner gone, the house seemed to carry on, telling them to stay off the lawn and threatening to take their candy like the owner had taken their balls and other toys that sailed onto his property.

They lingered until Kenny broke the spell, stepping first on the sidewalk, then off of it, jumping over the waist-high picket fence and approaching the house. His left arm cocked back and with a terrible stillness hung there for a second. Then, like Mel Parnell on the mound at Fenway pitching that no-hitter against Chicago back in July, Kenny let loose with a fastball and the egg sailed quicker than they could follow. With a mighty splat it exploded against the front door. Their collective breaths, which they had been unaware they were holding, burst out from them in an explosion of laughter and cheers.

"Steeeee-rike!" yelled Mikey, who then lobbed an egg at the second floor, but hitting a window on the first. The yoke slowly ran down the pane, streaking it with yellow, providing the only color the house had.

A volley of eggs from Big Kenny, Kenny, and Mikey followed, each landing on the house with a loud smack of cracking shell and splattering albumin. They did not notice that Tommy and Roger had hung back. Nor did they notice the silence surrounding them, so intent were they on showing Mr. McDonagh's house it had no power over them anymore.

Roger saw a light come on at the side of the house. As if someone had been inside and come out through the porch door next to the garage. His first instinct was to freeze.

"Guys" he whispered. "Guys!" he tried again when they ignored him. "I think someone's coming."

Kenny shot a look at him. "Cops?"

"Dunno."

Silence reigned. Then a snap of a branch. Someone had stepped on it at the side of the house.

"Should we cheese it?" asked Mikey.

They considered this. Then Kenny said, "If it were the cops, they'd be out here by now chasing us. I bet it's Eddie O'Connor and his friends. I got one egg left. I'm gonna nail them."

Kenny was the starting pitcher for his Little League team, so they boys knew if anyone could make good on that promise, it was Kenny. He looked at the light, aimed the egg, pulled back and let go. It sailed true and hit something just slightly above and behind the light. The boys heard it hit, but saw nothing.

Roger realized that the light illuminated nothing. They could see the light itself, but it was not showing them anything around it.

"Guys... I think we should...," and the light began to move towards them. Slowly swaying back and forth it slipped along the side of the house. Finally, as the light broke past the corner, the light of the moon showed them what it was.

Mr. McDonagh, wearing the suit he had been buried in, stood there, holding a large gourd with a candle in it. Raw egg slid down his suit coat. The first thing that occurred to Roger was, "Oh, that's why the light didn't show us his face—it was inside something." Then reality slammed home.

The boys screamed and then were silenced. It was not fear that held them to that place, but something stronger. The hatred of this old man for the children of his neighborhood had become a palpable force. It held them to the ground. Mikey began to cry. Big Kenny struggled to pull his legs up with his hands. Kenny stood defiant, but was out of eggs.

McDonagh's voice, when he spoke, was crabgrass and the grave.

"My… yard… What lands in my yard is mine…." He held up the candle and began to move towards Kenny, who was the closest to him.

"What lands in my yard IS MINE!"

Kenny finally broke and began to scream and cry and struggle to get away from the nightmare shuffling towards him.

Time slowed for Roger. Mr. McDonagh was stiff and his movements slow and awkward, but he moved relentlessly forward, raising the gourd to see the face of the boy as he approached. McDonagh's clawed hand reached out for Kenny, relentlessly moving toward his chest. McDonagh's suit was not dirty, though. Roger realized he had not climbed up out of the grave. But the egg hit him, so he was real. Tommy was right. Hell wouldn't have him, so now he wandered the Earth.

Suddenly, Tommy was moving. Moving fast. The knife was out of its sheath before Roger even realized Tommy was moving. How was Tommy moving? Why was he not stuck like the rest of them?

Hanging back before, he now leapt over the fence, placing himself between Kenny and Mr. McDonagh. Crying out, "*Imeacht as an saol seo!*" he swept down with the knife and missed Mr. McDonagh entirely. The knife was planned in the ground, sticking straight up. Mr. McDonagh grinned malevolently down on Tommy and Roger knew his new friend was dead. He should have never invited him to Halloween, never agreed to egg the house, never come out this night.

Then Mr. McDonagh's smile slipped. He stopped moving. The candle in his gourd began to gutter. Tommy looked up into the dead eyes looking down on him. "*Imeacht as an saol seo*, Jack. Hell might not want you, but neither does North Hamden. Not anymore. This is not your yard. This is not your house. The dead own nothing. What lands in this yard is not yours. Not anymore."

A look of pure hatred passed across McDonagh's face, and the candle grew dimmer. Then he turned. He walked down the front walk of the house, passing the boys on either side of him. Though they were terrified, they kept laughing.

He moved down the street, carrying the gourd. He stopped one last time to stare daggers at the boys and look at the house, almost wistfully. Turning away again, he shuffled down the street, looking like a very old man, lost and frightened.

The boys finally stopped laughing and stood there numb for who knows how long. Finally, Big Kenny screwed up his courage and tried to move his feet. He found he could move easily. Roger, Kenny and Mikey followed, running to Tommy, who pulled the knife out of the ground and cleaned it on his thigh before putting it back in the sheath.

"What did you do?"

"What just happened?

"What was that?"

The questions were a torrential waterfall that Tommy stepped back and away from, putting up his hand to quiet the boys.

"Wasn't Mr. McDonagh's first name John?"

What kind of question was that? "Uh… yes," said Roger.

"Hm." Tommy seemed to finally understand.

"Tommy?" Roger prodded. "Do you know what that was?"

"Mr. McDonagh."

The boys looked at each other. "Obviously, yes. But what was he?"

Tommy sighed, looked at the moon and turned back to them. "I don't know. But I told you that the veil is thinnest this time of year. He is Jack. Maybe not the original Jack-o-Lantern, but he has become one."

Big Kenny's brow furrowed. "I don't get it."

"You told me he was mean to kids and took their stuff and he lived here a long time, right? So, when he died, Hell didn't want him. He came back here to keep taking things from kids and I think tonight, since we were on his lawn he meant to take our lives. Stabbing a black-handled iron knife into the ground is a counter-charm to Jack-o-Lanterns. I told him that since he was dead, this was not his home anymore, so he had no claim to us."

"What was that you said to him?" Mikey asked.

"It's Gaelic," Tommy told him. "It means, 'Depart from this life.'"

"So where'd he go?"

"I don't know. Neither Heaven nor Hell will take him. He can't stay here. I expect he will walk the Earth until doomsday, but he won't bother kids anymore."

Big Kenny sat down on the lawn. "How do you know all this?"

Tommy chuckled to himself. "Well, I'm Irish. My Gran told me."

"How come we don't?"

"Because, dummy," snapped Kenny, "we're American."

The boys grabbed their sacks of candy and moved back towards the street.

"Thanks, Tommy," said Roger, and meant it. Somehow, Mr. McDonagh didn't seem scary anymore. He was just a sad, old man.

"You lent me a costume," Tommy said, indicating the buckskin fringe. "Guess that makes us even. Happy Halloween, right?"

Big Kenny still seemed confused. "So Mr. McDonagh isn't dead?"

Kenny hit his arm with his candy sack. "Couse he's dead. He's a ghost now, but Tommy just licked him good, and we egged his house and showed him," he crowed. They boys all smiled.

Roger looked back and saw Tommy had left the knife in the ground. He turned and ran back. "Hey, Tommy, you left your knife!"

"NO!" Tommy yelled as Roger leapt the fence and knelt to pull the knife out of the ground.

As soon as the blade was free of the soil, Roger felt a strong hand on his shoulder, pulling him up and towards the house and heard a voice low and close in his ear, "What lands in my yard is MINE!"

The Reckoning: Hidden Remains

Spencer Carvalho

In the late 1800s, there was a town called Bogart that had a serious problem. Many of the town's residents were disappearing. With fewer citizens, there were less taxes, and Mayor Crumble realized that decisive action was needed. He took up a collection and sent away for a specialist.

Jericho Heller rode into the town of Bogart at dusk. Just as the sun began to fade, he appeared over the horizon. Mayor Crumble advised Alexander Campbell, the town doctor, to wait for Jericho's arrival. He noticed that Jericho's horse appeared sickly and decrepit. It appeared odd to Dr. Campbell, but stranger still was the metal helmet that the horse wore. The helmet was in the shape of a horse skull and completely covered the horse's face except for two eyeholes.

Dr. Campbell waved down the traveler, who stopped by him. Now Dr. Campbell could see that Jericho was entirely clothed in black. His boots, pants, jacket, gloves, and hat were all black.

"Are you Jericho Heller?" asked Dr. Campbell.

"Indeed I am," said Jericho.

"My name is Dr. Campbell. I was advised to meet you. We are waiting for you in Chokers."

Jericho got down from his horse.

"Chokers?" asked Jericho.

"It's the name of the local dining establishment," said Dr. Campbell. "It is named after its owner, Samuel Choker."

"Unfortunate name for a dining establishment."

Jericho tied his horse to a post and untied his pack, which he threw over his shoulder. Dr. Campbell looked at Jericho's horse.

"Pardon me for asking, sir, but what's with your horse? He looks like he's on the verge of death."

"He is dead."

"Pardon me?"

"He's a zombie horse."

"What's a zombie?"

"Undead."

"Surely, you jest."

"Nope."

"Why in heaven's name would you want an undead horse?"

"He doesn't get tired and I don't have to worry about him dying beneath me."

"Why is he wearing a helmet?"

"That's more of a muzzle, to keep him from biting me or anyone else."

"Never the less, I'll get him some oats."

"He doesn't eat oats, only meat. Preferably horse meat, if you've got it."

"Sir, are you pulling my leg?"

"Nope. I'll feed him myself later. We wouldn't want you getting bit."

Jericho followed Dr. Campbell into Chokers. There were a five people in there waiting for them. One was behind the counter. Three were sitting together in a group and the fifth was standing. All eyes turned to Jericho as he entered. The man who stood was a rotund gentleman wearing expensive clothes. Jericho made the correct assumption that he was the mayor. Mayor Crumble walked over to Jericho with the intention of shaking his hand.

"Hello, Mr. Heller. I'm Mayor Crumble. Welcome to the town of Bogart."

The mayor held out his hand. Jericho put down his pack and shook the mayor's hand. Jericho was wearing leather gloves, which Mayor Crumble thought felt weird against his bare skin. They didn't feel like normal riding gloves to him. They felt more like human skin.

"I must say, I thought you would be older," said Mayor Crumble.

"I'm older than I look," said Jericho.

Jericho turned his attention to the other people in the room.

"Hello," said Jericho. "I'd like to get started quickly, so how about I get something to eat and you can all tell me what's going on."

Jericho sat down at a table near the three sitting people. The three men shared a family resemblance.

"Howdy," said Jericho.

Two of the three men nodded. The other just stared of into space.

"These men are the Grendel brothers," said Mayor Crumble. "There's Jethro Grendel, Jasper Grendel, and Jebediah Grendel."

"Your parents sure like alliteration," said Jericho.

The Grendel brothers said nothing. Jericho assumed that they didn't know what the word alliteration meant.

"Let me get this straight," said Jericho. "You three are all deputies and all brothers, right?"

Jethro nodded.

"I'm going to take a guess and say that your father is the sheriff of this town," said Jericho. "Am I right?"

"Their father was or is Gabriel Grendel," said Mayor Crumble. "He's gone missing, too."

The man from behind the counter brought Jericho a bowl of stew and a glass of water. Jericho carefully looked at the water before he drank it to see if it was dirty.

"Are you Samuel Choker?" asked Jericho.

"The one and only," said Mr. Choker.

"Nice place," said Jericho. "Real quiet."

Mr. Choker went back behind the counter.

"Okay, so tell me what happened," said Jericho.

"It all started about a month ago," said Mayor Crumble. "People just started disappearing. For no reason, people just went missing. We have no idea why."

"Did you have any disappearances more than a month ago?" asked Jericho.

"Maybe once in a blue moon, but now more than half the people of this town are missing. This place is turning into a ghost town."

"Do you mean that literally or figuratively?" asked Jericho.

"Pardon?" asked Mayor Crumble.

"Are there actual ghosts in this town?"

Mayor Crumble laughed. When Mayor Crumble saw how serious Jericho was, he stopped laughing.

"I would appreciate an answer," said Jericho.

"Uh, there are no ghosts in the town," said Mayor Crumble. "Not to my knowledge."

"This is ridiculous," said Jethro. "Why is this man here? We can handle this ourselves."

"Clearly you can't," said Jericho.

"Well, why do you think you can fix things?" asked Jethro.

"Because I'm a specialist," said Jericho.

"And what makes you so special?" asked Jethro. "Are you a detective or one of them Pinkerton boys?"

"No," said Jericho. "I'm more of a modern mage."

"What's that mean?" asked Jethro.

"I can do things and acquire knowledge using supernatural or nonrational means."

"What?" asked Jethro.

"I specialize in strange and unusual things," said Jericho.

Jericho turned to Mayor Crumble.

"I would like a map of the town," said Jericho. "I want to map out all the places where people went missing."

Mayor Crumble left to go get a map. Jericho looked over at Jasper Grendel who was staring of into space.

"What's his story?" asked Jericho.

"He was off on patrol with pop when he went missing," said Jebediah. "He wandered back into town on foot. He hasn't been right since."

Mayor Crumble came back with a map. They mapped out the homes of the missing people and when they went missing.

"And you haven't found any bodies?" asked Jericho.

"No," said Jethro.

"That's odd," said Jericho. "Well, it's definitely not some kind of animal. It's not a werewolf or zombies. Definitely not ghosts. We're too far away from salt water for it to be sirens or mermaids. It could be a curse or possibly wendigos. Are there any suspects?"

"Yin Lee," said Jethro.

"Who's that?" asked Jericho.

"A local China man," said Jethro.

"You mean he's Chinese," said Jericho.

"That's what I said."

"No. Actually, you said… never mind. Why do you think he's guilty?"

"I just don't trust him. He has shifty eyes."

Jericho looked around the room at the other people.

"Please tell me he's the only one in the town this stupid," said Jericho.

Jethro stood up.

"You better watch yourself," said Jethro.

"No," said Jericho. "You better watch yourself you incompetent, racist waste of life. You want to be violent with me, fine, but you'll be the one that gets buried. You remember that."

"Gentlemen, gentlemen," said Mayor Crumble. "I'm sure we can be civil."

Jericho looked at the map and pointed to a spot on it.

"Is this the last place where people went missing? The Helsing ranch?"

"Why, yes," said Dr. Campbell.

"I'll start there. Maybe I'll find some clues."

"We can head out at dawn," said Jebediah.

"No," said Jericho. "I'll go now. It should be dawn by the time I get there."

"We can be ready within the hour," said Jebediah.

"That's okay," said Jericho. "You guys stay here and guard the town. I'll take the doc."

"Excuse me," said Dr. Campbell.

"What if I find someone alive," said Jericho. "They could need doctor care."

"I guess," said Dr. Campbell. "I'll get my medical bag."

"I'll go with you," said Jericho.

Jericho finished his glass of water and followed Dr. Campbell. Jericho made sure to grab his pack before he left Chokers. Dr. Campbell's doctor's office was within walking distance.

Jericho was impressed at how clean the building was.

"You've got a nice place here," said Jericho.

"Why, thank you," said Dr. Campbell. "I also have a variety of tonics and vigors."

"Do you have any vampire blood?"

"Uh… why no. I can't say that I do."

"Too bad. That's the key to a longer life.

Dr. Campbell grabbed his medical bag and was about to leave when Jericho stopped him.

"Hold your horses," said Jericho. "Do you have a gun?"

"No, sir," said Dr. Campbell. "I have no need for one."

"Well, you do now."

Jericho reached into his pack and pulled out a sawed off double-barrel shotgun.

"This here is a double-barrel shotgun," said Jericho. "Now, I'm assuming you don't have a lot of experience with shooting?"

"No, sir."

"Well, then this is perfect for you. You barely need to aim with this. It doesn't have a long range, so it wouldn't be great in a gunfight, but it works great against anything that uses claws or teeth. Even if bullets won't kill it, it will at least stun it long enough for you to get away. The big drawback is that it only holds two bullets at a time."

Jericho opened the sawed off double-barrel shotgun. He pulled out two bullets from his pack and loaded them. He then closed up the gun and handed it to Dr. Campbell.

"See there," said Jericho. "Easy enough."

Dr. Campbell looked over the sawed off double-barrel shotgun.

"Now the most important thing for you to remember is to not shoot me," said Jericho. "Is that clear? Don't shoot me. You want to shoot someone else, go ahead, but not me. I really don't care for getting shot."

"I won't shoot you."

"Good. Do you have any questions?"

"Why, as a matter of fact I do. Why do you wear so much black?"

"It makes me look dashing."

"Really?"

"No, not really. It makes it easier for me to hide in the dark. I tend to rely on stealth. Somewhat like the ninjas of feudal Japan."

"An educated man."

"There ain't nothin wrong with smarts."

They got up on their horses and rode to the site of the last abduction. They arrived at the Helsing ranch around dawn. Dr. Campbell watched Jericho as the sun rose.

"What?" asked Jericho. "Were you expecting me to burst into flames when the sunlight hit me?"

"The thought crossed my mind."

"We can go the rest of the way on foot."

They got down off their horses. Jericho made sure he had his back turned to Dr. Campbell. Jericho stood there with his back turned to Dr. Campbell for a few seconds. Jericho turned around and walked over to Dr. Campbell.

"Still have your sawed off shotgun?" asked Jericho.

"Of course."

Jericho reached into his pocket and pulled out a box, which he handed to Dr. Campbell.

"What's this?" asked Dr. Campbell.

"The bullets in your gun are fakes," said Jericho. "These are real."

"Why did you give me fake bullets?"

"I barely know you. I wasn't going to give you a gun and turn my back on you until I knew you could be trusted. Now, you've had plenty of opportunity to shoot me and you haven't, so it stands to reason that you bear me no ill will. Now, there could be trouble in the Helsing ranch and I definitely want you armed before we go in."

Jericho pulled out two pistols, which he kept on his hips.

"Stay close to me," said Jericho. "And remember, don't shoot me."

Dr. Campbell followed Jericho inside the Helsing's home. The house was empty. Jericho got close to the ground and searched the house.

"What are you doing?" asked Dr. Campbell.

"Looking for a trail," said Jericho. "I found it. It's hard to see, but there's a little bit of blood."

Jericho crawled along the ground out the back door of the home. Dr. Campbell followed Jericho until he stopped at the Helsing's garden.

"The trail ends here," said Jericho. "The ground was recently disturbed. There's something buried here."

The two men found tools in a nearby shed and started digging. They dug less than six feet deep when they found the remains of the Helsing family. Their skin and organs had been removed. Only bones were left. Jericho pulled the bones up out of the hole to better examine them.

"These bodies weren't down here long enough to decompose," said Jericho. "Something removed the skin and organs. Probably to eat it."

"How were you able to do that?" asked Dr. Campbell. "How did you find the trail to the bodies and learn all this stuff?"

"My grandfather taught me. He was a medicine man."

"You're Indian?"

Jericho looked up at Dr. Campbell.

"I'm American. India is across the Ocean. I am part native on my mother's side."

Jericho went back to examining the bones.

"I know what did this. It was an Atshen. Atshens are cannibalistic spirits. They live inside people and transfer bodies by biting. When they take over a new person, the person acts, walks, and talks different. Remember how quiet Jasper was? My money's on him."

They rode back into town. It was close to dusk when they arrived. The men hitched up their horses.

"Now getting to Jasper may be difficult," said Jericho. "I have to get past his brothers."

"Can't you just explain what happened to them?" asked Dr. Campbell.

"The Grendel brothers don't really seem like the rational and reasonable type. They probably won't believe me until I show them the truth, and even then they might prefer to pretend that I'm lying. Where do you think the Grendel brothers are?"

"Most likely they're at the sheriff's office."

"We need to separate the boys. You need to go in and tell them you found bodies at the Helsing ranch. Then you lead them to the ranch. I'm not sure how many of the brothers will go with you. Even if it's only one, that's one less for me to worry about."

Jericho watched from the shadows as Dr. Campbell went into the sheriff's office. A little while later, Jebediah followed Dr. Campbell out. They got on their horses and went off in the direction of the Helsing ranch. Jericho sneaked behind the sheriff's office and peered in through a back window. Jericho had his pistols out.

"Hold it," said Jethro. "What do you think you're doing?"

Jericho turned and saw Jethro holding a double-barrel shotgun pointed in his direction.

"Most men can't do that," said Jericho. "Sneak up on me that is."

"I asked you a question."

"I'm afraid you wouldn't understand if I told you."

"You come sneaking around here you better have a good reason."

"Has your brother seemed different since he's been back? I don't just mean quiet. I mean strange. He hasn't said anything since he's been back."

"He's shook up."

"He's not your brother. Your brother is gone. The thing

that's been killing people is called an Atshen. It's a spirit and it now lives inside Jasper."

"You're crazy."

"Atshen's are cannibals. Have you seen Jasper eat since the night you lost your dad?"

Jethro thought for a moment trying to remember if he saw Jasper eat anything since that night.

"You're talking crazy," said Jethro. "Lose the guns."

Jericho placed them on a nearby barrel.

"You move inside now, you hear?"

Jericho walked inside the sheriff's office. Jericho saw Jasper sitting at a table near the window, staring out at nothing. Jethro pointed to the table with his double-barrel shotgun.

"Sit down," said Jethro.

Jericho sat at the same table as Jasper. Jasper turned to look at Jericho, but not in a human way. His eyes moved first and then his head. Jasper just stared and Jericho stared back.

"You wouldn't believe what he's been saying," said Jethro. "He called you an Atshen."

Jericho's eyes went wide and his heart started pumping fast, because he knew things were going to get bad quickly.

"I think you should offer him something to eat," said Jericho. "Have him eat and prove me wrong."

Jethro grabbed a bowl and filled it with stew cooking over the fireplace. He placed the bowl in front of Jasper. Jasper just kept staring at Jericho.

"What's the matter?" asked Jethro. "Ain't you hungry?"

Jasper smiled. He then jumped at Jethro with his mouth open. Jethro raised his shotgun and fired, but Jasper knocked the gun aside and the blast hit Jericho in the chest. The blast knocked Jericho to the ground. Jericho was struggling to breathe as he watched Jasper eating Jethro. Jethro struggled at first, but then stopped squirming. It was a few seconds before Jericho realized he was shot with rock salt. He pulled himself up which caught Jasper's attention. Blood smears covered Jasper's mouth and there was a crazed look in his eye. Jericho pulled out his knife.

Jericho remembered his childhood. When he was much younger, his grandfather showed him a dead body. His grandfather cut open the body and showed all the places to cut in order to cause the most damage.

Jasper lunged at Jericho. Jericho backed up and grabbed Jasper's wrist and then sliced the tendons in his arm. He then stabbed the knife through Jasper's other hand. Jericho pulled the knife out, but twisted it as he did to cause more damage. When Jasper moved in to bite him, he shoved the knife up through the bottom of his mouth. Jericho grabbed Jasper's hair while still holding the knife handle and directed him to the fireplace and kicked him into it. Jasper screamed through a mouth still stabbed shut. Jericho went for the double-barrel shotgun. As soon as Jasper got out of the fire, Jericho shot him in the chest sending him back into the fire. The rock salt wasn't enough to kill Jasper and death by fire is slow, so Jericho used the double-barrel shotgun like a pole and kept Jasper from getting out while he burned. When Jasper stopped moving, he got his pistols. Jericho shot Jasper's corpse in the head a few times just to be sure he was dead. He also shot Jethro's corpse in the head just to make sure he didn't come back as an Atshen.

Jericho got Mayor Crumble and explained what happened. He wasn't sure if Mayor Crumble believed him, but the mayor was willing to pay for Jericho to leave. He didn't want to have to explain this to Jebediah, so as soon as he had his money, he was off to the next town.

Halloween Bully

Edward M Wolfe

It started on Halloween night.

Daniel was at a party that he didn't really feel like being at, but it seemed foolish to turn down going to a party on a holiday. What would he do instead—sit at home and watch TV, by himself? He told himself there was zero chance of meeting a woman at home. But then he argued, he could meet someone escorting her kids door to door. Right. Like that's what he wanted, someone who already had kids. The party offered better chances of ending his single streak.

After sticking around for nearly two hours, thoroughly not enjoying himself and not seeing any dating prospects since none of the single women interested him, he slowly worked his way toward the door. He tipped his red, plastic Solo cup all the way up, finishing off his beer and took one last look around to see if anything could possibly make him change his mind. There was nothing.

Twelve minutes later, Daniel was driving slowly through his neighborhood, careful to avoid hitting any miniature witches or goblins that might come running out into the street from between parked cars. As he drove, he looked around at the houses that were made up for the holiday; white streaming gauze hanging from a tree, plastic jack-o-lanterns glowing with electric light, a few real pumpkins that were carved and lit with candles.

He thought back to the last time he had gone out dressed up as a kid on Halloween. He had grown up poor and frequently had to wear a homemade costume. When he was very young, he didn't know the difference between homemade and bought in a store. But the older he got, the more he noticed how fancy and professional the other kids' costumes looked compared to his and his sister's.

It was still easy enough to put out of his mind though as he enjoyed the night and harvested sweets that would last him for months. One day, everything changed. He was old enough to escort his sister around without parental supervision. He had reached the magic age of twelve and his parents no longer required him to have a babysitter. On Halloween that year, he argued that no babysitter at home should equal no babysitter while trick-or-treating. His parents relented and allowed him and his sister to go out alone after a brief lecture about safety, looking both ways before crossing streets, and so on.

Daniel was waiting for the two standard warnings that they couldn't possibly include in the speech: Come home when it gets dark, and don't take candy from strangers. He thought it was funny that they weren't going out *until* it was dark, and they were to do nothing but take candy from strangers. But he didn't voice those thoughts. This was a milestone event that he didn't want to risk having rescinded.

The night had gone perfectly. He and Rebecca had nearly full bags of candy and were heading home, not even stopping at any more houses along the way because they had so much candy already, and both of them had aching feet from walking far more than they were accustomed. If they followed the streets back home, it would take them twice as long as it would if they cut through the local park, so Daniel headed toward the park.

His family lived in a middle-class suburban neighborhood, and it was as safe as any normal neighborhood could be that was gated or walled off with security guards blocking entrances like Daniel had seen when they drove around looking a Christmas lights last year.

Half-way through the park, there were several picnic tables under a slatted roof. Daniel saw two dark figures standing next to one of the Hibachi grills near one of the tables. Instinctively, he steered his sister on a wide path away from the strangers. One of them left the darkness of the roofed area and began heading his way. Daniel started walking faster and took his sister's hand to make her keep up with him.

"Hey! Come here for a minute."

Daniel knew the voice without even turning around to see who it was. There was no mistaking Billy the Bastard and his fat, mean voice.

"Keep walking," Daniel commanded.

Rebecca trotted to keep up with her big brother. She

sensed from the tone in his voice and their increased pace that something was wrong. But she wasn't scared. Daniel wouldn't let anything bad happen to her.

They were crossing into the darkest part of the park, halfway between the light pole near the grills and the nearest streetlight by the sidewalk where Daniel and Rebecca would turn to head toward their street only one block away. They just had to keep walking and ignore Billy. Maybe he'd give up and go back to where he came from.

Daniel wondered later how a fat kid who was so out of shape could come up behind them without a sound. One second he was walking through the grass, and the next, he was face down with the wind knocked out of him. He struggled to breathe, but it seemed impossible. Just when he sucked in what felt like a lifesaving breath, it was knocked out of him again by Billy stomping on his back and laughing like a stupid, fat demon.

He turned to see if his sister was okay. She was lying beside him, facing him with her mouth open in a silent cry. She couldn't make a sound because she was also trying to breathe as her body tried to cry. Daniel was filled with rage. How dare he hurt a little girl? What kind of person could do that? He would gladly take whatever Billy had to dish out if he would just leave Rebecca alone.

As soon as his diaphragm stopped its spasm, Daniel sucked in a deep breath and screamed, "Leave her alone! She's just a little kid!" His voice came out way higher than normal, but he didn't think about that at the time. He was scared to death of Billy, but he was also so angry with him, he'd be willing to fight him (and lose) if he could just get up from under his big fat foot.

"What are you gonna do about it, ya little baby? Are you gonna cry all over me?"

Daniel hated knowing that it was true; he was crying. He wasn't making any sounds, but hot tears were running down his cheek and dripping into the grass. He tried to toughen up inside and make his tears stop, and make his voice sound bolder than he felt.

"I just think you should pick on someone your own size, instead of a little girl."

"Greg! Danny boy just admitted he's a little girl! You gotta hear this."

"I wasn't talking about me, you fat bastard!"

Daniel and Rebecca screamed in unison as Billy jumped up several inches and then landed on them where he had been standing on them before. Their breath whooshed out of them and for the third time, Daniel couldn't breathe. As he waited for his breath to come back, he grabbed fistfuls of grass and raged internally. He shouldn't have said anything. His sister would pay just as much as he would for anything he said or did that angered Billy. That was unacceptable.

The only way he could offer her any protection at all was to completely give in to Billy. To be a good big brother, he had to humiliate himself and not be her hero. He hoped she'd understand later that it was all he could do. He hated Billy even more now than ever before. Taking away his sister's admiration of him was crueler than simply beating him up. He swore he'd get revenge somehow, some day.

"I'm sorry. I didn't mean it. Just tell me what you want."

"That's more like it. Now say you're nothing but a little girl."

Daniel clenched his teeth. *Please don't make me look like nothing in front of my sister.*

"Go on! Say it!"

He knew if he didn't, Rebecca would get hurt again. She was crying now and her voice was tearing him up inside. He needed to get her away from here.

"I'm nothing but a little girl."

Billy laughed his stupid laugh again. Daniel could tell it wasn't even a real laugh. That's part of what made it sound so stupid. *Ah ha ha. Ah ha ha.* He wanted to punch Billy in his fat face.

"Will you please let us up now?"

Billy tried to think of how else he could take advantage of the situation, but he was distracted by the two overloaded bags of candy lying in the grass. He couldn't wait to see what was in them.

"After you say it again. Say you're a little girl. And a fag!"

Daniel almost blurted out how stupid that was. It didn't even make sense. But Rebecca's crying kept him focused.

"I'm a little girl, and a fag."

This struck Billy as genuinely funny and this time he laughed for real.

"Oh gawd, Greg. You just missed the funniest thing."

He stepped off of the prone kids and gathered up their Halloween bags, still laughing.

Daniel was relieved to feel the pressure come off his back

and that he could breathe much easier. He knew he had made things better for himself and for Rebecca by degrading himself for the amusement of that fat moron. He stayed down, unsure if getting up would cause Billy to resume his assault. But he didn't want to further embarrass himself by asking Billy for permission to get up.

He couldn't tell if Billy was walking away or not. Somehow, he was very quiet in the grass. He craned his head around to look behind him and saw two figures next to the grill the way they were when he had first entered the park.

He got up quickly and pulled his sister up.

"Come on!" he said, and they ran together toward the light.

When they reached their street, Daniel slowed to a stop and bent over to catch his breath. He looked at his sister, feeling shame and guilt.

"I'm sorry, Rebecca. I had to let him take our candy so he'd leave us alone. And I couldn't fight him because he had a friend there and it would've ended up being two against one."

Rebecca looked into his eyes, biting her bottom lip. Her left cheek had dirt and grass stains on it. The front of her mummy costume was wet. He picked off blades of grass and asked, "Are you okay? Do you hurt anywhere?"

"My back hurts," she said in her sweet little voice, and she sniffed, trying not to cry.

Daniel pulled her close and hugged her. He cried silent tears, thinking of how he had failed to protect her. She was so small and innocent and didn't deserve to ever have anything bad happen to her.

"You'll feel better in a little while. I promise."

But she didn't. The pain got progressively worse until a few days later their parents took her to the hospital. Daniel was taken to stay with an aunt for a few days.

Daniel peripherally saw a small light moving rapidly in a short arc. It was a glow-stick coming toward him in a kid's hand from ahead on the left. If it hadn't been for that, he probably wouldn't have even seen what happened next. There was a kid running along on a collision course with a little Cinderella and her mother just off to his left. The mother and daughter looked like they were done trick-or-treating and were either walking home or to a parked car.

The kid with the glow-stick was carrying a pillowcase burdened with a tremendous amount of candy. Daniel thought it was a good thing he was running because the kid could stand to burn a few calories. He looked about fourteen years old. Dark blonde buzz cut. At least twenty-five pounds overweight, and a look on his face that Daniel was sure he'd seen many times before. It was the look of a self-centered bully who had no regard for anyone else in the world but himself and his own cruel desires. He could practically be Billy's kid, all these years later.

Daniel lightly braked his Dodge Durango to a crawl and watched the boy as he ran right up behind the little blonde girl. The kid extended one of his arms toward the girl's back as he slowed down, but still impacted it with enough force to send the girl flying forward and down onto the asphalt that she and her mother had just stepped onto.

The next few seconds occurred quickly and mindlessly for Daniel, like a montage of sights and sounds. He saw the girl's face lift up from the street with blood running down from one of her eyes—he stopped the Durango and slammed the gear lever into park—the boy picked up the girl's plastic orange pumpkin and in one motion tilted it into his open pillowcase— Daniel reached for his door handle—the mother quickly went toward her daughter with her mouth open in shock and fear— Daniel opened his door and stepped out—and the montage slowed down as he focused his attention on the boy.

The kid dropped the pumpkin and cinched his pillowcase, holding the top end with one hand while sliding the other down to the bulk of the candy several inches below and began to spin the pillowcase around.

Daniel yelled, "Hey!" as loud as he could, intending to emote a sense of force and authority. He could hear both the mother and daughter crying behind him and that fueled his rage; a rage that had burned for fifteen years.

The kid stopped for just a second as he turned to look at Daniel over his shoulder. And he smiled. Daniel couldn't believe it. The little bastard smiled at him as if he had just accomplished something impressive. Then he started to run. One second later, Daniel ran after him.

The kid was overweight, but determined to get away with his loot. He took off faster than Daniel would have thought possible. All of the anger, guilt and shame from that Halloween long ago drove him forward like a lion. It was as if he was transported back to the past and he was chasing Billy the night he hurt Rebecca. Some part of his mind knew that this was different, but another part said it was the same.

It was always the same - human predators preying on the weak. And the weak were always decent people. Smaller, smarter, nicer, and unable or unwilling to defend themselves out of fear.

The bullies were always the same, too. Big, mean and dumb. Projecting their self-hatred on those they envied and could never be like. So they traded self-esteem for a sense of power; lying to theirselves that over-powering their victims made them somehow superior to those they victimized.

Daniel had never fought back before, but that was about to change. Something broke inside him. Something that kept him restrained within the bounds of society's rules; the same rules that let bad guys get away with hurting people. No one was supposed to take the law into their own hands. You were supposed to take your beating, then report it to the officials who may, or may not obtain justice for you.

The image of that tiny Cinderella's face hitting the pavement merged in his mind with the image of Rebecca's mouth open wide in a silent scream and it pushed him over the edge. This little girl's night of joy and candy harvesting with her mother turned instantly into a night of blood, pain and tears. With Rebecca, the bleeding was internal, so he'd never seen it. Maybe if someone *had* seen it, she would've been taken to the hospital sooner. Maybe if he had somehow fought back that night, she'd still be alive today.

Giving it no thought at all, Daniel leaped for the kid's back as he stretched out his arms, aiming for the kids shoulders. Daniel connected and his weight brought them both down, skidding on the street with the kid serving as a buffer between Daniel and the blacktop.

"Get offa me!" the kid screamed. The pitch of his voice was high and close to tears. Daniel got to his feet, breathing hard through his clenched teeth. He reached down and picked up the pillowcase. Some of the candy had scattered onto the street, but the case was still very heavy. It occurred to Daniel that the kid had probably stolen most of it. And that made him even angrier as he visualized little girls throughout the night being slammed from behind by this punk.

The kid turned over and pulled himself up into a sitting position and saw Daniel coming right at him. He started to scoot backwards, looking up at Daniel's enraged face, first with cocky defiance and then raw fear as he began to understand that the tables had been turned. Someone bigger and stronger than him was the predator now.

Daniel stomped on the candy that had spilled from the pillowcase as he approached the kid, turning it under his boots. "You stupid, worthless, fat, little piece of crap!" he growled.

"Lea' me alone!" the kid cried.

Daniel almost felt a second of pity for him. His chin was scraped badly from his slide on the street and was bleeding onto his ripped and stained t-shirt. His hands had pebbles embedded in them and blood was oozing out around the pebbles and gravel. Just when Daniel thought that maybe this kid had gotten enough punishment, the image of the little girl flashed into his mind again, followed immediately by the image Rebecca's face the last time he saw her as his father had carried her out to the car on the way to the hospital; crying from the internal injury that no one knew was there.

"You think it's cool to hurt people? Knock them down and steal from them? How do you like it now, you little bastard!?" he asked quietly, but with years of pent up rage boiling inside him.

Unbelievably, the kid started to deny any wrong-doing, "I... I didn't... I didn't..." and his words were cut off by Daniel kicking him once in the head. The kid flew back, his head hit the asphalt with a thunk, and he stayed there, not moving. Daniel turned around and ran back to his Durango. He got in, dropping the pillowcase on the passenger seat and put the truck in Drive with one hand as he pulled the door shut with the other. He drove past the kid who was still lying on the street apparently unconscious, and he used a side-street intersection to do a U-turn.

He saw the young blonde woman closing the rear passenger door on the driver's side of the car she and her daughter had been approaching, and then she quickly opened the driver's door.

Daniel turned off his headlights and came to a stop. The woman was startled and turned around, fearing that the young attacker had returned to inflict more harm upon her and her daughter.

"Please, don't!" she exclaimed as Daniel quickly rounded the front of his truck and ran toward her. She backed up against the passenger door and held out her hands in front of her as if to ward off this Halloween evil and protect her hurt and scared little girl in the backseat. Daniel approached the still open driver's door and tossed the bag of candy onto the passenger seat.

He wished he could say or do something to help them, but he knew there was nothing he could do. Besides, he had just committed a violent crime and it was stupid of him to have stopped and returned the stolen candy to the little girl.

He ran back around his truck, got in and took off, leaving his headlights off until he rounded the corner, hoping that his license plate numbers were not too visible. As he drove away, he was eventually able to unclench his jaw and his breathing slowed to a normal rate. Still later, his adrenaline wore off and his hands stopped trembling. And when he thought about it late, late that night, lying in bed, he felt good about what he had done. He felt really good.

That Halloween was the first time.

Mr. Cool's Final Halloween

Jay Seate

Jim Bob Jackson was a cynic in addition to being a cool dude. Religion was for those looking for infinity insurance before the big siesta. Love? Maybe someday. He might not give a rock star or a movie icon a run for their money, but he did have some righteous wheels and pretty good vocal pipes to croon the chickie-poos with. Could have been a dancer. He could jump and jive with the best of them in high school, but instead of pursuing either talent, he chose to put his dad's platitudes to the test and become Mr. Cool, as some of the high school simpletons used to call him.

"Son, with your looks, you'll have the pigeons eating out of your hand and begging for more," his pop told him.

Born with a strong, yet angelic face girls trusted, Jim Bob had become the *Don Juan* of Linden High as a senior. His rep had slipped a bit over the next couple of years. Reality had set in with menial post-school jobs and with the fact that nothing very exciting ever happened in the town of Linden. Buster's, a small drive-in restaurant, was about it. Once in a while, kids from the junior college up in Rayburn drove through and stopped for a burger. Those girlish sweaters stretched tightly over torsos and the smooth brown legs dangling from shorts could sure rev Jim Bob's engine. He might just go up to Rayburn and enroll next year. A lot of those coeds could be talked into the back seat of a car, he reckoned.

Something to contemplate another time. Tonight was Halloween. His party costume was a variation on a theme he had used for a number of years. Once he'd worn an old football uniform. Another year, he donned a hockey jersey and a goalie mask aka Jason from *Friday the 13th*. This year, he felt less creative than ever, settling on his high school letter jacket and counting on his charm and good looks to create a successful evening.

Creative enough for the dunces in this little burg, he thought as he pulled in front of Tania Connelly's modest home. His Chevy's chrome pipes revved one final bang of horsepower before Jim Bob cut the engine, gave his hair the once-over in his rear view mirror and sauntered through the screen door into Tania's living room.

Inside were the predictable assortment of immature high school hairies, oddballs, dropouts, and graduates trying to figure out a way to get out of town, the same as him. The assemblage participated in one of two activities. Some had formed into gossipy groups while a few monsters, witches, and princesses laughingly wiggled in the middle of the room to a boom box that blasted out Golden Oldies. Jim Bob couldn't help but smirk with the knowledge that he had slept with most of the girls who were dancing or running around being drama queens.

Tania Connelly leaned against her couch, holding a plastic cup of beer and talking to another one of his conquests, Debbie Shaffer. Tania wore her tired, pink leotard with ballerina accessories. Debbie sprawled across the sofa in an almost identical black leotard highlighted with black cat ears and a tail. They stopped gabbing long enough to look at Jim Bob as if sensing his presence. Tania wiggled her fingers at him and Debbie produced a tight-lipped half smile before they turned away and resumed their girl talk.

"Losers," Jim Bob mumbled. "Leftovers from the Jim Bob Jackson fan club." He headed for the beer keg.

"Hey, Jim Bob," someone called.

"Frankie," Jim Bob answered the oversized human unenthusiastically.

"Went all out on the costume this year, huh?" Frankie chuckled. "Can't stand to hide that handsome puss, can you?"

"Stick it where the sun don't shine, Frank-tank. That red devil outfit of yours has been around as long as Tania and Debbie's moth-eaten stretch pants."

"That ain't no way to talk about your past lay-me-downs, Jim boy. You should show a little respect. The boogie monster might up and bite your ass."

Jim Bob smiled at that. "Poor, ole Frankie. You're jealous. Let me grab a beer and see if there's anything worth hanging around for."

"Sure thing, Mr. Cool. Maybe the letter jacket will still work."

Jim Bob sidestepped Frankie and pumped a cup full of foamy Budweiser, the king of beers. He watched the revelers shuffle around the carpeted living room as best they could in their homemade costumes. His eyes swept the room. Tania and her cronies had hung orange and black crepe paper from the ceiling's corners to its center where a jack-o-lantern dangled in place of a reflective, mirrored ball. A few recycled, cardboard skeletons decorated the walls.

Jim Bob downed his beer, then squeezed the keg's nozzle again until his cup ran over and idly wondered if anything would ever happen in this poor little excuse of a town more interesting than the act of pursuing some chickie-poo to sweet talk into the back seat of his souped-up jalopy.

An ancient ballad began to play and most of the demons, freaks, and pirates found angels, fairies and female bloodsuckers to dance with. Jim Bob sipped his suds, resigned to the fact that no new blood had found its way to Tania's party when a set of long, spindly fingers crept onto his shoulder. He turned with a start. A slender figure stood behind him. Her black hair fell almost to her waist. Within the ghostly white face, her dark pupils, as shiny as beads, seemed to reach into his soul, and he was momentarily, helplessly spellbound.

"You are Jim Bob Jackson, are you not?"

Her silky words partially broke the spell. "Ahhhh, yes ma'am," he answered as if addressing a person many years his senior.

She seemed familiar somehow, but behind the Vampira white make-up, long wig, and blood red fingernails, Jim Bob knew something impressive lived, someone infinitely more interesting than anyone from the usual crowd.

Be as cool as the bottom side of the pillow. Jim Bob thought of his father's words when it came to women. "Love 'em all son, before one of 'em traps you," his dad often said and Jim Bob took the advice to heart once he realized what his good looks and a little bull could accomplish. "You're not from around here," he said to the stranger.

"No, but I know someone who is and they said you always show up at the Halloween party."

While she spoke, Jim Bob's eyes slid over the rest of this vision's body. The words, "Holy Toledo" rested behind his lips, wanting to spill out. She was shrouded in a tight black, floor length dress that matched her raven hair. The dress's v-cut neckline revealed the better part of milky white breasts. He remembered the character in the old television series, *The Adams Family.* He thought the broad's name was Morticia. Then he thought of the more recent Elvira who used to host those schlocky horror flicks. This woman reminded him of those two TV celebrities, but she was younger and hotter than the actresses.

Jim Bob gaped unabashedly. *A choice morsel such as this doesn't pass through Cabbage-Patch every day.* "Who's this person you know?" he asked.

"A close friend. We can talk about her later."

Her chest heaved when she spoke. Jim Bob watched her long fingers brush back her hair. "Let me get you a beer." He gestured at the keg.

"No thanks, I'd rather take a walk, get away from this crowd. That's the way she would want it."

The woman leaned in his direction and touched his arm. Jim Bob was rewarded with an excellent cleavage shot. His chain rattled. He didn't care about her friend. This *femme fatal* was the most provocative creature he had ever had a shot at. "I don't even know your name."

"Walk me to your car and I'll tell you everything. I could use a little company right now, unless you'd rather stay here and flirt with one of these little gypsies?"

He was more than willing to roll with the flow and he prayed he was getting the vibes he thought he was. "I would be honored to accompany you out of here."

No one seemed to notice as the couple walked outside to the yard, which had become a temporary parking lot. They walked past the first row of cars to Jim Bob's Chevy. He leaned against one of the fenders and struck a pose thinking about getting up close and personal with Elvira. He plotted a hasty strategy as he waited for the woman to speak.

She stood in front of Jim Bob, just beyond his reach. "Now, about my friend," she said. "You and she were pretty close for a while."

"So, she told you to look me up? That's great," Jim Bob offered. The lady in front of him was a Code Red. Jim Bob would babble about this friend for a while if that's what it took to get inside her slinky dress.

"Her name is Barbara Bobbitt. You do remember her, don't you? Although with all the girls you've been with, it might not be easy."

"Barbara? Yeah, I remember Barbara. She left town a while back." *Make a move*, he thought, *but stay cool.*

"At least you remember."

"Sure. So, what can I do to show you a good time?" The words slithered from Jim Bob's mouth.

"Well, golly, Jim Bob. I guess you can show me what you showed Barbara. I'm sure many a girl has looked dreamily into your eyes and you've given them what you wanted them to have." The woman's eyes drifted south.

She's looking at my crotch. Holy Jesus-on-wheels.

"Open up your jacket."

He complied, reminding himself to stay cool a while longer and wait for the right moment.

She put her hand on Jim Bob's shirt and pressed her palm against his chest, feeling the accelerating rhythm of his heartbeat. He looked at her long white fingers, luminescent in the moonlight, each tipped with a crimson fingernail. He pictured them wrapped around his most precious organ.

The mystery lady moved her hand to Jim Bob's thigh and squeezed. She looked at the night sky. "It's another beautiful night, much like the one when you were with Barbara."

"I guess," Jim Bob said. He made his move. He turned the woman's face toward his to kiss her, no longer caring what her name was or why she was here.

"Wait," she said. "Let's have a toast first."

"What are we toasting?"

"How about dead people?"

Jim Bob grinned. "Whatever. It *is* Halloween, huh?" *Whatever it takes to make it with you, my dear,* he gleefully mused.

"Unbuckle your pants, will you, Jim Bob?"

"What? Out here?"

"Why not?" A pale tentacle of light from the porch filtered between automobiles, splitting the woman's torso in half, highlighting her breasts on either side of the shaft, each begging to be fondled. A white, spindly finger traced a line across his cheek. "Barbara said you were beautiful. Have you pleasured many sweet, young things?"

"Some."

She looked into his expectant eyes. "Trick or treat, Jim Bob?"

"Treat," he answered excitedly.

She stepped back. Jim Bob watched as her fingers disappeared beneath the black wig. Her hands pulled the wig away to reveal an unspectacular tangle of short brown curls. A small smile, and not a particularly attractive one, carved the corners of her mouth. "Let's make one more toast," the woman said. "This time, let's toast to Barbara."

"It's your turn to undo something now," Jim Bob said impatiently, starting to feel less cool and somewhat defenseless with his jeans unbuckled.

"Sorry, Jim Bob, but I'm afraid it's a trick rather than a treat."

The woman put her hands on her forehead. She slowly peeled the pancake makeup—a mask—off in one solid piece.

Underneath were vaguely familiar features. The sense of déjà vu he had felt inside the house returned.

"And it's the worst trick of all. Payment for one of your sins," she said calmly with just a hint of pleasure. "You're about to experience hell on earth, my friend."

"What's this all about? I haven't done anything to you."

"That's where you're wrong, Jim Bob. You did something very bad to me." The woman now spoke as if she were talking to a child. "You made love to me and made me pregnant."

He looked into eyes which had turned pale blue, no longer dazzling or entrancing. "Barbara?" It *was* Barbara. "But… no… I… might…."

"No might, you had sex with me, but didn't have the decency to use protection. You said it would be all right. You have quite a reputation, you know. A handsome kid like you should be more careful, more considerate of girls who trust you, that give themselves to you."

Jim Bob tried to extricate himself from the bumper of his car, but some power pinned him there. "I will… be… careful."

"I don't think so. Not then, not now, not ever. You may not care to know what happened to me, but I'll tell you anyway." The corners of the woman's mouth curved down, transforming her countenance into something feral and frightening, spitting her words at Jim Bob. "I went away to have my baby, but I never had it. You have any idea what it's like to be an unwed mother in a traditional family like mine, a small town like this? Of course you don't, you selfish dolt. I knew what it would be like, so I killed myself rather than go through all the stigma of someone in my situation. It's all because of your sweet talk and your uncaring soul."

Jim Bob was no longer Mr. Cool. He was scared. Why couldn't he move? Why didn't someone come out of the house and investigate, but if they saw him with this woman, they would think it was just good ole Jim Bob showing off. On the verge of tears, he could only hope this was some kind of cruel joke. Maybe Barbara had come back to town and his dirt-bag friends put her up to this charade. Maybe his old man wanted a good laugh at his son's expense. Maybe....

Barbara's face began to change. She was no longer the mousy little girl behind the make-up of a sexy siren. Her features were rotting away, running down into her dress.

"Don't you want to touch me all over like before?"

"Help!" Jim Bob screamed. His cry only blended with the pounding rhythm of the rock-n-roll standard, *Shout*, as it blared from the boom box inside Tania Connelly's house.

"Anyone who might have been looking saw you come out alone because I don't exist on their plane. Only you, darling Jim Bob, can see me. I can become whatever I need to become for you to understand your crime. I've made myself visible only to you."

Barbara removed her dress. Jim Bob expected to see more rotting flesh and bloody bones, but instead, he saw nothing. The form of this shapely creature no longer existed, only the hideous head and hands with those long, spindly fingers remained. They reached out from the dark and brushed his cheek. He cringed and prayed for this nightmare of all nightmares to rattle him back into consciousness. *This has to be a hideous dream, has to be, and it's very un-cool.*

"Are you ready, my love? Are you ready for the rush of a lifetime?" Barbara crooned.

"This joke's gone far enough. I've been drugged," Jim Bob cried in one final attempt at macho, trying to regain some cool, even now.

The dripping skull looked at him and laughed. "It's a joke all right. The joke is on you. Those on the other side are waiting to administer punishment while you give some thought to my dead baby and my bleeding wrists."

"Don't hurt me," Jim Bob pleaded. He didn't know he was crying until he felt the hot tears running down his cheeks. No more bravado. No more cool. "Please. I never meant—"

"Yes, you *did* and I mean to do what I'm going to do. Enjoy what's left of your last Halloween."

Jim Bob put up his hands as if they would hold off the hell that had found him. His screams went unnoticed as the phantom's fingernails, as long as knives now, slashed. Her teeth ripped and tore at his flesh and nerve endings.

Someone dressed like a confused caveman turned from his dance partner to look at the figure beyond the screen door on the front porch. "Hey, everybody, look at Jim Bob. Cool change. Who are you now, one of *My Bloody Valentine's* victims? Trick or treat, right?"

Everyone looked at Jim Bob and laughed until his severed hands fell out of his letter jacket onto the porch. He tried to say something, but could only gasp for air as his most precious organ was lodged in his throat.

Suddenly, one of his former conquests screamed as Jim Bob fell through the screen door, turning the carpet beneath him the same shade of red that Barbara's fingernails had been. His final Halloween seemed poignant somehow, being the victim of the same apparatus that caused Barbara to end her life, and then haunt dear Jim Bob into a premature grave.

There were no teenage Halloween parties the next year or the year after that. Only the tiny voices of the small goblins saying "trick or treat" echoed through the small town's lonely streets. But the townspeople, stuck in their humble burg, began to whisper about the unsolved fate of the town's former Don Juan, and those who had attended Tania Connelly's last Halloween party began to embellish the tale of the trick played on poor Jim Bob Jackson, a.k.a. Mr. Cool.

Afraid

Thomas Beck

He awoke in complete and total darkness. He could not see his hand in front of his eyes. Trapped in a tight place, he had been positioned on his back. He could barely move. His body was cocooned in silky wraps and he was not able to stretch his arms in any direction. He didn't know where he was. Unable to it up, his mind reeled with confusion. He had no idea how he became trapped in this icy and silent world where darkness ruled. His fingers felt stiff and so very cold. He could barely move them. Slowly, he drifted back into nothingness.

When he regained consciousness, he was sprawled on top of faded green and dying grass. A jungle of gray granite tombstones, mausoleums, and crypts closed in to surround him. A chill wind moaned softly through a large oak tree and whistled eerily through the cracks of the crypts. Confused, his eyes searched for some kind of an answer. He could make no sense of it and why was he in a cemetery? Everything seemed so unnatural, unreal, and different. He felt as though he was looking through someone else's eyes. He concentrated, but he couldn't remember anything at all. How did he end up there?

He sat up, bewildered.

When he did, everything came rushing back like a slow-motion nightmare—the sounds of screeching brakes and shattering glass. He relived the horrible pain in his head and remembered an ambulance whisking him away. He heard the wail of the siren echoed in his ears. A picture of him staring up from a hard table into a bright light at the hospital popped into his head. That picture faded. It was all that he remembered until he woke in the deep, cold darkness.

This was his first day out of the grave. The darkness he remembered was the inkiness from being stuck underground. He had a hard time getting out of that sealed box. It held him in the total blackness.

"Mom! Dad!" he called. There was no answer. Loneliness filled and escaped as tears. He didn't want to stay there, not alone.

After several days of collecting his thoughts and energy, he found a way to escape. He managed to break out of the darkness in his underground prison.

Free from the icy hold of the grave, he quickly found that he wasn't alone. Even though he was no longer bound under six feet of dirt, he was still gripped with pangs of fear. Everything he heard about cemeteries was that they were horrible and scary places filled with scary things. It was a hard for a newly departed ghost as young as him and without his parents to endure it all. It almost made him wish he could return to hide in that horrible dark box.

Everything was new to him. He awakened in a new world or maybe with just a new view on his old world. He still remembered all of the usual places that surrounded the graveyard. The things that he saw were all familiar to him, but in an out-of-focus, other-worldly way. His mom or dad weren't here to help or protect him and so many of the things that he saw made him afraid. Even though he felt different, he didn't feel as though he was dead, whatever that was supposed to feel like. It had never happened to him before.

Under the ground, beneath the fresh-mown sod, he saw thousands of slimy, worm-filled, rotting things, and putrefying flesh. When he was alive, he never would have guessed that all those things were there, waiting for the next person to end up in their underground world.

It had been even colder and darker below the ground than he ever could have imagined in his young mind. he didn't know how long he had been was stuck in the coffin; trapped inside, before he was able to pull his ghost-self together and escape its smooth, satiny wrappings. He shuddered when he thought of the creepy, crawly things that were held at bay outside of that box. Why had his family allowed him to be stuck in such a nasty place? He didn't like those things or to even think about them. Perhaps, they didn't know that they were lurking down there.

He was happy to have escaped the darkness, but wished his mom or dad was there. It was a fear of the unknown, the loneliness, and the strangeness that caused him to tremble.

Being a ghost did have some advantages, but not many for sure. At one time, his physical body restricted him. He had to use doors. Now, he could walk through walls. He was able to float in the air and not have to use the stairs. He quickly learned that he could disappear when he wanted to avoid anything bad. And he saw some very, very bad things there among the cold granite tombstone forest.

Lurking behind and inside most of the icy mausoleums were the undead. Everywhere else, in between the monuments, were large, powerful, and hideous demons as well as grim gremlins, ghouls, and angry ghosts. He peeked with one eye from his sheltered hiding place behind his headstone until he was sure that they had gone before he would reappear. There had been several close calls. One was so close he could smell the Devil's putrid breath. He almost ran into the fiend while escaping a hairy demon.

While he hid behind a headstone, he noticed that the granite bore his name. It had been etched on the tombstone. Beneath it, on the recently turned ground were several large baskets of wilted flowers.

He had to believe what had been carved in the pale granite surface. His finger slowly traced the words that had been etched in the stone; his name, his date of birth, and the date of his date of death. He had been ten years old. It felt so odd that he could read the words through the transparent flesh of his finger.

He missed his mom and dad, longing to hear their comforting voices, but they weren't there to help him or hold him. He wished he could see his sister, but not here. It was intensely cold, dark, and frightening among the tombstones at night. He had no idea what he should do. There was no one for him to ask. He was afraid to approach anything that prowled the cemetery.

The freshly carved date read October third. Halloween had to be close. Maybe that was why there were so many ghosts, ghouls, gremlins, and demons hovering around the cemetery. He didn't know.

It had been hard for him to accept the fact that he had died. But, nothing else made sense. He finally understood that he was no longer alive. The words that were carved in stone over his grave told him that. He couldn't ignore the facts when they were deeply chiseled in hard, cold detail.

He was glad that he had been buried near his home. At least he could remember the places and neighborhood that had once been familiar to him and played. He knew his way to school and the way to his home from the cemetery. When he was alive, he used to walk past the graveyard every day with his friends. Who would have thought that he would be stuck inside the graveyard's black wrought iron fence so soon?

His buddies and he could have taken the shortcut through the graveyard at anytime, but they avoided going beyond the heavy, black wrought iron gate. Not one of them dared to enter or to walk that path, even in the daylight. He was still afraid but now he had no choice.

His fear grew as he thought of spending another night in that dismal cemetery without his mom or dad. As dusk fell, his nerves were on edge, listening for the faintest sound or the slightest movement. As he leaned against his headstone he jump at each sound, sometimes he shook uncontrollably.

No matter how small the noise, the blackness magnified the sounds. An acorn when it dropped, the scurrying feet of a mouse, or the flutter of a bat's wing, startled him and made him cringe in terror.

As the shadows deepened, evil came alive. Most were demons, spooks, ghosts, and ghouls. The pale silvery moonlight shimmered on the spectral figures giving them a more frightening and ghastly appearance. Because they changed their shape and size like normal shadows, he had been caught unaware and was almost caught by one of the demons.

Adjusting to his ghostly state was a slow process. First, he learned how to fly, then how to move things. He found that he didn't have to go around things, he could go through them. It was a tight squeeze, but he found that he could hide inside of a tree trunk.

As usual, he watched his friends walk on the sidewalk, near the iron fence barrier of the cemetery. They were on their way to school. It was one of those chilly autumn mornings, filled with wisps of shifting, patchy fog. His buddies would appear and disappear in the mists, almost like they were spirits themselves. It was late enough in the year and early enough in the day for it to still be dark.

An old oak tree grew in the middle of the graveyard. It was nowhere near the walkway or the fence. Its thick gnarled limbs still wore autumn colored leaves. He could hear the acorns dropping through the drying, dying foliage. Hearing his friends' voices combined with the sounds of the dropping nuts gave him an idea, just to amuse himself. He threw an acorn toward them as they drew near.

The acorn landed close to their feet. They stopped, looked at the acorn at their feet. They looked at each other, then gave a strange, distressed stare through the bars of the ornate black fence before hurrying away. If he hadn't been so sad about his own passing, he probably would have laughed.

Gaining strength, he ranged farther and farther away from the graveyard, looking for a safe haven. He found the way back to his home. His family wouldn't be able to see or hear him. He didn't have much form and was little more than a few small wisps with tatters trailing behind him. But he could visit with them and that thought comforted him.

All sorts of Halloween decorations filled the porches and lawns along his old street. Halloween was close.

His front porch was bare. There were no jack o' lanterns, pumpkins, and no bundles of corn stalks. He stopped the locked front door. It was an ingrained habit for him to use that door, but as he reached for the knob, he remembered that there was no need for him to grab the knob to open it and slipped through

The house was much quieter than he could ever remember. There were no sounds from the television and no music coming from the radio. The rooms were dark. Mom sat in her rocking chair, holding his sister. Little Hannah had fallen asleep in his mom's lap. Absently, his mom stroked Hannah's hair and rocked back and forth. He heard the familiar squeak of the rockers on the carpeting. Mom stared straight ahead, looking at nothing.

Dad perched on the edge of his large, green recliner chair. His dad's reading glasses rested on top of the small table at his elbow. His father seemed to be looking at a photograph of his son that rested on the fireplace mantle.

He heard his dad sigh. His father's hands rubbed the worn leather of his son's baseball glove. His dad leaned back and rested his head against the back of the seat.

His ghostly form floated up the stairs going into his bed-room. They hadn't changed anything at all inside. The room was the same as the day he died. He touched the painted plastic model cars on the top of the chest of drawers where he had left them.

He remembered the day his dad and him stripped, sanded, and reassembled that dresser. The chest of drawers had been his father's when his dad had been a child. He lovingly rubbed his hand over the smooth, shiny surface. Only the baseball glove was missing and he knew that his dad was holding it.

Sitting on his bed, he looked around. His bulletin board still held some of his drawings, a birthday card Hannah had made for him, and a blue, first prize ribbon. He'd won it for a model plane that he'd built with his dad helping him.

He was worried. He needed to find a way that would let them know that he was safe. They needed to know that he still loved them.

He floated across the room to his toy box. The lid was still up and open, just like he left it. The sight of all his toys inside gave him an empty feeling. He knew that he'd not be able to play with them anymore.

Buried near the bottom was his favorite teddy bear. He hadn't slept or played with it since he was a baby. It was battered and had been re-sewn several times, but his younger sister loved it. She would sneak Teddy out of his room every time she had the chance. She'd hold the bear, play with it, and sleep with it, if he didn't notice that the bear was gone. It was missing an eye, but it was soft from its many washings. The softness of its body begged to be cuddled. He knew what he wanted to do for Hannah.

It was a struggle for him to pull that stuffed bear out from under the other toys, but he managed. Half lifting and half dragging it, he moved Teddy to his sister's bedroom and placed it on her bed where she'd be sure to find it. He patted Teddy and said, "Goodbye, dear friend."

He told the bear, "Let my sister know that I love her and that I'll miss her. Hug her back when she hugs you, Teddy."

Back in his bedroom, he wondered, what he could give his dad. What could he do to let him know that he had visited and that he loved his dad? He began to look at the things that he loved. Inside of his desk drawer were several marbles, a pencil box, his penknife, a kazoo, and a few seashells. That was it.

He took the small penknife from his desk drawer. It had been a gift for his eighth birthday from his granddad, Alfred. He carried the knife to the hall closet and slipped it into his father's jacket pocket where his dad would be sure to find it when he went to work. Patting the pocket, his specter inhaled deeply. He wanted to remember the familiar, tangy smell of his father's cologne.

"I love you, Dad," he whispered.

Now, came his biggest challenge. What could he do to let his mom know that he was there and that he really cared for her?

The laundry basket was on the floor beside his dresser. He's promised his mom that he'd put his clothing away. That was before the accident. His clothes were still there, pointing a silent, guilty finger at his unfulfilled promise.

His socks were balled into pairs on top of his folded shirts and pants. He smiled. It was a private joke between his mom and him.

He was sometimes careless as to where he had tossed his socks. His mom always asked him when she did the laundry, "Honey, I found another sock that doesn't have a mate. Where did you put it?" Or she would say, "You must have eaten one of them. Why can't you put them in the clothes hamper together? I can't figure out what you do with them."

The one good thing about being a ghost was that he could look for things where he couldn't go before. He searched the whole house, floating from the top to the bottom. He looked everywhere that he could think of—behind dressers, inside storage bins of closets, and under his bed. He even found one stray sock behind the dryer.

He collected every sock that he could find. He even discovered ones that had been lost from the time that he was a baby. One by one, he placed them in the dryer.

Finding all of those socks, she would have to know that he had visited. No one else could have found them. It was the one special joke that only the two of them shared. All of the missing socks were home.

"I love you, Mom," he mouthed.

Home—when he thought of that word, he was overwhelmed with feelings of loneliness and sadness. It filled his heart. He felt so small, so frightened, and so alone. Now that he lived in another world, there would be no place for him to stay with his family. Although he yearned to stay, he could no longer live there. Though he was home, he was still lost and very unsure of himself. Where could he go?

No, not back to the cemetery. Never. He couldn't face all of those horrible creatures and vile things roaming through the tombstones again. It was too much for him to bear. It was too scary, too evil and creepy among the gravestones. He started to cry.

Hearing a soft whisper, he stopped sobbing to listen closely. It was a familiar voice that he hadn't heard in years.

"Billy."

"Grandma." His tears stopped when he recognized who it was. She had died several years ago. He saw her reach her and toward his barely formed one.

"There you are my little man. I came back to help you so you wouldn't get lost. Come with me now. It's time for us to go home. You know I love you."

Holding Grandma's hand, he was no longer afraid.

Under a Hunter's Moon

Timothy Bateson

October 31st, 2013

A janitorial closet served as my hiding place, until the museum staff locked up for the night. The simple lock disengaged in seconds, and I made my way down the corridor. A solid oak door blocked my progress, as I reached into a backpack. This presented a challenge, but I resolved not to be defeated.

Pulling out my lock-picking tools, I set to work. I glanced over my shoulder a couple of times, thinking I heard movement from around the corner. The night guard was making her rounds, and I wanted to avoid running afoul of her. If she discovered me so close to obtaining my target, it would be disastrous.

Less than a minute after starting, the tumblers clicked into place. I eased the door open, slipping into the room housing the touring exhibition. Green light from the emergency exit sign, cast a pale glow over my shoulder. I shouldered my backpack as I placed a folded piece of paper between the dead-bolt and the strike plate, preventing the lock from engaging. I tested the door and it required more than a casual effort to push open—more than satisfactory.

The door opened into the rear of an exhibition room. Dim overhead lights shone down on several displays. Dim moonlight shone through the honeycombed skylight, causing filaments of shadow to overlay the displays, a little like dark cobwebs. The clouds were so wispy that there was little chance of them obscuring the moon.

The displays highlighted various predators and prey of Washington. Different lighting effects created a feel of the wilderness, and unsettled the nerves of the average visitor. Years of hunting at night meant that I wasn't even the least phased.

I glanced around, getting my bearings, and took in the life and death struggles that surrounded me. To the left a rabbit ran from a cougar. To the right several pheasants flew from bushes, pursued by a raging boar.

Despite the familiarity of the other scenes, the central dis-play caught my attention. The woodland recreation was so realistic that I detected the scent of dampness in the soil. Two hunters hid in the bushes, pointing their rifles at a third figure. Though she wasn't human, I knew both aspects of her natural human and wolf.

Her wolf form was posed as if running from the hunters. As I reached out to touch her paw, I remembered how things had turned out on the night portrayed. My fingers made contact with perfectly preserved fur, and the sensations flooded back from that Halloween night.

The air turned damp, the scent of the forest after a rainfall filled my nostrils, and the sensations of grass and mud between my toes. Tears welled up, blurring my vision, and memories came flooding back. As I looked up through the skylight, the moon became fuller and brighter—a Hunter's Moon that shone through the trees. The room faded.

October 31st, 2001

The wolf lay panting for a moment, before rising unsteadily. An old injury often made her transformations painful. On this occasion, it left her breathless for a few moments.

I gave her time to gather herself, trying to ignore the scent of alcohol that wafted up with her every exhalation. Thanks to the lupine heritage I shared with this woman, my ability to distinguish odors was sharper than the average humans. It made it easy to pick out the aroma of her favorite whiskey.

I glanced over my shoulder, making sure our clothing would not be spotted by the casual observer. I fought back a stab of shame at their poor condition. Shape-shifters often wore loose clothing, but my mother had been buying from thrift stores ever since my father abandoned us. It would break her heart if she knew just how much teasing I endured from the other members of the gang, but I loved her regardless.

My companion gave me a silent nod, and I started my own shift into wolf form. I dropped to all fours, and rose onto my fingers and toes. My joints and muscles rippled, as my entire physiology changed in a process I have never understood.

As my transformation finished, my perceptions of the world both narrowed, and expanded at the same time. While my sense of smell had always been sharp, my wolf form was aware of a wider range of scents than my human form. The scent of the female beside me became as identifiable as her facial features and the red tints in her coat. My wolf eyes were unable to pick out the same range of colors as my human eyes would have. Reds had shifted into a muddy blur, yellows into creams, and blues were more vibrant. The reduced color depth didn't pose a problem since I was far more attuned to the slightest of movements around me.

I looked up between the overhead branches and saw the clouds part, revealing a clear full disk of light. The moon shone down on the damp grass, causing it to glisten. I had often gone hunting under the full moon. It made seeing the prey a little easier, and I loved spending the time in wolf form. But tonight was also Halloween, and a blue moon—the second full moon of the month. There was no choice about changing to wolf form. The Hunter's Moon—the one time of the year that a lupine could not avoid his inner beast.

I stretched out my limbs, and pawed at the ground, reveling in the sensation. I had skipped dinner in anticipation of tonight's hunt, and my stomach tightened at the thought of biting into juicy prey. If we didn't manage to catch anything, I would be going hungry until breakfast, and my stomach growled at the thought.

My companion had several years on me, but she was as eager to hunt as I. The speed with which she accelerated from a standing start belied her injury. Her maneuver was unexpected, and I would have found myself running in her wake, if I hadn't picked up my own pace. We both kept ourselves in good running form, and my youth was a definite advantage. I pulled alongside her flank in a few long paces, both of us were alert for signs of movement, or other hint of prey.

Killing an animal the size of a small deer would leave too much meat. Instead, we planned on catching something smaller. Our target might be more elusive, but it would make a manageable meal. We ran for several miles, before picking up the scent of suitable prey.

I caught a brief flash of movement off to my right, and watched as the rabbit darted across the trail, and I slowed a little. My companion caught the hint, and turned a little ahead of me, as I turned on the rabbit's other side, so the two of us ended up flanking it. We harried our prey hard, snapping at its hindquarters. Several times, it tried to evade us, and we adjusted our tactics to accommodate. The chase ended as our prey ducked into a hole at the base of a burned out tree stump, leaving us standing there exhausted, chests heaving.

Click-clack!

The sound of a pump-action rifle round being chambered, bought my mind back to the clearing. I watched my companion's head snap around toward the source of the noise. I was unable to see the hunter, but I had pinpointed his location. The sound gave away his position, even though his scent remained hidden from me.

The wind direction shifted, and I realized he wasn't alone. I smelled at least two of them now. The scents of gun oil, leather, and sweat drifting toward me on the breeze. I tried to spot the second hunter. As I did, my companion began moving forward. One, two, three long strides toward the first hunter, and then she gathered herself to leap into the brush.

Crack-BOOM!

The blast echoed through the trees as the second hunter fired. The shot coming straight out of the bushes, its path untouched by the breeze.

Time seemed to slow.

As the shot rang out, I was already stepping away from the sound. My mother's head snapped to the side, as the bullet ripped through her neck, before embedding itself in a tree.

I watched in horror as the impact drove my mother sideways. Spatters of blood missed me by inches. My mother landed a few feet away from me. Somehow, she kept her feet under her, landing in a crouch. Blood dripped from her wound, but it didn't look as bad as I expected. For a moment, I thought that the bullet had clipped her rather than penetrating.

Locking her legs in challenge, she stood between me and the hunters. Her chest puffed up, and she started to growl, but the noise that came out was barely a rattle. Blood dripped from her jaws as a look of pain and surprise crossed her face.

I can't imagine the force of will that kept my mother upright. But that willpower seemed to be fading, as she staggered once, and then collapsed onto her side. Blood started to pool around her head and shoulders, soaking the ground, and her fur.

Shock and horror held me in place for a moment, and then I found myself taking a step forward. I found myself operating on instincts, not believing what I had just seen. Nor was I ready to accept my mother's death, or that I would have to leave her. She lay so still, her chest barely moving, as her life drained away into the ground.

She must have sensed something, because her eyes flashed open, and she focused behind me. It was the very last action my mother took. Her head dropped, her chest deflated one final time, and the last of her breath left her body.

I followed the direction of her gaze, and spotted the barrel of a rifle poking through the bushes. A third hunter. This one hid upwind of us, and had managed to stay undetected. Either my mother and I had stumbled into a well executed trap, or the hunters were looking for other prey. The opportunity to bag themselves a wolf had presented itself, and they took it.

Insanity seemed to take control of my body, as the beast within bypassed any consent my brain might have given. My heart and mind turned icy calm, as the raging beast prepared to give reign to its anger at my mother's death. The beast drove down all fear, common sense, or thought beyond the urge to kill. Beyond any doubt, I would die in the attempt.

I watched as my paw rose, and I took a step forward, followed by another. Like my mother, before me, I was going to try to take down as many of these killers as possible, before they killed me in return.

Never, since my earliest transformations had I allowed the beast to take complete control. It was like watching from outside my body. I started accelerating into a sprint, and muscles bunched up to power the leap my speed was fueling. I felt numb to the guns, especially the one at my back. My mother's killer was going to feel the grip of my jaws at his throat as I tore my claws through his guts. The kill would have to be quick and decisive. I couldn't allow his companions a chance to react.

The moment before my paws would have left the ground, the third hunter took his shot. Stone shrapnel and earth struck my hindquarters, as the ground to my left exploded.

The shock and pain were enough to thaw the ice in my veins. The world snapped into sharp focus, and I shook my head to clear the ringing in my ears. I needed to escape before the first hunter took a shot at me. I turned on the spot, like a cornered beast, seeking escape from a cage.

A deer path looked to be the safest exit from the clearing. That meant having two guns pointed at my back. And that was a gauntlet that would normally terrify me. In its favor, that route put a tree between me and the one hunter who not yet fired. I had no idea what lay in that direction, but I saw no alternatives. I poured my terror into my muscles, and raced from the clearing, as I tried to shake off shock, and outrace certain death. I dodged over uncertain ground, and leaped over a fallen tree. The whistling of a near bullet miss reminded me why I was running.

I ran for more than a couple of miles, before I started feeling guilty about leaving my mother behind like that. Regardless of the fact that she was now dead, she'd stuck beside me through everything.

Thinking about everything my mother had done for me, I resolved to give her a decent burial. I might not have been able to get revenge on her killers. But I would make sure they were unable to take the credit for a wolf kill, or put her remains on display in their homes.

As I came to the decision, I realized that I had been heading back toward the clearing where I had stashed our clothes. It was as if something in me reached out toward the familiar, and safe. I could have tried howling for assistance from the pack, but I couldn't assume that anyone would have been in range to answer such a call. I would recover my mother's body tonight—alone. The odds of being able to do so would decrease over time.

There was one place that I was certain that I would pick up the hunter's trail. I steeled myself for the potential horrors that I might have to face. Setting a cautious pace, I tried to keep all my senses tuned to my surroundings. A single surprise was all it had taken to put me in this position.

When I reached the clearing, the hunters had left, but their scents were still fresh. Scattered around the kill sight were signs that they had hastily moved the body. A couple of scraps of rope and tarpaulin suggested that they may have wrapped the body for transport.

This was good news in terms of being able to track the killers. The lack of other remains also indicated that there had been insufficient time to gut the carcass. They would be carrying it whole. My mother weighed about a hundred and forty pounds, and that would slow them.

As I sniffed around, I found traces of my mother's blood on the one remaining path out of the clearing. My nose told me that the hunters had all traveled together. They were likely heading back toward a wider trail used by campers to carry backpacks and hunting supplies deeper into the woods.

I followed them while maintaining my distance. The hunters were not able to travel fast, because they were carrying my mother's corpse between them. As I had suspected, they had wrapped it in a blue tarpaulin and secured it with a length of rope. Two of them would carry the body, while the third was weighed down by the weapons and ammunition.

Several times, I thought about attacking the hunter with the weapons, but the risk was too great. He had all the guns and only one of which needed to be ready to fire.

So instead, I followed them all the way back to their truck. As they were loading up, I kept to the shadows, and tried to memorize their faces, the make and model of the truck, and the license plate. My mother's body was tied to the bed of the truck with bungee cords, and the guns were locked into boxes above the wheel wells. The three hunters climbed into the cab of the truck, and started the engine. I watched as one take a last look at their load, and nod to the driver, before they started back toward the main roads.

The drive was slow at first, because of the roughness of the path, and I found it easy to trail them at a reasonable distance. Not one of them showed any signs of having seen me in the rear view, but I kept off the path wherever possible. I crossed the path once to get better cover as they rounded a bend and the gravel gave way to tarmac.

After another couple of miles they turned onto one of the main roads that skirted the edge of the woodlands. They turned right, gunning the engine, and accelerated out of the junction. Another vehicle came racing up behind the truck, its sirens blazing, and the roof mounted lights flashing away. I saw the truck break, and noticed that one of the taillights was out.

The two police officers climbed out of their car, hands resting on their sidearms. The taller one stalked toward the driver's side of the truck. His colleague walked to the rear of the vehicle. As the other officer spoke to the driver, I saw the brake lights, and indicators flash several times. A quick nod confirmed that the tail light wasn't just cracked, but not even functioning.

From my vantage point, the conversation at the front of the truck sounded friendly enough. The driver looked to be cooperating with all requests for information, and paperwork.

The second officer raised the tarpaulin covering the guns and the wrapped wolf corpse, and everything changed. I heard the driver's tone get very defensive, and the first officer took a rapid step backward, moving the driver's documents to his left hand. His other hand rested on his pistol, thumb poised to snap the safety off.

As I watched, the second officer stepped away from the truck, and made his way back to the patrol vehicle. He reached in for the radio, while keeping his attention on the truck, and his partner. A second vehicle was requested to pickup a wolf corpse, and help take the hunters to jail.

I lay down, forced myself to watch the scene unfold as the hunters were ordered out of the vehicle and onto the roadside.

When the second patrol car arrived, everything from the bed of the truck was loaded into its trunk, and the hunters divided between the two vehicles. I suspected that my mother's body would end up being used as evidence in any criminal charges, and then be destroyed.

The two patrol vehicles pulled away from the truck, leaving it at the roadside. Since there was little chance of following them, I closed my eyes, and lay there, the shaking growing worse, and gave in to the grief and despair.

I settled back on my haunches, and let the beast speak for me. My howl split the air, calling to the skies. The pain and rage in my voice echoed back to me from a multitude of sources, carrying many miles, before dying away. A couple of voices joined mine, as other pack members picked up on my call. In my heart, I could have sworn that my mother's joined with them.

The tears flowed, as I curled in upon myself, shifting back from wolf to human. The blurry darkness was comforting as I lay there, hugging my knees to my chest, rocking myself.

I don't know how much time passed before the familiar sound of paws approached through the undergrowth. I knew that I had to pull myself together. Rolling myself into a sitting position, I started to uncurl, my limbs protesting from having been held in one position for so long. As I sat up, trying to persuade my fingers to loosen their grip, I felt a pressure falling on my shoulder.

I wiped away my tears with one hand, and looked upward. My other hand, reached out to remove the tightening grip, even if I had to break the owners fingers to do so.

My fingers encountered a huge hand, and the scarring left by years of hard work. Maybe the hand's owner sensed my intentions, but the grip tightened as he crouched and looked me in the eyes. I could see his own pain, buried behind the concern. I'd lost a mother, and he had lost a pack member.

As I looked up, the bright full moon threw the man's face into sharp relief.

October 31st, 2013

The room snapped back into focus as I blinked, and turned away from the spotlight that framed Art's features. He removed his hand from my shoulder, letting me rise under my own power.

"Richard, do you know why I told you about this exhibition?" I could hear the accusation, and understanding in his voice.

"How did you find me?" I brushed at the dust on my knees.

Art smiled. "How do you think I found out your mother's remains were coming back here? The night guard has always had a soft spot for the pack, even though she's not one of us. You'd do well to keep in her good books. She was the one who recognized your mother's wolf form, and called me."

"I know you didn't intend for this to happen, but I won't risk losing her again. You know what happens to the exhibition once it's run is finished? It gets broken down, and hidden away again, until the next wolf scare. Then they unpack it and remind people why these things happen."

"The cities are taking hunting ground from the wolf and lupine populations. That's the lesson displays like this are intended to teach, but that's not what happened in your mother's case."

Art steered me toward the display railing, and he leaned against it, his gaze on what remained of my mother. His big hands indicated the expanse of the scene, and he was silent for a moment.

"Your mother never told you about the rogue lupine that was hunting the public trails, did she?"

I shook my head. There were a lot of things my mother hadn't told me, including why she decided to hunt in that particular area, when it wasn't our usual territory. Looking back on it, I hadn't even thought about the lack of territorial challenge that our presence would have warranted. It had been a full moon, so every lupine in the city would have been in wolf form, and almost all of us choose to hunt on those nights.

"Needless to say, we couldn't have a lupine drawing attention to the rest of us. Police reports showed something unusual about the wolf, and the killings. That's how it got my attention."

"Because we never interfere in the affairs of the wolves?"

"Except this time, there was a public outcry, and demands for the city, or state to announce a cull on the wolf population."

I nodded, seeing where this was going. "So the pack stepped in and took out the rogue to prevent the cull from being approved." I followed the train of logic a little further, "They never voted on the cull, so my mother thought it safe to go hunting?"

"Except, I suspect your mother went out looking for those hunters. I got wind that several groups of hunters had been talking about finding the killer wolf, and claiming it as a trophy." Art turned to me, and looked me square in the eye. "Your mother knew this, and was looking to end her own pain."

"Is that why she stank of alcohol? I suspected she'd been drinking again, but she seemed sober enough."

"She was never the same after your father left. I could have taken you home that night, but I couldn't bring myself to leave you there with all those memories. Did you know your mother cried herself to sleep?"

I looked at him, his words bringing back a vivid memory. "She was crying over an old photo of her, me and my father, together. She even asked me to stay home while she went and hunted, but I didn't want to be caged. I'd been at home too many nights, and I wanted to run."

"You can't blame yourself for what happened, Richard. No lupine likes being confined, but you were 12 years old, too eager to spend all your time in wolf form."

I leaned out and stroked my mother's fur, and knew that despite the depression and drinking, she had loved me. But she had given her life, so I had a chance to live. Even if she had gone out there to end her own pain, she had managed to see past it. In the end, she had defended the one thing in her life that still held importance… Me.

I put my hand on Art's arm, indicating I was ready to go. He stopped another moment, as if saying his own good-byes to my mother. Then he picked up my backpack, and handed it to me.

"Time to get back to the present. Isabella will let us out the side door. No-one need be any the wiser."

Home for Halloween

Kelli A. Wilkins

Kyle cradled the giant pumpkin in his hands as he walked down the street. His thin arms jutted out from his black vampire cape, and he bit his bottom lip as he concentrated. *Not far to go, now,* he told himself. The heavy gourd stretched his aching muscles all the way to the ground, but it was worth it.

Mrs. MacLaughlin had thrown a Halloween party for his fifth grade class today. She'd read ghost stories and talked about the history of Halloween while they made paper cut-outs of ghosts and Jack O'Lanterns. After lunch, they ate bat-shaped sugar cookies with black icing and sang a Halloween song about five little pumpkins sitting on a gate. At the end of the day, everyone got a bag of candy to take home, and the king of all pumpkins was raffled off to one lucky kid. He couldn't believe it when his name was called. It was the first thing he'd ever won.

Kyle stopped to take a break and squinted toward the setting sun. A breeze ruffled his hair, and his cape swirled in the wind. The maple trees had tossed off all their leaves last week. Orange and brown husks skittered around his feet.

He loved autumn. The crisp air held a sense of magic and wonder. Part of him longed to linger, to take it all in and make this perfect moment last forever, but he had to hurry home. Tonight was special. It was Halloween.

Every Halloween, Mom forced him to sit at the kitchen table and eat dinner like it was a regular night when all he wanted was to race out the door and start trick-or-treating. Mom didn't have to be at the diner until nine tonight, so they could stay out even later than usual. Even though he begged every year, Mom never let him go out trick-or-treating by himself. "Too many maniacs creeping around," she said.

A car horn blared from behind him, and he turned as an old green Buick pulled to the curb.

"Hey kid, need a ride?"

Kyle smiled, displaying a full set of vampire fangs. "Tommy! What are you doing here? I thought you were at college." He lumbered over to the car with his pumpkin. "Look what I won at school. Mrs. MacLaughlin had a Halloween party. She didn't even assign homework because it's a holiday. Will you take me trick-or-treating tonight?" Kyle paused. "Does Mom know you're home?"

Tommy stepped out of the car and took the pumpkin from Kyle. "Sure, we'll go out. I promise. You'll have to find me a costume. Is Mom working tonight?" he asked as he nestled Kyle's prize behind the driver's seat.

"Yeah, but she's not going in until nine," Kyle answered, hopping into the car and tucking his cape around him. "There's a monster movie marathon on tonight. Can we watch it?"

"Sure, why not? But I need to talk to Mom first."

"How come you're home now?" Kyle asked as they pulled into the gravel driveway a few minutes later. Tommy hardly ever came home, especially during the week. The drive from the state college took five hours, and his car wasn't very reliable.

"I wanted to surprise you and Mom and have a good Halloween, but I can't stay long," he answered.

Kyle glanced at his brother. Tommy wasn't acting right. Something was wrong. Maybe he had failed a class or had gotten into trouble. But whatever it was, it didn't matter right now. Tommy had come home, and it was Halloween night.

"Let's get Halloween started," Tommy said as he got out of the car.

Kyle raced up the porch, his cape flapping behind him as he flew into the house. "Mom, Mom, hey Mom, guess what?" he shouted as he tossed his empty bookbag on the beige couch.

"I'm in here," she called out from the kitchen.

He bolted down the hall. Mom stood at the stove mixing a pot of macaroni and cheese. She looked up as he entered the room.

"Mister Evans called me in early tonight. I have to be at work by seven, so I already started dinner. If we eat right away we can get some trick-or-treating done before I leave."

Kyle leaned against the table and frowned. Every time he

wanted to go somewhere or have fun, Mom had to work. No matter how many hours she put in at the diner, it seemed like they never had enough money. He knew missing out on the fun stuff and never being home made her feel bad. People thought because he was a kid, he didn't understand things like grown-ups did. But none of that mattered tonight. He grinned so hard his plastic fangs popped out of his mouth.

"Kyle, what is it?"

"Tommy came home today! After dinner we're gonna carve the pumpkin I won and he'll take me trick-or-treating and—"

Kyle followed his mom as she brushed past him and dashed into the living room.

"Tommy! My God, you are here. How are you?" She threw her arms around him. "I didn't think I'd see you until Thanksgiving. Why didn't you tell me you were coming home? You should have called."

He shrugged. "I didn't know it myself until today. I guess it's a nice surprise, huh? Look at this." Tommy lifted up the pumpkin. "Kyle won it. He told me all about the great Halloween party Missus MacLaughlin threw at school," he said as he placed the gourd on the coffee table.

"Why don't you go upstairs and find me a costume, Kyle? See what's in the hallway closet. There's probably a bunch of old clothes and stuff in there," Tommy suggested.

"Okay!" Kyle bounded upstairs.

Tommy followed his mother into the kitchen and poured them both a cup of coffee. He flopped into a chair and spooned sugar into a blue mug. He waited for his mother to turn off the macaroni and sit across from him.

"How's school?"

"It's okay." He sat back in the chair and studied his mother. She looked older than she had in August. He noticed streaks of gray in her brown hair, and her eyes had dark circles under them. She seemed tired, almost worn out. "I'm sorry we fought last week. I shouldn't have hung up on you."

"I know, honey. It hasn't been easy around here." She sipped her coffee. "It seems like I'm always working, but it's for a good reason. You need to finish college. If I have to argue with you about what's best, then I will."

Tommy gazed around the blue and white kitchen where he had eaten breakfast thousands of times. The back door led to a small yard. An old tire swing hung from the oak tree. When he was Kyle's age, he had buried Pepper beneath that tree. He glanced at the white clock over the refrigerator. It was already three-thirty. He didn't have much time.

"I know working two jobs is hard, and I didn't want to add to your burden. I appreciate all the sacrifices you made so I could go to college. But Kyle's here and he needs you. You're all he has now."

His mother brushed a lock of blond hair away from his forehead. "You're so grown up." She smiled. "Believe me, honey, I know. I feel bad for Kyle. I want to spend more time with him, but I'm always running from one job to another and leaving him by himself or with a neighbor. He understands, and he knows a lot more than he lets on. He's one smart kid."

Tommy leaned across the table and clasped her hand. "That's why I'm here. I came to see Kyle and have a good

Halloween with him." He took a thick white envelope out of his jacket pocket. "I also came to give you this."

"What is it?" his mother asked as she took the envelope.

"Almost three thousand dollars. I saved it up for next semester's tuition and books. Today I found out I won't need it, so I'm giving it to you. That's one reason I came home."

Her mouth dropped open. "Won't need it? Why not? Something's happened, hasn't it?"

He stared into the back yard, too nervous to face her. Even if he wanted to, he couldn't tell her—or Kyle—the truth. He had arranged it so they wouldn't find out until after he was gone.

"I applied for a new work-study loan. I didn't want to get your hopes up, so I didn't say anything until I knew I got it." He forced himself to smile. "The point is, I don't need the money now, and I want you to have it. Take Kyle away on a weekend trip or pay off some bills so you don't need two jobs." He paused. "It's all I have to give you."

"Look what I found!" Kyle ran into the kitchen carrying a bent tri-corner pirate hat, a black eye patch, and a plastic sword. "Do you wanna wear these?"

Tommy laughed and pretended not to notice his mother's worried expression. "Sure, I'll wear 'em. Why not? It's Halloween."

Tommy cut a circle around the edge of the pumpkin stem and pulled off the top.

Kyle peered inside. "It's dark in there." He reached into the hollow and pulled out a clump of pulp and seeds. He held the mess out to his mother. "Want some?"

She grimaced and shook her head. "No thanks."

The doorbell rang, and Kyle tossed the stringy innards on the table as he ran to the door.

"Kyle, wipe your hands. You know, Tommy, we should save these pumpkin seeds. I can bake them...."

A chorus of "Trick-or-Treat!" echoed through the house.

"You say that every year, and every year, we never do," Tommy replied as Kyle returned eating a candy bar.

"Hey! Those are for the kids," Mom protested.

"So? I'm a kid," Kyle argued. "We got three were-wolves, two ninjas, and a princess." He rolled his eyes. "Lots of kids so far, and it's only six-thirty."

Tommy scooped out a handful of wet pumpkin seeds. It felt good to be home. College had absorbed too much of his precious time. He could have been here enjoying his family and having fun instead of being stuck in the library, studying.

He carved two cat-slit eyes into the Jack O'Lantern. "Missus MacLaughlin sure knows how to pick a perfect one," he commented to Kyle.

"Yeah, she's cool. She decorated the classroom and told us the history of Halloween. Tonight is the one night of the year where the doorway between the land of the living and the land of the dead is open. Dead people can come back and walk the earth. You know, like zombies."

"Kyle," his mother exclaimed. "Don't say things like that."

"Well, he is right," Tommy agreed, nodding.

She rolled her eyes and shook her head. "Sometimes I wonder about that MacLaughlin woman. Okay boys, I've gotta go. Stand up and let me take some pictures."

Tommy put on the pirate hat and adjusted his eye patch. He pretended to look scared as Kyle stood on a chair and tried to bite his neck. After a few more pictures, they both posed next to the Jack O'Lantern.

"Kyle, take one of me and Mom." Tommy wrapped his arms around his mother and hugged her tight while Kyle snapped the picture.

"Okay, Tommy, I have to run." His mother pulled away and took her purse off the counter. "Have fun and be careful. Remember, it's Halloween. Kyle, don't give your brother any grief." She walked through the house toward the front door. "Be careful of cars, don't eat all your candy before I come home, and—"

"Watch out for maniacs," Kyle recited. "Okay, Mom, I know."

"I'll be back between eleven-thirty and twelve, unless I can get out early," she added, as she opened the door to another chorus of "Trick-or-Treat!"

Tommy watched his mother hand out candy from the orange plastic bowl as she juggled her keys and purse. Seconds later, the front door closed and she was gone. His heart sank. Why did she have to work tonight of all nights?

"Hey, this Jack O'Lantern looks cool. Maybe next year

we can buy one of those pumpkin-carving kits and make a really scary one." Kyle ran his hands through the pile of pumpkin guts and was silent for a few seconds. "When are you going back?"

Tommy glanced at Kyle, then carried the carving knife to the sink. He didn't answer right away. "I told you, I can't stay long. I'll have to go soon." He looked at the clock to avoid Kyle's steady gaze. Mom was right. Kyle understood more than everyone thought he did.

"Let's hurry up," he said, breaking the somber mood. "You don't want the girls in princess costumes getting all the good candy, do you? I'll put the big guy on the porch and leave Mom a note."

"Alright, I'll get the pillowcases. They hold more candy and the bottoms don't rip like those stupid plastic bags," Kyle replied as he left the kitchen and headed upstairs.

Tommy carried the Jack O'Lantern to the front door. He didn't want to disappoint Kyle on Halloween, but he couldn't get into a lengthy discussion about why he came home. He didn't have much time.

He opened the front door and yelped. The faceless black hood of Death loomed in front of him. Seconds later, he realized Death wore white sneakers and carried a plaid pillowcase heavy with candy.

"Sorry, didn't mean to scare you," a deep voice said. Death pulled its hood back and turned around. "Dennis, come on." A timid dragon about four years old peered around the porch railing. Death grinned. "My son's a little frightened."

Tommy gave the man several handfuls of candy and forced himself to laugh. "It's okay. It's Halloween. We're all entitled to one scare."

*

"Where to first? Missus Sharpe's house?"

Kyle shook his head. "Nah, she gives out little boxes of raisins and takes too long to get to the door. Let's go to Albert Street. A guy who lives in an A-frame house lets you take candy from a real coffin!"

Tommy chuckled and tightened his grip on the faded Spiderman pillowcase he carried. He was almost embarrassed to be seen with it, but it was the last remnant of his favorite sheet set. When he was little, mom tucked him into bed and told him to imagine he was Spiderman until he fell asleep. It seemed like a lifetime ago.

He watched the silver stars twinkling in the black sky. A sliver of yellow moon peeked out from behind a cloud. Trees swayed in the breeze, and dried leaves rustled on skeletal branches. He breathed deep and inhaled woodsy-smelling smoke. Someone had lit a fire. This was a perfect Halloween night.

"Are you homesick, Tommy?"

"Why do you ask?"

"I don't know. You seem sad." Kyle shrugged. "Is college hard?"

"No. It's not too bad if you go to class and do your

homework. Do you do your homework now?"

"Yeah, Missus MacLaughlin says every time we all do our homework she'll give us a surprise. Usually it's cookies or an hour of free time outside."

As they walked up Apple Grove Road, Tommy watched children dressed as elves, aliens, and cowboys passing them with sacks of candy clutched in their fists. He longed to go back to a time when life was carefree and he didn't worry about Kyle, his mom, anything. It felt nice to pretend to be a kid again for a few hours.

"How are things at home? Is everything okay?" he asked.

"Sure. Mom's not around much, but I get to stay up late and watch TV if my homework's done. Why?"

Tommy trailed behind Kyle as they strolled up the flagstone path leading to a well-lit porch. He rang the doorbell. "Just checking. Big brothers are supposed to be nosy," he joked. A middle-aged man answered the door.

"Trick-or-treat!" they cried out in unison. Tommy waited for the man to give out the candy and close the door before he continued.

"I want to make sure Mom's okay. People have to help each other out. You help Mom, right?"

Kyle took out his fangs, unwrapped a candy bar, and bit off the end. "Yeah. I do my chores; take out the garbage, pick up my stuff, clean my room."

"Good. Families should stick together. Like if Aunt Betty came to stay with Mom for a while, you'd help out, right?"

Kyle rolled his eyes. "Aunt Betty smells funny. Why would she visit? She lives in Arizona."

"She came out and stayed with us when Dad left. You don't remember because you were little. But that's when I knew I had to take over and help Mom out whenever I could." He glanced away. "Now, it's your turn."

"Why?"

Tommy switched the Spiderman pillowcase from one hand to another and took a deep breath. "I won't always be here and—"

"You mean you'll be at school, or when you graduate college you might move far away for a good job, right?"

Tommy looked down. Kyle gazed up at him expectantly. He hated avoiding his brother's questions and giving him half-truths. Kyle wanted an honest answer, but he wasn't about to break his heart—not tonight.

He cleared his throat and nodded. "Yeah, something like that. But you never know how life will turn out. So you should always make the best of it. Enjoy the little things, your pumpkin, Halloween, riding your bike. Things change and plans don't always work out like we figured."

He stopped walking and leaned against a tree. "I know it sounds corny, but people should make the most of each day, before it's too late." A group of kids streamed by, laughing and pretending to scare each other. "So let's have fun tonight. Where to next?"

Kyle grinned and put his fangs back in his mouth. "Let's go over to Miller's Pond Road. My friend John lives there. He'll give us extra candy."

✳

"You have to come home for Halloween next year, too," Kyle said as he popped a handful of candy corns into his mouth.

For the last two hours, he and Tommy had walked around town collecting candy and talking about everything: school, movies, comic books, and maybe even getting a dog. It was great having him home for Halloween, just like old times.

"I'm glad you had fun. I know how much you like Halloween, and I wanted to spend it with you," Tommy replied as they walked up to the house.

"Hey, look." Kyle pointed to the driveway. Their mother's gray SUV was parked behind Tommy's green car, "Mom's home early! Let's show her our candy."

"You go on ahead."

Kyle bolted up the porch and rushed into the living room. Mom spun around and motioned for him to be quiet as she pressed the phone closer to her ear. He started rooting through his pillowcase for the cinnamon gum she liked.

"I don't understand officer—"

He stopped hunting for the candy and stared at his mother. This wasn't good. She sounded strange, like she was mad—or very afraid.

"How did it—"

Kyle watched as his mother picked up the note Tommy had left next to the phone. It fluttered in her trembling hand.

"You have the wrong person. He's here, he came home. Don't tell me you found him in the car this afternoon! What kind of sick joke is this?"

A chill ran down his back. He'd never heard Mom sound so strange. Something bad must have happened. All night, he'd had a sick feeling in his stomach. Maybe Grandpa had been hurt. Mom wiped a tear from the corner of her eye with the back of her hand, smearing makeup across her cheek.

"Wait, hold on." She turned away from the phone and sniffled. "Kyle, where's Tommy? Go get him for me. Bring him in here." She took a deep breath. "There's a man on the phone who's trying to tell me Tommy never came here today."

Kyle dropped his bag of candy and sprinted outside. The screen door slammed behind him and he gasped. Tommy's car was gone, but Mom's gray SUV still was parked in the same spot. He scowled. How could that be?

"Tommy! Come back!" He dashed into the street, hoping to catch sight of taillights in the distance. The dark road was deserted. Maple trees at the end of the gravel driveway rustled in the Halloween air.

Kyle turned to go back into the house and stopped. Tommy's Spiderman pillowcase lay next to the Jack O'Lantern.

Remembering Natalia

James Park

What's that, Wolfgang? Yes, yes, I know. It's been quite some time since I've stopped by. Life, it's been a little crazy as of late, and I've been struggling to make sense out of this bizarre and unusual world in which we live. But you seem happy, and it appears that business hasn't been half bad. I admire that, for I, too, know the joy of a successful entrepreneurial venture.

Tonight, I think I'll help myself to a seat at the bar. I could use some good company, if you don't mind.

What's that?

Oh no, I don't think I'll be trying anything new, just the usual. Let's start off with a gram and a glass of water? And who knows, if it goes too quickly, I might just splurge and buy some more. Say, how 'bout that chunk right there? Yes, yes, that one. Let's cut it down the center and have ourselves a look.

Nice and yellow on the inside, just the way I like it.

What's a teaner going for?

One-fifty?

I'm sold. Toss it on the mirror and I'll be good to go for awhile.

Wolfgang, I must admit, you have an extraordinary memory. It's quite kind of you to ask. The plumbing in my apartment has been a thorn in my side for what feels like ages. Most of the trouble pertains to the bathtub—*stupid thing wouldn't stop backing up*—but I've managed to pinpoint the source of the problem, *finally*. I reported it to the landlord before leaving on vacation, and was hoping that, just maybe, he'd have it fixed before my return. It wasn't. These things seldom are. Sometimes you just have to take the bull by its horns and, well . . . you know how the expression goes.

My trip, you ask?

Well, my most recent expedition to a foreign land left a sour taste in my mouth. *Spat!*

I wish I could tell you that I discovered excitement, but alas, I wasn't in the frame of mind to enjoy the pleasures at hand. Excursions taken to forget a lover are never as satisfying as journeys shared when the flame is fully lit. Oh, I'm sure I must sound awful; please, don't hold it against me. When you're as loaded as I am, it's so unbecoming to act ungrateful. But after your heart's been ripped from the vessels to which it supplies blood, pleasures that you take for granted—activities such as sex, drugs, and the accumulation of material possessions—become quite insignificant. To be wealthy with youth and the passion of first loves is what we all desire most, but at my age, these experiences only exist in the past. I understand that I'm amongst the fortunate, for I can at least cling to my stock portfolio as I stand at the brink of becoming elderly, deathly frightened that the persistence of time will propel me into an oblivious realm of senility. And if that's what the piper has in store for me, then *que sera, sera.*

What more can I do? Tangible wealth is all I have to fill that great big hollow void where happiness once rested.

But even with my possessions, I feel helpless and out of control.

At this point, I must regain the ability to steer my life. Of this, I am unmistakably certain. My excursion to the Netherlands was nothing more than a lazy attempt at letting others dictate *my* desires. Amsterdam is an appropriate city for such carelessness. There's no point in forming preconceived expectations about the women you hope to meet, for they're only interested in selling you what they have, not necessarily what you want. They won't cater to specific tastes unless it's drugs you're after.

Drugs, oh drugs, oh glorious drugs.

They have them all in Amsterdam—*all the voices that call your name*—from hard-to-find strands of cannabis sativa to dangerously potent grams of diacetylmorphine. And you can even find them in the most convenient of places. But, if it's women you're after, it's best to leave your expectations at home, for specific makes and models are not readily available. I know what you must be thinking; the red light district has all types—all ages, all colors, all sizes, all perversions—and this much is undeniably true. But if you have precise specifications for your woman of the night, well then, Wolfgang, the next ice age may very well blow through before you make her acquaintance.

When you walk into a madam's pantry these days, it's a take it or leave it situation. There's no haggling over price if she's not what you fancy. Either bed the woman or go next door, those are your choices. I picked a different pantry each night, at random, swallowed my pill and then settled for whatever they were selling. I suppose it's rude of me to complain, for the world is filled with common men unfit to afford such luxuries. There's a workingman waiting for the bus at every street corner, and I'm glad that I no longer wait amongst them. But when you're grieving the loss of a lover, not even the most talented of the de Wallen women can free your thoughts from despair.

In hindsight, I should have traveled to Japan, for if you want forbidden desires presented to you in a detail oriented manner, then Japan is without doubt the Mecca of your choosing. Seriously, Wolfgang, I've been there before and the diligence with which they dazzle you is nothing short of astonishing. Try it sometime, I urge you. Just walk into one of their whorehouses, give them the minutia of your choosing, and by George, they deliver. Sure, you can go for that old Japanese staple and order a room full of schoolgirls, and it will be a rewarding experience, but if you're ever in the land, I beg you to challenge them, make them work for your money. You can demand a pair of Siamese twins joined at the hip, a Laura Palmer lookalike, or a portly woman dressed in a suit of armor, and then all you have to do is relax with a drink as they scurry about, jumping through hoops until your request is fulfilled. The Japanese pride themselves on this strange breed of hospitality.

I'll go back there someday, maybe sooner than I intend, for the experience is simply invigorating. But right now I have to let my psyche heal. Given my current condition, it's unlikely that even the most expensive of their yellow-skinned treats will be able to wash the burden of Natalia from my tainted memories.

My heart still mourns our broken love.

I have riches. I can journey to far regions of the world, but what I want more than anything tangible is the ability to enjoy new adventures with Natalia. The sights we witnessed hand-in-hand—from the Hunyad Castle of Romania to the Monte Cristo Homestead of Australia—were simply breathtaking. The scrapbook of my mind is filled with scenery that wraps beauty and chaos into single memories, and within these memories are escapades that Natalia and I embraced together.

As you're certainly aware, she possessed a peculiar affinity for ghosts, and my willingness to encourage this fascination led the two of us to haunted locales the whole world over. I'll never forget the Hyatt Hotel in Taipei or the Hammersmith area of London. Natalia was downright frightened each and every second, but I for one failed to acknowledge anything unusual about those trips, and I bloody didn't give a damn. I was happy just having Natalia by my side, making love to her in unfamiliar parts of the world.

I'll never forget the time we visited Bhangarh, India. It

was by and large the most unsettling experience of my life. Upon arrival, we each felt sick, overcome with strange feelings of anxiety that were nearly debilitating. The locals claim there was a presence amongst us, that we were not welcomed by the spirit. Frankly, Wolfgang, I found the food more disagreeable than any alleged haunting, but I exercised my manners and didn't protest. It was mostly for Natalia's sake, really. She wanted to see ghosts, to collect evidence that we'd experienced something extraordinary. So I went along with it, only because it made her happy, which subsequently made me happy.

We took trip after trip, and though Natalia wanted to believe that ghosts and evil spirits stirred behind every misplaced pebble, I, for one, wasn't buying it. I only bought the plane tickets, the hotel rooms, the food. *Que sera, sera.* As long as Natalia sought refuge in my arms whenever her illusions scared the piss from her bladder, well then, Wolfgang, I was eager to partake in any adventure she desired.

We drove to Ohio last fall, for no other reason than to enjoy midnight walks along Walhalla Road. Natalia told me all about the Mooney Mansion, some nonsense or other about a doctor going insane and slaughtering his own offspring, only to drag their bodies outside and hang them from the Calumet Bridge. I wasn't having a word of it, I mean seriously, who would? But I humored Natalia; I listened and I pretended to believe. And as we made our way hand-in-hand along Walhalla Road, there was a part of me that started to wonder. It was more than just the sheer eeriness that radiates all about Walhalla in the midst of night. I tell you, the owls along that stretch of road are not what they seem. The trees seem to be hiding something.   And every footstep you hear, no matter how distant, feels like it's right beside you.   When we peered up at the Mooney mansion, we saw something.   At first, it was nothing more than pale blue light in every window.   Hardly worth writing home about.   But I glanced up at the attic window, and Wolfgang, I swear on my mother's grave, I saw a man upstairs with an axe, just as the legend describes.

The sheer sight of Dr Mooney's ghost made our legs quiver, but still we lingered, feeling secure in each other's presence. Though frightening, the escapade paled in comparison to our experience at Nagoon Park, just outside of Manistee.   We were so in love at the time, consummating our private pleasures in a public park after closing.   God only knows what approached us, but it didn't cower in seclusion behind the walls of a mansion. Oh no, this presence came right up to us.   It disturbed our moment of passion in such a glacial manner that we fled the scene in only a partial state of dress.   I tell you, Wolfgang, whatever it was, it touched us, we felt it, and it didn't want us coming back, *ever*.

So, she had me convinced; perhaps one or two of the destinations we visited was haunted.   I'm not too stubborn to admit it.   Besides, our love took us other places, too.   It wasn't all about alleged ghosts and unknown spirits.   It was about exploring the strange and mysterious world in which we live.   I tell you, Wolfgang, there's nothing quite like the Hebrides of Scotland.   Standing there with my love, I felt like I'd come to the edge of the world.   It made me feel like a man, as if wrapping my arms around Natalia was a chivalrous act that kept her safe.   And weekends in Paris.   Nothing rivals the experience of engaging in immoral acts of affection in the city of love. These days, I'd even settle for that cheap imitation of Paris submerged beneath the tacky underbelly of Las Vegas, if only it would allow me to hold Natalia's hand one last time.

It's quite unfortunate, I tell you, that those days are forever vanquished. But there was a time when we did more than just explore the world together; we used to climb inside each other's minds. Natalia knew how to make me forget the minor irritations that plague my life. The drain in my bathtub that wouldn't stop backing up, footsteps coming from the apartment above, or just the misfortune of being neighbor to a man like Edward Hegstrand; these were things that Natalia forced me to file away in the back of my mind.

I know, I know, I know, you've heard me complain endlessly about Edward Hegstrand—*who hasn't?*—but living below a womanizer is no easy task. He liked to entertain women into the wee morning hours, playing his grand piano and carrying on with complete disrespect for polite society. I suppose he's just blessed with good genes, 'cause he didn't seem to age one bit the entire time I knew him. Not one wrinkle, not one grey hair. And then there's me, an aging man who takes what he can get. I suppose it's not completely hopeless. Though it proved to be temporary, I did manage to capture Natalia. Perhaps, I'll manage to perform such a feat again, Wolfgang, just perhaps.

Wouldn't it be wonderful, to procure the company of another woman who's by far too young for the likes of me. I dream of it happening just one more time before my pills stop working. And hopefully the Edward Hegstrands of the world will learn to keep their hands to themselves.

I won't bore you with any further details of how that damned womanizer stole the most recent love of my life. It's all behind me now. But what I can't comprehend is why Natalia left me for a man who doesn't appreciate the virtues of monogamy. We'd heard the footsteps from above many times. Women sauntered into his life by the dozen, then just disappeared, as if unimportant to the man.

It must be that a combination of curiosity and ego got the better of Natalia. I can't imagine what else would have driven her into the arms of that smug little bastard. I know how women are. She was interested in experiencing whatever it was about him that attracted so many women, and she also wanted to prove that she could tame his beast, become his one and only object of desire.

And we both know that she failed miserably. Everybody knows that.

Que sera, sera.

I try not to lose too much sleep over it.

Life is filled with so many worries. I suppose it's unfair of me to waste all of my frustration on Natalia. Certainly, the agony she left me with was emasculating. It's irritating enough listening to a man entertain different women every night, but when sleepless nights became entrenched with the sound of familiar footsteps frolicking above, depression immediately takes hold.

I tried to busy myself with domestic activities in hopes of relieving my mind, but how many books can one person possibly read?

Television?

Please. It's so not my style.

And you can only go snow skiing so many times a month before complete and utter paranoia takes hold . . . nothing personal, Wolfgang.

I opted to occupy myself with chores.

I know what you must be thinking, a clean house is a sign of wasted life, but I needed something with which to busy myself. I cleaned out the cupboards and organized the drawers, and I started making daily phone calls to the landlord. But it didn't matter how badly I complained; he couldn't stop my bathtub from backing up. Nobody could. The landlord called for outside help, and a whole slew of plumbers gave it their all. They came in with those big snakes they send down stopped up drains, then told me that the problem was fixed. And for a little while they were right, but time after time it would back up all over again. So another plumber would be sent out, and then another, and then another.

For the rent I pay to live in that complex—*luxury apartments my ass*—I shouldn't have to tolerate malfunctions of that nature, not for such an extended period of time. It was bad enough that my view was ruined, at least temporarily. I couldn't set foot on the balcony without hearing Natalia's voice seeping down from above. And I could picture them both, indulging in candlelight dinners on the terrace, the taste of wine on their tongues as they kissed. In isolation, I learned to ignore sunsets; they probably watched them together, and then held each other beneath full moon illuminations.

My only salvation was that Natalia's foray with Edward

Hegstrand was quite short. Compared to our relationship, it was merely a fling. One day, out of the blue, I stopped hearing her footsteps. It was only a matter of days before the trample of other women's feet replaced Natalia's. This was a clear indication that she'd left bigger wounds for me to mend than she'd left for Edward, and this misfortune made me bitter.

Que sera, sera.

I was again disturbed by piano music and laughter at all hours of the night, but at least the laughter belonged to women I didn't know.

I never contacted her, Wolfgang. Not with my pride intact I didn't, and I never asked Edward what happened. I was just relieved that they'd split. The abrupt turn of events provided me with the simple courtesy of being able to mend my broken heart in isolation.

And so the story goes. Nothing more to say.

At this point, I probably shouldn't ramble anymore, but rather I should apologize for my lack of manners. We haven't seen each other in some time, and here I sit engrossed with my own personal problems.

You must have stories of your own to share, don't you, Wolfgang?

But first, could you be a good man and pour me another glass of water? I'm afraid the drip has left a rather impure taste in my mouth.

And if it's not too much trouble, I sure could use a tissue.

Thank you very much, Wolfgang.

Now, where was I?

Oh, yes. Alone at last, without the pain of Natalia's feet

stomping around up above. It was a tremendous relief. But the speed with which Edward Hegstrand moved on to other women—*followed by even more women after that*—only served to downgrade my own personal struggle. I found myself longing to just up and get away, to disappear; so naturally, I started planning a vacation. Some faraway adventure was long overdue and I deserved a getaway that didn't revolve around haunted houses. Even with this minor stipulation, Wolfgang, the possibilities felt limitless.

At first, I pictured myself in Key West, taking refuge amongst the anonymous parade of tourists stumbling up and down Duval Street. It seemed like a fitting destination; the southernmost point of the States is where most over-the-hill Americans travel to lose themselves in a stream of alcohol. But the more I thought about it, the more unsettling the proposition became. The brothels in that neck of the woods are ghastly, to say the very least. The girls are nothing more than haggard chain-smokers with sun-stained skin and poorly manicured nails. I tell you, Wolfgang, it takes a good dose of alcohol to enjoy yourself in the company of those leathery whores. Really, I don't know what's more nauseating about the island, their subpar selection of flesh or those annoying little roosters that crow all night long.

For me, it was off to Amsterdam, curious to discover what the city has to offer now that my beloved Yab Yum is no longer in operation. But I tell you, Wolfgang, sometimes it's best to travel with low expectations. Thoughts of Natalia continued to plague me, and as a result, the marijuana didn't smell as fresh, and the working girls didn't appear as attractive.

Once you rekindle the type of love you thought you would never again experience, only to watch her run from your arms in order to partake in a meaningless fling, the impersonal decadence of purchased pleasures just feels artificial. I was going through the motions of discovering new joys, only to learn that the joys I sought were not new to me.

There was no sense of exploration, no unexpected excitement.

Prostitution is not a young profession, just as I am not a young man.

Que sera, sera.

I returned from my trip jetlagged and forlorn, and to my surprise, I encountered a sight that forced the most genuine smile ever worn to inhabit my face; Edward Hegstrand was moving out. He didn't say much about it—we'd never engaged one another in lengthy conversation—just that something from his past had caught up with him.

"It's time to move on," he told me, and then returned to his business.

I wasn't exactly sure what he was running from. He wore a young face, the kind of face that suggests he doesn't have the type of past that causes one to flee. But I gave little thought to the details of his situation, for I was happy just to see him packing. The sight of him pulling out of the parking lot and then fading into nonexistence will reside in my memory until senility does me in.

Having endured a lengthy flight, I decided that I owed myself the relaxation of a hot shower. I recall having mixed emotions as I stepped beneath the running water. The womanizer was gone, for good, but my own emptiness seemed to outweigh the splendor of his departure. There I was, a lonely man, showering in an empty apartment where the drain didn't work properly. I know, I know, just a minor irritation, but in my current state of worthlessness, minor irritations do nothing more than reinforce feelings of despair.

Seriously, Wolfgang, I felt like my life had gone down the drain. And the notion made it difficult to concentrate.

I ignored the accumulation of water at my feet, and began to wash. Soon, I found myself just standing there, motionless and spacing out, staring at the pool of soapy water in which I stood. But as I stared, I saw something come up from the drain the appeared out of place. I bent over and picked it up for closer examination, and to my horrified dismay, discovered that I was holding a human bone. It appeared to be from the hand, most likely one of the phalanges, and was quite small.

It never before occurred to me that Edward Hegstrand would be involved with such iniquity, but the evidence rested in my palm.

Natalia had small hands. There wasn't one inch to her body that was disproportionately large. Such a tiny woman she was, and one can only imagine that when Edward Hegstrand initiated his sordid little game of Jack the Ripper, she didn't possess the strength to muster much of a fight.

You see, Wolfgang, a life really had gone down the drain, of that much I'm sure. But the life wasn't mine, Wolfgang. Oh no, it wasn't mine. And I know beyond doubt that it wasn't just Natalia's life either.

How can I be so certain, you ask?

The answer is actually quite simple, and can be measured by more than just the frequency with which my drain malfunctioned.

On certain nights, I still hear the grand piano playing, and on those nights I'm again disturbed by the soft pitter-patter of female feet. And from time-to-time, it's not unusual to be awakened by womanly laughter.

I know what you must be thinking, and I know what others will say. They'll tell me I'm at the early stages of dementia, or that maybe I've put too much of this wretched powder up my nose. People will say what people will say. Some of them don't even think you exist, Wolfgang, that you're nothing more than a ghost, or just a figment of my imagination. They take me for a crazy old man who likes to get loaded on alkaloids and talk to himself. But I shrug my shoulders at such nonsense. My imaginary friends may give me grief, but it's only a matter of time until a new neighbor moves in, and I'm certain that whoever that neighbor might be, he'll agree with me; the ghosts that Edward Hegstrand left behind are not few in number.

I've begun to wonder if maybe, just maybe, Natalia's ghost will be so kind as to enter my apartment. It probably won't happen, but I still have my fantasies, and this scenario has made its way into the fold. I think of her constantly, the love I still have for her. In its own strange little way, our flame still burns. The days since Edward Hegstrand left have reminded me of the days when Natalia and I traveled the world. When I step out on my patio, I can hear a voice seeping down from above, and it's a voice that I recognize.

Masks

Fred C. Adams

"They can't take Halloween away from us!" Eddie thumped his bony fist on the cafeteria table and the silverware danced on his tray. Mark, Billy, Sam, Jason and Paul all nodded in agreement.

"But they did," said Paul angrily poking at his meat loaf with a fork. "Reverend Dawson says so, and that's how it goes." His face was almost as red as his hair with indignation.

"Aw, man," whined Sam, pushing his glasses up his nose with a sausage of a finger. "I had my costume all ready and everything."

"Who were you going to be this year?" Billy jibed, "Jabba the Hutt?"

The others laughed and Sam glared at Billy. "Maybe you could rub olive oil over your zits and go as a pizza, Billy."

"Maybe you could hold a hula hoop around your gut and be the planet Saturn," Jason added. "Or just put two flashlights in your armpits like headlights and be *a* Saturn."

"Hey, guys," said Eddie. "This is serious stuff. No school Halloween party? That's crap! Where's the *Reverend*"—he rolled his eyes—"get off telling us we can't have Halloween? It's not just the school party; he's preached the last two Sundays that it's a pagan holiday and we shouldn't celebrate it at all. No party, no trick-or-treat, no costumes, no jack o'lanterns—zip."

"We aren't the only Christian school that shut down Halloween," said Paul. "Pillar of Fire started this last year, and now Sacred Covenant, First Christian and a couple of others have jumped in."

Jason moaned, "Why did our parents have to send us to this place?"

The Apostolic Academy was one of eleven Christian schools that had sprung up in Barlow County like mushrooms in the nineties, sponsored by nondenominational churches and peopled with the children of the faithful. Parents were promised a first rate education for their children delivered in a spiritual atmosphere far away from the corrosive influence of the heathens who overran the public schools and their godless teachers. The school was an annex to the original building and soon outgrew the church itself. Reverend Arthur Dawson was its principal, English teacher, and chaplain, and the jobs bled into each other like three colors of paint until one set of aesthetics, principles, and tactics gave a monochrome tint to his performance.

"I think this whole thing was Rodney Miller's fault," said Billy. "If he hadn't shown up at the party last year dressed in that Grim Reaper outfit with the bleeding skull mask—"

"Naah," said Eddie. "Dawson can't stand to think that any church or school is holier than his. "Like last spring when the music police started grabbing our iPods and checking what music we had on them. First Christian started that, and in a week, Dawson was calling our parents and causing us grief."

"Yeah," said Mark, winding his striped necktie around his finger. "It's bad enough we have to wear these stupid uniforms. Even Pillar of Fire doesn't make the guys wear white shirts and ties. Might as well just put a noose around our necks."

Across the cafeteria, Reverend Dawson sat down with his tray at the faculty table and the other teachers stopped their banter while the Reverend made a great show of saying grace. His shock of white hair swirled in a style reminiscent of Porter Waggoner, and his bushy eyebrows bobbed when he spoke as if they had lives of their own. And right under his chin, in a perfectly wimpled knot, hung the same striped necktie the boys all wore.

Nicky, the new guy sidled over with his tray. Everybody nodded and he sat down. He started at Apostolic Academy that September, and the guys were just beginning to accept him. A kid from a single-parent home, he lived with his dad and he was pretty cool. He always seemed to have the latest new game on his cell phone, or the hippest graphic novel hidden behind *Ivanhoe* during library period.

"What really ticks me off is that it happened this year," Said Jason. "Next year we'll be in the seventh grade and too old for the school party and it wouldn't matter anyway. We're getting ripped off."

"So what do we do about it? What can we do about it?" Sam said.

Nicky looked up from his tray. "You guys talking about the no-party?" Heads nodded all around. Nicky's dark eyes narrowed. "Have one of your own."

"Aw, man," said Jason, "If Dawson says no Halloween for the flock—" He turned pointedly and looked to the Reverend as his voice twisted the word into one of sneering contempt. "My parents would never let me do something like that."

Nicky leaned forward, lowering his voice. "Who says they have to know? Keep it a secret. Just have a party for the seven of us." Glances shot around the table.

"What if our parents find out?" Mark leaned forward, interested but still wary. "What if Reverend Dawson finds out?

"What are they gonna do?" Eddie jumped in. "Excommunicate us? Punish a bunch of kids for acting like a bunch of kids? Besides, Dawson needs our parents' money to run this place, every stinking dime of it."

Nicky grinned. "If we can keep the whole thing quiet, we can have a great party and we'll know we won't be held down." Eddie took note of Nicky's segue into the inclusive "we," but If the others had misgivings about it, it didn't show.

"Yeah," said Eddie, taking command. "Let's do it." Heads nodded all around. "Just us. Too many people and the word'll get out."

The bell rang and as the boys rose with their trays, for the first time that day all of them were smiling.

That Sunday Reverend Dawson followed his homily, as he often did, with comments for the good of the congregation, announcements of who was in the hospital, and what fundraiser the school was running any given week. Today he folded his arms and looked over the congregation for an uncomfortably silent minute.

He frowned, his green eyes blazing over his starched white shirt. "I am saddened that some students, and I might add, some parents have spoken out in opposition to our prohibition of Halloween activities this year. Why should Christians celebrate an abomination descended from the pagan holiday Samhain?" He spat the words like venom. "Human sacrifice, devil worship!" He paused to sweep the congregation with his baleful gaze. "The children—I might understand the allure of candy, dressing up, playing party games, but parents?" The word hung in the air as if it were a net poised to drop on the offenders. Some of the adults squirmed in their seats, while others ratcheted their noses a degree higher in the air.

"Salvation!" Another shoe-drop pause. "Is no party game!" Dawson's face reddened, contrasting his shock of white hair. "Will you bob for apples in the Lake of Everlasting Fire? Remember, it was the apple that Eve used to lead Adam astray. You'll wear no mask on Judgment Day, and the flames of Hades will burn the apostate rags from your soul." After another uncomfortable silence, he bowed his head for the benediction, and Eddie stole a look to the row behind where Nicky sat with his dad. Nicky looked up and winked.

The next day at lunch, Billy had some good news. "Hey, guys," he said, excited, "my Uncle Fred and Aunt Betty left for Florida yesterday and they won't be back until Thanksgiving. I can swipe the spare keys from my dad's dresser drawer and we can use the house for the party."

Eddie looked skeptical for a moment. "I don't know. People could see in the windows and if nobody's supposed to be there, maybe they'd call the cops. Does it have a basement?"

"No, said Billy, but it has a garage behind the house. If we cover the windows, nobody could see in, and there's a fence and bushes. If we bring stuff in through the alley, nobody'll notice, especially if we do it after dark."

"I'm glad we're doing this," said Mark. "Did you know that some of the parents wanted to have an 'anti-Halloween party' at the school? Games, food, just no costumes or Halloween stuff."

Eddie snorted. "I heard. Dawson shot that idea down, too. He said having any party at all on Halloween is just another way of celebrating it. Well, they can't take Halloween away from us. Right?" Heads nodded all around. "You better believe it."

The next ten days were spent in covert operations. The boys covered the garage windows and the glass panes in the overhead door to keep out prying eyes. Piggy banks were emptied, allowances were pooled, and the boys went about quietly buying everything a good Halloween party could need and smuggling it into the garage. If the neighbors noticed the activity, none of them mentioned it to anyone.

The garage walls were hung with black and orange crepe paper and overlaid with cardboard skeletons, witches and black cats. Rubber bats hung from the ceiling on fishing line and ghosts made of white plastic bags pinched around balloons fluttered spectrally every time someone walked past. Arms and legs made of stuffed shirts and trouser legs lay in corners spattered with red paint. A long table sat against one wall for snacks. As the holiday neared, the food supply grew; chips, candy bars, popcorn balls, candied apples, all in bright cellophane wrappers. A big plastic cooler was dragged in from Uncle Fred's basement for the drinks, and a tub to bob for apples in defiance of Reverend Dawson's rant. Halloween was only two days away.

"Anybody having any trouble getting out for the party?" Eddie was taping up a movie poster from *Friday the 13th* next to one for *Dracula*.

"Naah," Jason said. "I'm supposed to be going to your house to play video games. I kinda think my parents have it figured out, but they don't agree with Dawson. I heard my mom talking about it on the phone to somebody. She thinks he should let us be kids."

"Yeah," said Sam, looking up from the pumpkin he was carving into a leering ghoulish face, "My mom bought my costume for me two months ago. She came in my room and saw me looking at it hanging on my closet door and said it was a shame I wouldn't get to wear it. I think she may know it, too, but she didn't let on."

In fact, if any of their parents noticed anything unusual for the past two weeks, none of them said anything to their offspring, or to each other. If the scissors or the duct tape went missing for a day or a six pack of soda or a bag of potato chips wandered off the basement shelf, moms and dads dismissed it with a wink. After all, boys will be boys, and what was the harm anyway? Maybe Reverend Dawson was being too harsh.

It was only Halloween.

And then the garage was ready. The evening before the party, they gathered to admire their handiwork. The party room looked better than anything their parents and teachers had ever done at the Apostolic Academy, and it gave the revelers satisfaction, both that they had done it themselves and that they were spitting in Reverend Dawson's eye without getting caught. They stood in the middle of the garage and turned full circle, admiring their handiwork.

"Wow," said Jason. "I can't believe we did all this." Fluorescent paints glowed in the cold radiance of black-light bulbs, swirling ghosts and flames that seemed almost to pulse. A boom box under the food table poured out eerie moans, creaks and howls, whistling wind and clanking chains.

"And one last touch," said Nicky. He pulled a small controller fob from the pocket of his jeans and pushed a button. A strobe light began pulsing erratically like blue lightning. The boys moved their arms and legs in sweeping gestures, laughing at their jerking limbs.

"That is the coolest thing yet," said Mark. "I can't wait for tomorrow night."

"I told you they couldn't take Halloween away from us," Eddie said. "This will be the best Halloween ever." Eddie was wary at first about Nicky easing his way into the group and thought maybe he was trying to take his place as the ringleader. The party idea was Nicky's, and he got all the credit for that but Nicky deferred to Eddie on every detail of the setup, the decorations and the food. He wasn't bossy or pushy about anything. And Eddie had to admit, the strobe light was a nice touch that didn't occur to him. Yeah, Nicky was all right.

Dark came early Halloween night, and the boys arrived alone or in twos on their bicycles. They changed into their costumes in separate rooms in the house so nobody knew exactly who was who, except of course for Sam. As the party began, only six of them had arrived, and for a while, nobody was sure who was missing. Then they started talking, and by their voices, recognized each other. Nicky was the only hold-out.

"Do you think he punked out?" said Billy, dressed as an intricately detailed *Star Wars* storm trooper.

"I hope not," said Eddie, around a mouthful of jagged fangs. Eddie came as Marlowe the über-vampire of *30 Days of Night*. "He's got the controller for the strobe light. Anyway, the party was his idea. He'd better be here."

The flickering candles in the jack-o-lanterns threw dancing shadows around the room. Jason found he couldn't eat with his Freddy Krueger mask in place, so he cocked it up on his fore-head. Sam, as Davy Jones from the *Pirates of the Carribean*, had the same problem with a face full of tentacled beard. Skinny Mark was Gollum unmasked, and Paul took off his Gandalf beard. Masks off, they dove into the food and the drinks, enjoying the delight of forbidden fruit. Eddie was right. This was the best Halloween ever. And even Reverend Dawson couldn't do a thing to stop it.

The side door opened, and what walked in made them all freeze.

It was tall, looming, in fact, with segmented insect arms that ended in saw-toothed pincers. Its red-cloaked torso seemed hollow; at its center, a dark maw ringed with sickly pink tentacles that undulated like the palps of a sea anemone. The face that perched atop the slender trunk was angular, its shape changing in the flickering light. Its nose, or was it a proboscis, or was it a tentacle, or was it a separate living thing, curled upward and danced like a cobra, nodding toward each of them in its turn. The eyes glowed amber. Then the oozing slit of a mouth opened and a keening wail like a band saw cutting oak emerged that made them all quake.

Nicky's voice sounded from the torso's maw. "Hi guys. Sorry I'm late. Did I miss anything?"

Eddie let out the breath he'd been holding for the last minute. "Holy—man, did you give me a scare."

"That has to be the coolest costume I've ever seen," said Billy. The others chimed in with their praise.

"Where did you get it?" said Jason.

"My dad helped me. He's pretty good at making things." Nicky reached up with a pincer and delicately caught the edge of a membrane just below his chin. He peeled away the alien face with a sound like wet Saran Wrap revealing his trademark grin.

"Wow, that's impressive," said Sam. "You said your dad helped you?" He hesitated. "He knows about the party?"

Nicky nodded. "Yeah, he knew all along, and actually, he thought it was a great idea. He's really good with masks.

Watch." He reached for his face and carefully pulled away another membrane, revealing a different face below it: Jason's.

"Whoa!" said Mark. "That is really cool. How'd he do that?"

"And there's more." Nicky pulled away another face, this time revealing Sam's, then Billy's, then in turn each of their faces, Eddie's last. Then Nicky pulled Eddie's face away to reveal his own again.

"That was some trick, man," said Paul, "but I gotta say it freaked me out."

"Just one more to go," said Nicky. He peeled his face away leaving the alien face from his entrance. Though they'd all seen it before, the boys cringed a little and fell silent.

Eddie laughed nervously. "Hey, Nicky, that's great. Uh, take off your mask and have some food."

The keening voice came from the mouth-slit. "End of the line, guys. This is the real me." He reached overhead with a pincer and tripped the lever that locked the overhead garage door. His yellow eyes glowed hungrily. The segmented arms reached toward the cowering boys. "And yes, I will have something to eat."

Nicky started toward them, pincers clicking shut on the air, and some of the boys laughed nervously.

"Hey, Nicky," said Billy. "Uh, the costume is cool and all that, but this isn't funny."

"Who said I'm joking?"

The realization dawned on all of them at once that pretend had become real.

"Lights!" the voice screeched. "Camera! Action!" The

strobe light came on, and in spasmodic motion, the Nicky thing stalked toward them, the only constant in the room its glowing eyes. The boys ran in panic from one end of the garage to the other. The food table upset and fell against the side door, blocking their exit.

A pincer shot forward and snapped at Jason's face with a sharp clipping sound, barely missing his nose. He wailed in terror and fell backward over the bobbing tub. Water sloshed out and the boys slipped and slid as they dashed from one corner to another from the Nicky thing.

Eddie picked up one of the pumpkins, its candle still burning, and heaved it at the Nicky thing's head. He missed, and the pumpkin burst against the wall, throwing the candle into the crepe streamers. In seconds, the garage was ablaze and seconds later, the costumes caught, turning the boys into screaming, writhing torches. The Nicky thing stalked through the flames untouched and threw the table away from the door. "Good night, guys," the band saw whined as the Nicky thing stepped out. "It's been fun." By the time the fire trucks arrived, the garage was a bonfire to rival any Samhain revel.

The newspapers were full of it the next day: Clandestine Party Ends in Tragedy. Minister's Ban Brings Fiery Death. Real Halloween Horror Kills Six. The congregation stood behind Reverend Dawson, but reactions from the public were mixed.

The following Sunday, the church was hung with black crepe—just black no orange—and easels stood on the dais with framed pictures of Eddie, Sam, Jason, Paul, Billy, and Mark. Their weeping parents sat in the front rows as Reverend Dawson droned on about mansions in Heaven and the will of God and the arms of the angels and honoring thy mother and father. Outside the church, TV crews waited ghoulishly to ambush the grieving and to pounce like jackals on the Reverend. His torment had only begun.

A few rows from the back, Nicky turned and looked up at his father who looked down at him with a reassuring smile. For just an instant, Dad's eye turned golden and winked.

The Hunt

IE Castellano

The bright full moon lit everywhere the eye could see. Staring at the soft silver in a sea of black, Teeg sighed. Glimpsing at Teeg, Meir shook his head. "What are you doing?"

Teeg jumped. He thought he was alone. "Just looking," he answered.

"At…?" Meir asked.

"The moon. We never just look at it anymore. It's so beautiful."

"Aw, Teeg, don't get all human on me," Meir complained.

"I'm not," Teeg said. "Sometimes, it's good to stop and stare in the moonlight."

"Uh-huh. Not tonight. We gotta go," said Meir.

Teeg's eyes searched the shadows. He clapped his hand over his mouth. "The Choice. It's tonight. We gotta go."

Meir rolled his eyes. Falling on all fours, they sprinted through the moonlit woods.

The circle had already begun to form. They took their places among their brethren. A shadow approached the circle. No one said a word.

It was Teeg's final year to be eligible for the Hunt. Hunters could only be chosen for three years. For the past two years, he watched others around him join the prestigious hunt. Desperately, he wished he could don Hunter's armor. Like his peers, he had been training his entire life. The Notkyn evolved purely to hunt.

Moonlight illuminated a bare foot inside the circle. Bronze chains and rings adorned the feminine foot.

On beat to a song Teeg did not hear, a woman danced into the circle. Strips of fabric shimmered in the silver light. Bronze bangles jingled a tune to which Teeg began to sway.

Her skin glistened with each step. The Huntrix did not make eye contact. She faced everyone and no one.

Her bare feet brought her to the center of the circle. Her body still moved to a beat only she could hear. Finally, her lips parted. Like whispers on the wind, names escaped her mouth.

Teeg leaned in close. He longed for the Huntrix to utter his name. Only her word permitted his admittance.

Softly, she said, "Quinn, Meir, Ky, Tin, Cine, Pri, Feen, Rhash, Teeg."

Hearing his name, he smiled. The dancing ceased. Those not chosen left the circle.

"You have trained under veterans. Weaned on legends. And now, you, too, have your chance to make your place among the stars," said the Huntrix. "Welcome to the Hunt."

Her brown hair whipped around her as she turned. The nine of them followed her path away from what they knew.

Meir punched Teeg's arm in excitement. Teeg could not believe it either. He was finally walking with the Huntrix. She would lead him to his destiny.

She brought them to Hunter Mountain. A man wearing dark armor met them at the base. "The Chosen," he said. "I am Kron."

The Huntrix disappeared while they were distracted. "This will be your home for the next three years, after which you may live wherever you'd like. Many, however, stay within the complex," Kron explained. "Regardless of living quarters, we train in this complex. It is only here where we can simulate hunting conditions."

They walked up stone steps with multiple corridors at all different levels. Kron stopped in front of an opening. "From this point, *I* am your direct superior. Down this corridor are your quarters. Each one of you has a trunk with your name on it in front of a bed. In the trunk, you will find armor and weapons. Change. We hunt tonight."

The Chosen ran into the corridor. A metal door slid open, revealing a small dormitory. Along the walls, rested beds with trunks at their feet. Teeg found his name carved into the top of the metal trunk. He bunked next to Meir.

Opening the trunk, he found dark armor. The material ran over his fingers like water. Immediately, he changed. The body suit-like armor covered him from head to toe. A removable piece covered his face, leaving only his eyes exposed.

Secured inside the lid was the most beautiful weapon he had ever seen. His fingers grazed the carved bone handle before unsnapping the leather straps. Grasping it, he marveled at the comfortable grip. With a snap of his wrist, the silver blade shot out from its bone casing. He quickly retracted the blade, then fastened the carved bone to his forearm.

Kron waited for them on the steps. Without a word, he led them further up the stone stairs. The crisp, night air glided around their armor. Moonlight crept into the staircase. Pausing a few steps from the opening, Kron said, "We are a hunting party. There will be no heroics. We stay together. We help each other. Keep an eye on one another. Do you understand?"

"Yes, sir," they all said.

They emerged on top of the mountain. Dark armor clad Hunters scurried into place. Kron led them to the back of the pack. Silence blanketed as the Huntrix inspected her Hunters.

Her armor did not differ from theirs. A bone handled weapon was strapped to her forearm. She carried a silver bullhorn by its dark strap.

When she took her place at the front, the horn echoed in the surrounding valleys. The Hunters attached their face coverings. Dropping to their hands and feet, they sprinted down the mountain.

Their speed kept them yards above the ground. While on the move, they resembled a pack of wolves, dogs or even men on horseback.

Adrenaline pumped through Teeg. He did not know where they were going or what he would face. Kron had them stop in a moonlit clearing with another party of Hunters. The rest kept running.

Following Kron's lead, they detached their weapons from their forearms. Blades snapped into place as they fell into formation.

Teeg inhaled deeply through his nose. He discerned lingering smoke from a bonfire mixed with drying leaves, wet grass and must. Not must. Ghost. The smell strengthened.

A low grumble reached his ears. His eyes roved in their sockets. His heart pumped faster. He spied a shimmer in the distance. It sped towards them.

Pri caught the shape on her silver blade. It burst, whispering a scream.

The sickening sour stench of ghost intensified. Translucent shimmers surrounded both hunting parties. Teeg forgot to breathe.

"Remember, you were trained for this." Kron's words gave them confidence. "On my signal," he said.

Teeg watched the ghosts converge on them. *This is just like training*, he repeated in his head. In training, they used technology that simulated the look of ghosts. When their blades cut through the manufactured shimmer, there were no screams, no ectoplasm oozing down the faux silver.

"Now," coordinated Kron.

They attacked the descending ghosts with gusto. Whispered screams resounded in their ears as ectoplasm blanketed the grass.

Teeg's first stab was easy. The goo on his blade glowed light green. Slashing the translucent shimmers did not end. It was as if the ghosts sacrificed themselves.

The meadow cleared. Darkness replaced the shimmering. Teeg's arm felt sore, but he had no time to rest. The air reeked of ghost. He was not sure if the sourness lingered in the ooze or if more approached.

A sinister laugh haunted their ears. Chests heaving, they scanned the clearing. Even Kron's eyes frantically searched for its source. The moon fell below the horizon, but night's grip held firm.

In the darkness, dots of translucent color floated over the grass. The Hunters readjusted their grips on their blades. Like fog, the dots rolled towards them. A faint, scream-like singing saturated their ears.

"Don't listen to it," Kron advised. "They want to confuse you. Stay where you are. Let the Wisps come to you."

Teeg digested Kron's guidance. Wisps were not simulated in training.

The Wisps danced across the landscape seductively, trying to lure them away from one another.

A blade next to Teeg lowered. He reached out his free hand. Grabbing Meir, he kept his friend near.

Slithering closer, the Wisps morphed into earthly forms. Bunnies, puppies, chicks, kittens, alluring women, anything that would cause the Hunters' blades to pause.

Their transformations played tricks on the eyes, but not on the nose. Teeg smelled their wretched odor. Inhaling deeply, his nose guided him. He punched Meir in the arm. Snapping out of the haze of a siren's call, Meir gave Teeg a determined look.

Side by side, they slashed and stabbed benign looking creatures. The screams of slaughtered Wisps carried on the wind. Teeg and Meir worked as a team, releasing the Wisps from the earthly realm.

Across the field, a Hunter from the other party plunged to her knees, convulsing. She ripped off her facemask. Blade still in hand, she vomited in the grass.

A translucent shape raced towards her, taking advantage of her vulnerable position.

"Voy!" Kron screamed.

She lifted her blade while the shape swooped. The shape spilt in half, gliding around the silver. Voy stumbled backwards as the halves penetrated her nose and mouth.

All movement in the clearing paused, except for Voy. She rose off the ground gracefully. Gravity released only her, then reclaimed her with such force, the earth rumbled.

Kron dove to her still form. Picking up her abandoned weapon, he slashed everything in his path with both blades.

The wind washed away the last of the screams. Scattered around the clearing, Hunters waited for whatever was to come next.

Teeg spotted a translucent face hanging over the meadow. Empty misery filled its eyes. Its mouth twisted with despair. A wicked, maniacal smile spread in the air.

A bullhorn blasted from the woods. The face faded.

None of the Hunters retracted their blades. They waited, ready to attack, until the pack returned.

Upon seeing Voy's body lying in the grass, the pack stopped. The Huntrix circled her body, then touched her forehead. A brass and silver coin-like object rested where she touched her. The tracking device would allow the Collectors to find Voy.

Almost black lightened to navy at the horizon. Fastening their weapons, they scurried back to Hunter Mountain.

Kron escorted his charges to their quarters. Both his and Voy's weapons were attached to his forearms. Unfastening his facemask, he addressed them. "Like all of you, Voy and I were chosen together. You form close bonds with whom you hunt. She was a dear friend and will be greatly missed." His gaze shifted to the floor for a moment. "In all my years of hunting, I have never experienced a Hunt like tonight. Our job was to get the stragglers, the runaways, not to deal with a full-blown attack. You have done well for your first night. You should be proud."

"Sir?" said Rhash. "If I may? How did she die?"

Kron's sadness could not hide. "They did something to make her sick. To make her remove her mask." He paused as the scene replayed behind his eyes. "They knew what they were doing. Get some rest. We hunt again at sun down."

He left the newly chosen to discuss their first Hunt. Walking through the stone corridors, the laugh echoed in his ears. They planned an attack on them. Had the Hunters become the hunted?

The corridors brought him to a chamber with a long table. Around it, Hunter Chiefs gathered, all of whom held a higher rank than he. The Huntrix sat at the head of the table. "Kron," she said, "please, recount your Hunt for us."

After taking a breath, his mouth spilled every detail of the night, including the haunting laugh. He, however, did not see the face looming over the clearing.

"We encountered very few ghosts," mentioned one of the Hunters.

"We as well," said another.

A flurry of chatter stormed the table. Kron ignored the other Hunters. His eyes focused on the Huntrix.

She listened to her Hunters complain. Her face showed no emotion. She was every bit a hard, calculating woman. When her lips parted, the chattered ceased. "Thank you, Kron. Your party will train in Sublevel G first thing."

He bowed his head, then took his leave.

First training in Sublevel G was unheard of for the newly chosen. But, Kron figured, if they were to survive, it had to be.

After what seemed like no sleep, Kron entered his party's quarters. "Up. Now. Armor. Weapons," he ordered.

Startled out of bed, they scrambled to slip into their armor. They stifled yawns as they lined up in the center of the room.

Following Kron through the corridors, Teeg could still feel last night's Hunt. No one asked where they headed.

They crammed into an elevator. Kron spoke, "We are training in Sublevel G. This is an advanced training level. Newly chosen normally do not enter this level until after six months of hunting. And never first thing. Sublevel G generates just about all the nasties you will hunt *ever*. You can get hurt down here. Be on guard."

The elevator opened. Uncertainty welcomed them. Kron led them through the second door down the corridor.

They filed into a vestibule. Beyond a glass wall was the darkest cavern Teeg had ever seen. "We are going to enter the training room as a group," Kron said. "Once you take your positions, I will start the simulator. Be ready." He ushered them through the glass door.

The caverned breathed. Standing near Meir, Teeg listened to the deep, rhythmic, dark breaths. His eyes searched the darkness for its source. "Where's that coming from?" he asked Meir.

"What are you talking about?"

"The noise—the breathing."

Shaking his head, Meir said, "I don't hear anything. Maybe you didn't get enough sleep."

"Maybe," Teeg conceded.

Shimmers appeared around rocks. Blades ready, they waited. The training room filled with the inescapable stench accompanying otherworldly beings. The smell nauseated.

Teeg suppressed the bile bubbling up his throat. His arm raised his blade. His head turned, following instinctually. As he sliced through a misty form, the scream rang in his ears. Ectoplasm dripped onto the dirt.

Feeling a presence behind him, he spun. He did not know if it were friend or foe. Seeing through the shape, he stabbed. He felt another. Spotting Meir, he said, "Behind you." Meir's blade slashed the simulated ghost.

They slaughtered simulations of things they had only heard of in tales. Teeg used his senses to combat all that surrounded him.

Another hunting party gathered in the waiting room. One

by one, they replaced those in the training room. When someone tapped Teeg's shoulder, he joined his party behind the glass.

"You made good work of the simulator," praised Kron. "Eat. Rest. We hunt tonight."

Teeg followed his partymates. In the corridor, the first door opened. The Huntrix stood in the doorway, watching them pass. Her hand reached.

Feeling a hand on his arm, Teeg stopped. Light brown eyes searched into his. Before he could utter anything, the Huntrix said, "Trust your instincts. They are never wrong. Sometimes, Notkyn retain more traits from our human ancestors than we like to admit. Use them to your advantage." She let go of him, then faded into the shadows.

He ran to catch his partymates before they entered the elevator. Riding up, no one said anything about his tardiness.

Once the sun had fully sunk below the horizon, the Hunters emerged on the mountaintop. They encircled Voy's pyre.

"Her life was noble—devoted to the Hunt. She will be well remembered," said the Huntrix. She lit a torch. Many of the Hunters shielded their eyes from the brightness. Transferring the flame to bottom sections of the pyre, she continued, "Let the fire release your soul and the smoke carry it to the heavens." The Huntrix watched the fire burn for a moment, then extinguished the torch.

"We dedicate tonight's Hunt to Voy," she said to her Hunters. "Hunt well." Taking her place at the front, she led them down the mountain.

Per instructions, Kron brought his hunting party to the

mid-pack.   They hunted in a wooded field with two other parties with much more experience.   Staring at their strong stances, intimidation crept inside of Teeg.

The sour stench of ghost slithered into his nostrils, preceding a mist that rolled between the trees.   Fog gobbled them. The dark armor of the other Hunters disappeared.   When the waning gibbous moon popped out from behind a cloud, the smothering gray blanket brightened.

The eyes of the Notkyn evolved to see in the darkness to discern the faintest of ghosts roaming in the night.   The encompassing brightness blinded them.

Trust your instincts.   The Huntrix's clear voice played in Teeg's mind.   He rooted his feet in the earth.   Through the leather soles, he felt the warmth from the dirt.   Teeg inhaled and exhaled until his skin could feel through his armor.   The muffled sounds of skirmishes surrounded him.   He paid no notice.   The fog felt wet against his armor.   He smelled dampness.

Wetness turned to cold.   Sour replaced damp.   He slashed. A whispered scream lingered in the fog.   His blade found another and then another.

After the moon moved behind low clouds, the unnatural fog lifted.   Dark figures fought around the field.   Some had fallen to the ectoplasm covered ground.

Teeg followed a large, translucent shape chasing Meir into the trees.   The woods breathed like the training room in Sublevel G.

Trying to slash the shape, Meir stumbled.   He swung again, then tripped over roots poking out of the forest floor.

Meir tumbled to the ground. He searched frantically for his blade.

The shape weaved between the almost dormant branches. Running on all fours, Teeg could not reach him fast enough. He transitioned to two legs. Detaching his weapon from his forearm, he hurled it. The silver sang as it sliced through the night.

Teeg heard the shape whisper a scream, then a thud. His blade lodged into a tree trunk.

Noticing Teeg, Meir sighed in relief. Teeg picked up Meir's weapon as he approached his friend.

"Thanks," Meir muttered. He secured the bone to his forearm.

Teeg climbed the tree to retrieve his weapon.

"We need to get out of here," Meir said. "Something is hunting us." He stood at the base of the tree. "I saw Rhash and Pri go down."

Jumping out of the tree, Teeg landed beside him. "We should get back to the others."

Meir adamantly shook his head. "We need to reach the Huntrix. The other way is a deathtrap."

Seeing the fear in Meir's eyes, Teeg nodded. They ran through the forest. At the edge of a field, they stopped. A cottage sat in the distance. The air smelled sharp with rain.

"She wouldn't choose hunting grounds so close to humans," Teeg said.

Agreeing, Meir said, "Let's keep going."

They jetted into the field on two legs, as they had to do within human range. Laughter crackled across the field. The air reeked of ghost.

Stopping, Meir and Teeg searched, keeping their backs to one another. A shimmering face hung over them. They snapped their blades into place.

Over the howls of the wind, Teeg could hear its dark breathing. They *were* being hunted. But, by whom?

"Show yourself, coward," Meir egged.

The face vanished. Sourness lingered. Goosebumps shimmered over Teeg's skin.

A man-like figure stood in the field. Dark armor, similar to theirs, covered it. A curved silver blade reflected light from the cottage. Its dark hand clasped the long staff of the scythe.

"Who are you?" Meir asked.

The figure did not answer. A haunting laugh echoed off the low cloud ceiling. The scythe's blade tipped towards them.

Teeg and Meir ran in different directions around the figure.

Still standing in its spot, the figure released another wicked laugh.

It seemed to be waiting, but Teeg did not know for what. Teeg kept running, keeping the figure in his sights.

Across the field, Meir stopped. In an instant, the figure reappeared in front of Meir. Its scythe ghostly sliced through his body. Frozen, Meir dropped his weapon. The figure transformed into a translucent, snake-like shape.

Teeg darted to Meir as the shape entered Meir's body. After it exited, Meir dropped to the ground as if cutting the strings of a marionette. Teeg stood over Meir's crumpled body lying in the tall grass.

Hearing the laugh, Teeg snatched Meir's weapon off the ground. He faced the face with blades in both hands. The sky dumped rain over everything. He stared misery in the eyes. The gray above lightened. The face disappeared.

Teeg waited. Rain pounded his armor. Beyond the clouds, the sun rose. Nothing came. He attached a weapon to each forearm.

Returning to Meir's body, he knelt in the wetness. Childhood memories of them pretending to be the best Hunters that ever walked into Hunter Mountain raced through his mind. He could not stop from remembering training together or the excitement of being chosen together. They were supposed to hunt with the Huntrix together. His fists pounded the earth, splattering mud.

A hand softly touched his shoulder. He looked up to see light brown eyes staring at him. They did not belong to the Huntrix.

Dark blonde hair enwrapped a sad expression. Her other hand clutched a black umbrella that shielded the rain and the rising sun. "You should get out of the rain," she said. Her voice sounded like bells.

Although dark gray clouds hid the sun, dawn arrived. Teeg never heard the bullhorn. He needed to get out of the daylight. Removing his facemask, he said, "I can't leave him here."

Gazing at Meir, she nodded. "There's an empty stall in the barn." Her hand slipped off his shoulder, but her comforting touch endured.

He scooped Meir's lifeless body off the wet earth, then followed her through the raindrops. Sheep scurried out of barn doors. He placed Meir on the floor of the empty stall. Numbness replaced all his senses. He could not believe Meir was gone.

"I'm sorry about your friend," she said.

"Thank you."

"He'll be safe here. You look like you've been up all night," she said. "Come, dry off and eat."

Surprised, Teeg looked at her. Her eyes revealed kindness and compassion. "Why? I'm a stranger with a dead friend."

She flashed a smile. "I saw what he did to your friend from my window. The Soul Eater has plagued this area for centuries. We help those who fight him."

His peers, if any survived, would mock him for taking help from humans. He felt as if he could trust her. She saw what many humans could not.

He covered his eyes as he followed her out of the barn. "I'm Rebecca."

"Teeg." He lowered his hand and his hood when he stepped inside the cottage.

Entering the bright kitchen, he squinted. An older woman stood in front of a stove while an older man walked in behind them.

"Mom, Dad, this is Teeg," Rebecca announced.

"Have a seat at the table, Teeg," Rebecca's mother said.

Teeg sat on a wooden chair. He had never been in a human house. His eyes adjusted to the brightness as food was placed in front of him. The three humans joined him. "Thank you," he said.

Her mother smiled at him. "Upstairs, there are dry clothes," she said. "We have an extra bedroom if you'd like to lie down for a while."

"Yes, thank you," Teeg said. "How can I repay you?"

"Don't worry about that now," her father said.

Rebecca brought him to the spare bedroom. "You being here has given my father hope that my brother's death will be avenged."

"When did he…?"

"Eleven years ago."

"I'm sorry."

"Thank you." She smiled. "In the trunk over there should be some old clothes that fit." She closed the blinds to darken the room. "Do you need an alarm clock?" she asked from the doorway.

"No. Thank you."

"One of us will be around if you need anything." She closed the door as she stepped into the hall.

Teeg hung his wet armor over a metal bar at the end of the bed. The room was not as dark as he would like, but it would do. When he closed his eyes, Rebecca's face replaced the darkness. Thinking of her, he fell asleep.

Awaking in the dim bedroom, Teeg had not slept long. The Soul Eater swinging his silver scythe haunted his sleep. He heard muffled voices. After getting dressed in the human clothes, he opened the door.

"…maybe five minutes. The body was there and then it

wasn't," Rebecca's father said.

"I'm sure there's a good explanation," Rebecca's mother countered.

Covering his eyes, Teeg descended into the bright kitchen where Rebecca's parents sat.

Rebecca entered, carrying a basket when her father asked, "Are you a Vampire? Your friend's body is gone."

"Dad!"

"No," said Teeg with his hand completely covering his eyes. "The Collectors found Meir's body and took him back to my people for his funeral tonight."

"Here," said Rebecca. Her hand gently forced something into his. "Sunglasses to protect your eyes."

Squinting, he fumbled with them. Her father continued his questioning. "Who are your people? Why are you sensitive to light?"

The dark lenses eased the brightness. For their hospitality, he at least owed them an explanation. "We call ourselves the Notkyn. We have evolved from humans to hunt those who stalk the night. Our eyes see in the dark. Our ears hear higher frequencies. Our legs run faster. Our noses smell ghosts before we see them. I have never been out during the day. We are taught that sunlight will diminish our sight, destroying our ability to see the dimmest ghosts."

"Why aren't you sleeping?" Rebecca's mother asked. She patted a chair.

Sitting, he said, "I keep seeing that silver scythe slashing Meir and I can't do anything to stop it." He buried his fingers into his hair. "I am exhausted, but I can't sleep."

Knowing Teeg's pain, her father touched Teeg's arm. "You need to work through your anger to have a clear mind. Come with me."

Teeg allowed Rebecca's father to steer him outside.

"We lost our son, Tim, to that monster," he said. "Nothing takes away the pain, but you can channel it."

The man knew loss, frustration and helplessness. Teeg wanted to learn from him. Wearing sunglasses, Teeg followed him around the farm. He cleaned out the stalls, brushed down horses, even helped him change the oil in the old truck. Every so often, he stole glimpses of Rebecca. When it was time to milk the ewes, Rebecca's father explained the process.

"To avoid being kicked when milking, we feed them first. The food is a great distraction while attaching the pumps." He demonstrated, then had Teeg do it.

Sitting at the dinner table with Rebecca and her parents, Teeg found clarity. He was a Hunter. He refused to be the hunted.

In the dark spare bedroom, Teeg slipped on his dry armor. Someone softly knocked. Opening the door, he found Rebecca.

Her light brown eyes grazed over his body before landing on his. "Are you hunting the Soul Eater tonight?"

"I am. And every night until my blade releases him from this world."

"Will I ever see you again?"

Obeying his urge, his fingers ran through her dark blonde hair. "I don't know what will happen to me."

She briefly closed her eyes. "I'll leave a light on for you, so you can find your way back in the darkness."

A deep desire to stay with her overwhelmed him. However, his duty to Meir, the Notkyn and her family pushed him. Downstairs, he thanked Rebecca's parents.

"You're welcome back anytime," her mother said.

With a warm handshake and a pat on the shoulder, her father said, "Good luck, Son."

Rebecca stayed on the stairs as he said good-bye. In the field, he glanced back at the cottage. Rebecca stood in the doorway. He smiled. Turning, he ran on all fours into the woods.

Stopping, he closed his eyes. Like in the fog, he relied on his other senses. He heard feet in wet grass. Bone released silver. Sick laughter resonated in his ears. He smelled leaves drying, wet bark and a sour undertone.

Opening his eyes, he followed the sour smell to a clearing. He stood behind the face as it watched Hunters battle ghosts. It waited, so he waited.

Whispered screams clung to the battlefield as Hunters slashed shimmers out of existence. The face morphed into the figure the humans called the Soul Eater.

Like milking sheep, Teeg postponed making his move until the figure was well distracted.

Its silver scythe tipped.

Teeg dropped on all fours. He waited for the chosen Hunter to stop moving.

The Hunter stopped. The figure vanished. Teeg sprinted.

With a cackle of laughter, the scythe poised to swing.

Teeg's arms pushed off the ground behind the figure.

Crossing them in front of his body, he snatched both bone handles. His wrists flicked. The silver blades sliced through the figure.

Laughter morphed into a wail. The scythe fell. The figure dissipated into the darkness.

Teeg faced the figure's chosen Hunter. Ripping off his facemask, the Hunter dropped to his knees, then vomited into the grass.

A bullhorn signaled the end of the Hunt. However, Teeg did not retract his blades.

The Huntrix stood next to him. She gave him a nod, then collected the dropped scythe.

He returned with his brethren to Hunter Mountain. Only Cine and Quinn remained of those chosen with Teeg. Inside their nearly empty quarters, Kron gathered Teeg.

Kron led him through the corridors to the long table at which the Huntrix sat with ranked Hunter Chiefs. Standing, the Hunters applauded.

When they returned to their seats, the Huntrix said, "The cunning Hunt is well rewarded, Teeg. You have earned the right to hunt in my party. Someday, you will lead a party of your own." She gazed at all the Hunters in the room. "Your prey, Teeg, I am sad to say was one of us—a ghost of a fallen Hunter from long ago. The scythe is well protected where no one can reach it. Get your rest. I will see you in the front of the pack tomorrow night."

Kron clapped him on the shoulder as they exited. Teeg barely felt it. He should have been exuberant. He got what he always wanted—to hunt with the Huntrix.

Cine and Quinn also congratulated him. He peeled off his armor. From his bed, he stared at Meir's empty bunk. He glanced at the other empty beds. Perhaps Hunting was not the life he wanted after all. His thoughts floated to Rebecca as he drifted off to sleep.

Waking early, he tiptoed past his sleeping brethren. Avoiding everyone, he climbed through a narrow opening to the outside. The setting sun displayed its last vestiges of orange light before navy eclipsed it.

Teeg stood near the top of the mountain. A waning moon rose above the valley. He just wanted to stare at it—bask in its beauty—if only for one night.

"Hunters such as yourself have seen much. Perhaps more than one should," said a clear, female voice.

His head turned. The Huntrix stood beside him. "I," he started.

"You don't have to explain yourself," she said. "Many a good Hunter, even legendary, chose to leave this life." Her light brown eyes sparkled in the moonlight. "The night is young. Good for a long journey. Take all you belongings. I don't want it cluttering the complex." The Huntrix gave him a rare smile.

As he sprinted to his bunk, he thought he heard an echo of her voice say, "Besides, you may need it again someday."

With all of his gear in a bag, he exited Hunter Mountain before most of them awoke. The bag slowed his travels, but he knew exactly where he journeyed.

Night began to yield to day. His eyes spied a small cottage. A light brightened one of the windows. He smiled.

Gravel crunched under his feet. The door opened, spilling light onto the gravel path.

Rebecca stepped out of the cottage. Pausing, she gazed at the man running towards her. "Teeg?"

He dropped his bag beside her. His arms wrapped around her, pulling her into an embrace.

"You returned," she said into his ear.

"You left the light on for me." His hand caressed her soft cheek. She closed her eyes at his touch. His lips found hers. Closing his eyes, dawn broke over the horizon.

About the Authors

Fred C. Adams

Masks

Fred C. Adams is a lifelong resident of Western Pennsylvania whose first publication occurred in 1970, and he has continued writing and publishing his work throughout his career as an English professor at Duquesne University, California University of Pennsylvania, and Penn State University's Fayette Campus from which he retired in 2011. His novel *Hitwolf* was published in July of 2014 and *Six Gun Terrors*, a supernatural western, was published in August, both by Airship 27 Press. His mystery novel *Dead Man's Melody* will be released by Airship 27 in 2015. His nonfiction book *Edith Wharton's American Gothic: Gods, Ghosts and Vampires* is pending publication from Borgo Press. A singer-songwriter, he also performs his original work at local venues including the Pittsburgh Renaissance Festival and the walk-through haunted attraction Castle Blood.

Timothy Bateson

Under a Hunter's Moon

Having spent time in the computers industry, customer service jobs, retail, and library services has given Timothy (Tim to friends) a lot of experiences. His interests include falconry, reading, writing, history, role-playing, sci-fi, fantasy and music.

Tim was born in England, raised in the London area, and earned a computers degree in Wales. In 2005, he moved to Alaska to marry Sandi, having met online through mutual friends. Tim rediscovered a passion for writing while reading and editing Sandi's own stories. Art is used in "Under a Hunter's Moon" with Sandi's permission, and appears in her fiction works as well.

http://timothybatesonauthor.wordpress.com/

Thomas Beck

Afraid

A father, grandfather, and nursing supervisor, Thomas Beck has lived in Southwest Pennsylvania his entire life, except for a stint as a naval corpsman. Writing from his home in the mountains near Acme, he draws on past experiences and creative thoughts to weave together baskets of tales for the reader.

Spencer Carvalho

The Reckoning: Hidden Remains

Spencer Carvalho has written short stories for various literary magazines and anthologies. His stories have appeared in anthologies like *the Barcelona Review, Keep Going, Imitation Fruit, Mused, Istanbul Literary Review, Almia, Inner Sins, Fever Dreams Ezine, Voluted Tales, Aphelion, Vine Leaves Literary Journal, Allegory, eFantasy, eSciFi, eRomance,* and *eFiction.* His stories have also appeared in anthologies like *Certain Circuits Volume 1, Another Wild West, Remembrances of Wars Past: A War Veterans Anthology, Tales of the Undead-Suffer Eternal: Volume 3, Undead of Winter, Fossil Lake,* and *Horror in Bloom.* For more, Google: Spencer Carvalho.

IE Castellano

The Hunt

IE Castellano is an American author and poet living in the Eastern United States. Falling in love with the mechanics of the English language at an early age, she started writing poetry before venturing into fiction. She loves history (especially ancient), mythology, archeology, and anthropology. Anything IE reads, sees, or does could wind up in one of her books in some manner. With her propensity to ask, what if, she writes speculative fiction—authoring the dystopian sci-fi novel, *Tricentennial*, and the contemporary epic fantasy series, *the World In-between*.

For news and a current list of her writings, visit her blog: IECastellano.blogspot.com.

Kevin Hayman

The Hearth

Kevin Hayman studied Media at the University of the West of England, where he took a keen interest in screenwriting. However, after reading Stephen King's *Skeleton Crew*, he realised the short story format and the horror genre in particular would be his preferred direction forward. During the day, he works as a cameraman for a video production company, leaving his evenings and weekends free to write. He is currently working on two novels as well as a collection of short stories. *The Hearth* represents Kevin's first publication to date. He lives in a small rural town in England with his fiancé and a black cat looking over his shoulder.

Jovan Jones

Bumps in the Night

Jovan Jones resides in Charlotte, North Carolina with his wife and children. His sources of inspiration for his work come from various facets of life. It is the pure joy of delving into the deeper stream of consciousness that inspires him to often write dark tales. Donald Goines, Iceberg Slim, and Clive Barker are some of the authors that have influenced him. He is the author of *Tears of a Rose* and a contributing author to Vamptasy Press' *Broken Mirrors, Fractured Minds.*

Renny Kalp

The Lightkeepers

Lifelong student of all things spiritual, Renny Kalp is a wife, mother, and salon owner who infuses a bit of the mystical into her writing.

Matt Kolbet

When the Wine Begins to Sour

Matt Kolbet teaches and writes near wine country in Oregon. His work has appeared in *First Line Magazine*, *Defenestration* and *Three Line Poetry* among other places.

Jacob Lambert

Stranger Nights

First place recipient of the Scott and Zelda Fitzgerald award for short story, Jacob M. Lambert has published with Dark Hall Press, *Midnight Echo: The Magazine of the Australian Horror Writers Association*, and more. He lives in Montgomery, Alabama, where he teaches music and is an editorial assistant for *The Scriblerian and the Kit-Cats*, an academic journal pertaining to English literature of the late seventeenth-and early eighteenth-century. When not writing, he enjoys time with his wife, Stephanie, and daughter, Annabelle.

Patrick MacAdoo

Masquerade

Patrick MacAdoo is the author of *Damn Zombies*, published by Severed Press, 2014; *Bigass Squirrels*, published by May December Publications, 2013; and *Weeyatches*, published by Damnation Books, 2012, as well as several short works in various anthologies. www.patrickmacadoo.com

James Park

Remembering Natalia

James Park lives in Columbus, Ohio with his gorgeous and delightfully articulate wife Ngouanephone. He's been featured in a number of genre fiction publications, including *Dark Moon Digest*, *Ghostlight Magazine*, and *Cemetery Moon*. New work is scheduled to appear in upcoming issues of *Infernal Ink Magazine*, *Night to Dawn Magazine*, and *Massacre Magazine*. He has also contributed work to the upcoming anthologies *The New Whakazoid Circus* and *Lost in the Witching Hour*.

Jay Seate

Mr. Cool's Final Halloween

Winner of Horror Novel Review's 2013 Best Short Fiction Award, Jay's stories inevitably turn to the macabre. They may be told with hard core realism or humor, but it gets the pulse racing enough to pull his corpses from the grave. His stories appear in numerous magazines, anthologies, and webzines. Many of his works can be found at www.troyseateauthor.webs. com and on amazon.com.

DJ Tyrer

A Night Behind Bars

DJ Tyrer is the person behind *Atlantean Publishing* and has been widely published in anthologies and magazines in the UK, USA and elsewhere, including *Sorcery & Sanctity: A Homage to Arthur Machen* (Hieroglyphics Press), and issues of *Anthology 29*, *Tigershark* and *Carillon*, as well as two novellas available on the Kindle, *The Yellow House* (Dynatox Ministries) and *Acting Strangely* (Jazzclaw Publishing).

DJ Tyrer's website: http://djtyrer.blogspot.co.uk/

Kevin Wetmore

"Stingy Jack" and the Boys

Kevin Wetmore is an author, actor, director and professor based in Los Angeles, although originally from New England. In addition to numerous short stories, he is also the author of *Post-9/11 Horror in American Cinema* and *Back from the Dead: Reading Remakes of Romero's Zombie Films as Markers of Their Times.*

Kelli A. Wilkins

Home for Halloween

Kelli A. Wilkins is an award-winning author who has published more than 90 short stories, seventeen romance novels, and four non-fiction books. Her speculative fiction has appeared in *The Sun*, *Weird Tales*, *Dark Moon Digest*, *The First Line*, and in several anthologies, including: *Wrapped in White*, *Mistresses of the Macabre*, *Haunted*, *The Four Horsemen: An Anthology of Conquest, War, Famine & Death*, *Frightmares: A Fistful of Flash Fiction Horror*, *What If...* and *Dark Things II: Cat Crimes: Tales of Feline Mayhem and Murder.*

Kelli publishes a blog (http://kelliwilkinsauthor.blogspot.com/) filled with excerpts, interviews, writing prompts, and whatever else pops into her head. She also writes a monthly newsletter, Kelli's Quill. Kelli invites readers to visit her website, www.KelliWilkins.com to learn more about all of her writings.

Edward M Wolfe

Halloween Bully

Edward M Wolfe was a field reporter for one of the first independent news websites in the late 90s, and later worked as a city beat reporter on the Oregon coast. His latest novel, *Reaching Kendra*, is a story about what happens when true love is interrupted by terrorism, and other religious beliefs.

He lives in Tulsa with two human children, and two canine children who all love his writing, and tolerate his guitar playing.

www.ingramcontent.com/pod-product-compliance
Lightning Source LLC
Chambersburg PA
CBHW051253210726
48287CB00002B/487